Fingertips, light as the brush of a butterfly wing, stroked her face. Warmth spread throughout her body in a radiating fashion from her heart. She closed her eyes and languished in the sun. Immense love washed through her, and Madeline was certain she had never felt as adored before. In a moment of satiety, she opened her eyes to see the clear blue ones—though a watered-down version, chalk drawing instead of oil painting on canvas—of William Gray staring back at her.

He smiled at her. "You can see me, can't you?" he whispered.

"And why would I not be able to?" she asked.

"Because I've been dead for more than a century."

Praise for Renee Canter Johnson

"Renee Johnson is a natural storyteller with a graceful elegance of style."

~*Janet Hulstrand,*
Writing from the Heart, Reading for the Road
~*~

"I want to give thanks for Renee Johnson—her writing raw, sublime, and beautiful, is (there is no other word) a gift."

~*Justen Ahren, author of A Strange Catechism, founder of Italy writing retreat, Orvieto, and director of Noepe Martha's Vineyard Center for Literary Arts*
~*~

"[*THE HAUNTING OF WILLIAM GRAY* is] A workout for mind and emotions as Renee Canter Johnson brings you back in time for an intriguing romantic adventure."

~*Jane Seskin, author*
Witness To Resilience: Stories Of Intimate Violence
~*~

"If anticipation killed, this novel would murder!"

~*Ellie M. Whittington, Journalism Major,*
Elon University
~*~

"Who knew I could love a story about a hostile corporate takeover so much? It was an unlikely place for romance, but author Renee Johnson pulled it off [in *ACQUISITION*]. I really wanted to know there'd be a happy ending, but this book kept me guessing about how, if, or when, until the very end. That, to me, is the true sign of a great romance and a great read!"

~*Tracy Thompson McPherson—visual artist*

The Haunting of William Gray

by

Renee Canter Johnson

The Haunting of William Gray

COPYRIGHT © 2015 by Renee Canter Johnson

Cover Art by *Rae Monet, Inc. Design*

The Wild Rose Press, Inc.
PO Box 708
Adams Basin, NY 14410-0708
Visit us at www.thewildrosepress.com

Publishing History
First Fantasy Rose Edition, 2015
Print ISBN 978-1-5092-0435-9
Digital ISBN 978-1-5092-0436-6

Published in the United States of America

Dedications

To my parents,
Wilburn Grady and Blanche Canter,
for instilling their love of travel within me
and teaching me to keep my mind open
to new experiences.
~*~
To my husband, Tony Johnson,
for understanding my desires for both
traveling and writing.
~*~
And to my editor, Maggie Johnson,
for providing me with guidance
and the opportunity to become published.

Chapter 1

It wasn't time yet. Madeline Waters peeped at her watch for the tenth time, trying to squelch her attack of nerves. Everything she had been working toward depended on the success of this meeting with William Gray.

Waiting at the coffee shop across from the Arts Council, she watched its van pull against the curb. Painted with multicolored flowers and lots of green leaves on the otherwise white background, it was impossible to miss. Tossing some cash on the table, she made a dash for the door and crossed the street.

"Hello," she called out to the lady standing at the front of the bus, assuming her to be the tour director. "I'm Madeline Waters. I believe you'll find my name on your list."

The young woman raked her eyes over her before glancing at her list of participants. "I'll check."

Madeline's heart fluttered as the possibility of being denied arose. Her broken-down car was in the shop yet again. *What if they forgot to add my name? What if—*

"Ah, yes. Here you are." She pointed to the list before handing Madeline a name tag. "You may board any time. We'll be leaving in about fifteen minutes."

"Thank you," she said and immediately climbed into the van.

Cars started filling the parking lot beside the building. Several people walked toward them. Madeline could think of nothing except the upcoming meeting. *What if he didn't agree? What if he refused her access?*

Keeping to herself, she chose the single seat over the back wheel well where it wouldn't be necessary to engage in conversation with the others. They were all taking the tour as sightseers, laughing and talking as the last name was checked off the list and the van pulled away from the curb. She wasn't really part of their planned outing; just going along for the ride from Georgetown, South Carolina, across the causeway, to one of Winyah Bay's islands.

The road hugged the coastline for a short distance and then fingered off into a bit of swampland before continuing into a shaded forest of black pines and live oaks. Spanish moss draped the overhanging twisted limbs lending a sense of foreboding to the trip.

In spite of her nerves, Madeline looked forward to seeing Pine Island's antebellum house, a multi-storied colonial with shaded porches on every side. The cupola at the top was rumored to offer sweeping views in every direction. She had seen it in the distance from the water, and in pictures, but never up close. Accounts from those lucky enough to have been guests of the owners throughout the years, described its spot in the bay in the same way one might a ship on a swath of green, floating from Winyah Bay to the ocean.

When the van pulled up at the tall iron gates, Madeline's breath caught in her chest. The driver punched a series of numbers into the pad at the base of a covered telecom and the mechanism clicked, releasing the gates' grips on one another. Creaking as they swung slowly open, anticipation built tension in Madeline's gut.

An eternity seemed to yawn before her as they waited for both gates to fully open. She clenched her fists, fingernails burrowing into her palms, until the van finally lurched forward. Madeline's heart thumped, and her breath was only a shallow intake with an imperceptible exhale.

Scanning across the landscape as they proceeded, Madeline stored every image into her memory bank. The ancient flowering shrubs, struggling against their confines within the low brick walls on either side of the drive, appeared to be aching for freedom. Here and there a brick bulged outward giving the impression the plant was poking out a toe. *Did azaleas really grow this large naturally?* she wondered.

They rounded a curve in the drive, oaks and pines in small groupings on either side, and suddenly a vision in white shooting to the sky rose before them. Madeline's heart nearly stopped. Her ears drummed with pressure.

The tour participants *oohed* and *aahed* and mumbled among themselves. Madeline was unaware of their actual words. Their voices became a drone, akin to a hive of bees buzzing off toward the azalea blooms. Or was it merely the humming in her head?

When the van pulled to a stop and its doors remotely opened, Madeline took a couple of deep breaths. She had arrived—finally. *This is it*, she told herself as she stepped down from the last stair onto the ground she had been waiting so long to see. Though she moved steadily forward, Madeline could barely feel her feet beneath her.

****

William Gray thumbed the green postcard providing proof of receipt of the letter he had sent via certified mail to Madeline Waters. She would either show up today, or he would be finished with her requests to pilfer through his ancestor's priceless personal journals.

They were still off limits to the public. While most of the documents in the Historical Society's possession were public domain, the journals had a specified number of years they could remain private. The Historical Society wouldn't store items with no public release date. Seventy-five years had seemed a long time twenty-five years ago.

If it hadn't been for Hurricane Hugo, William would have kept them locked in the vault at Pine Island. He picked up the photo album labeled "Hugo" from the credenza behind his desk. Flipping through the pages made his heart drop.

The house, originally built by Captain William Gray for his young bride, had survived many such storms over the years, but was nearly destroyed when Hugo roared through. As painful as it would have been to have lost the house, the thought of losing those priceless journals from the eighteen hundreds had been even more devastating.

His parents had been alive then. He had been so young, so full of hopes and dreams.

William slammed the album shut before he got to the pictures that always shattered him. *Why do I keep these horrible pictures? Why don't I toss them out, or run them through the shredder?*

Even now, after all these long years and great

losses, he couldn't part with the reminder of how he had once loved greatly. It seemed appropriate, however, to maintain them in the album reserved for the greatest destructive force to blow across the island in his lifetime.

Hugo had nothing on Julia McNair. Hurricane Julia, his nickname for her, had been equally as damaging. And for whatever reason, known only to *her*, she had broken his heart so thoroughly he had vowed to never love again.

But Julia wasn't the only great love he had lost. William pulled the desk drawer all the way out and retrieved his drawing of the vineyard and winery he had planned to start upstate in Greenville.

Seeing the layout once again brought a smile to his sullen face. It faded fast, as fast as a young man's dreams. He slammed the drawer shut and crossed the room to stare out the window.

William wasn't seeing the landscape. He was reliving what would have been his wedding day, the one that had left him broken and bitter. Julia apparently couldn't go through with it and hadn't explained it either. She just didn't show up. All he could attribute it to was his obligation to Pine Island.

William rubbed his face. It had become his destiny to relinquish every dream he had ever had for the sake of this old barn of a house, and the relics of his ancestors. And part of that obligation was hosting the annual party whose proceeds funded both the Arts Council and the Historical Society.

A flicker of sunlight on metal caught his eye. The van bringing the tour group had arrived. *Was Madeline Waters among them?* His stomach gave a small lurch as he tried to catch a glimpse of the people on board.

The Azalea Ball, which drew in the most elite of the area, still lacked a photographer. He needed someone to work the dance, its attendees expecting to see their faces splashed across the front pages of the newspapers from Georgetown, Charleston, and Myrtle Beach.

His mind raced back over the previous years' events and the long list of photographers whom he now refused admittance to Pine Island. Each had cost him plenty to ensure silence about the odd shadows mysteriously appearing in their shots and their observances of his own sometimes-strange behavior that he could never remember. So here he was, mere days from the ball, and no photographer booked.

Several suggestions from outside the low country had reached him. One he had considered for a brief period of time. The drawback was their lack of dependence on his benevolence, and therefore the potentially higher cost should it be necessary to obtain their silence.

William was determined his ancestor, the great Captain William Gray, for whom he was named, would never be reduced to a ghost story. Whatever the cost, he would make sure the fabled Captain Gray's best-known legend was not haunting the very house he had built and within whose walls he had lost a young wife and many children.

Madeline Waters wanted something from him, something he didn't wish to relinquish, yet she was also a photographer. Not particularly well-known for her work, she had a camera and knew how to use it—even if it was mostly in cataloging estate jewelry and fashion shows.

William paced and rubbed his chin, thinking and planning what he should say to both encourage her to attend as photographer, while maintaining control over what she might print about the photos. She could possibly be desperate enough to be willing to stay on the premises and complete the task he had long wanted to accomplish.

If she didn't show up though, no amount of planning would solve his dilemma.

Chapter 2

A woman of some age answered the door bell. Wearing a practical black dress, soft-soled shoes, and a white apron, she welcomed the visitors from the Arts Council into the foyer which stretched across the entire ground floor. "Welcome to Gray Estate on the privately owned Pine Island," she said, without much inflection in her tone.

Though her voice was decidedly southern, it had a bit of a monotone quality. *Perhaps that was what William Gray liked about her.*

"Thank you," said the guide. Turning to the group, she instructed, "If you'll all just follow me." She led them forward while reciting a bit of history of the area and the house they were standing in.

When Madeline remained by the door, the lady who had greeted them motioned for her to follow the others.

"Excuse me. But I'm not actually part of the tour. I rode out with them to meet with Mr. Gray." Receiving little more than a quizzical stare, she added, "He's expecting me. The name's Madeline Waters."

"Just a moment, please," the woman said, before climbing the stairs.

Madeline waited, experiencing an odd sensation. The hairs on her arms quivered. *Was someone there? Was William Gray watching her from above?*

Peeking around the staircase, Madeline saw the gallery of paintings. Her feet moved of their own accord, depositing her directly beneath the portrait of Captain William Gray. She'd been drawn to it by an invisible cord connecting her to the ancient mariner through her research.

He looked regal, even with the extraordinarily long sideburns framing his round face. Eyes the color of the Atlantic horizon had been painted with the optical illusion that made them appear to follow her.

Madeline let out a nervous sigh, recognizing it was the eyes in the painting of Captain Gray causing her angst. He had built this house, had once stood upon the exact same spot as she. The realization sent a shiver along her spine.

Feeling strangely connected to him, likely due to spending so many long hours reading documents pertaining to his life and family, she met his odd oiled gaze. "What kind of man were you really?" she whispered. Laughing at herself for talking to a painting, Madeline scanned the rest of the gallery.

The portrait of the current owner and sole heir, William Gray, hung there as well, failing to emanate the same warmth of his ancestor. Perhaps it was the lack of patina, or the skill of the artist, or maybe he simply didn't possess the same convivial spirit.

She studied his cocky expression. He appeared young and reckless, self-absorbed.

"Ms. Waters?" the aproned lady called.

Madeline jumped, startled. She peeped around. The rambling crowd of sightseers was dispersing for plastic cups of wine and small plates of cheese straws and sugar cake.

"Yes, I'm here," she called out to the woman. Her voice echoed up the hollow staircase leading to a pinpoint of light at its apex.

"Mr. Gray will see you now, in his study on the second floor." Stepping toward the sweeping staircase, she removed the velvet rope.

Apparently it was hanging there to discourage any who might be tempted to venture upward during the tour. The spectacular blooms of the azaleas during this two-week period of the year had given someone on the Arts Council the idea of private antebellum homes, in and around Charleston, opening their doors for visitors to enjoy.

Madeline slipped upward, entering a narrow doorway toward the left, as directed by the wave of the aproned one's hand. She found William Gray seated in a large, burgundy leather wing chair.

Rising, he pointed to the chair's twin as the place she should sit. "Ms. Waters?"

Disarming her with his hawkish gaze from crystalline blue eyes, he could have walked out of the portrait she had just seen downstairs. There was nothing different about his features aside from a few gray wisps of hair at his temples. He had remained stunningly handsome, though more angular and sharp than the painting suggested.

She extended her hand. "Thank you for meeting with me."

The grip of the muscled man in front of her made her weak at the knees as he encapsulated her palm with long, strong fingers. Madeline welcomed the opportunity to sit.

Although her research had garnered her many

details, it had not prepared her for such a powerful persona as William Gray maintained in the flesh. His presence dominated the room. Even the scent of sea water and sunshine on sand wafting in through the open window, lent itself to masculinity. Madeline could almost feel a pulse vibrating around them, coming from inside the four walls.

"I understand you are doing a paper on my family." He spoke with the southern accent often attributed to Charleston—its own particular blend of rolling long "a" sounds.

Madeline swallowed hard. "The Grays *are* rather notorious in the stretch of territory between Georgetown and Charleston."

"Is that so?" He lifted an eyebrow, the only facial movement she could discern.

"I think it is the combination of strong ethical beginnings juxtaposed with the rumors of murder and pirating at sea."

He chuckled, but it sounded unnerving coming from him. "I'd be very careful if I were you. Lawsuits of lesser slander have been known to be won here in South Carolina."

Madeline searched his face for a hint of humor in his comment. Finding none, she pulled the hem of her skirt over shaky legs to hide the sudden goosebumps popping out at his coldness. "Perhaps you could tell me what it is you object to in my thesis, and we could take it from there."

She wasn't sure why he would have such strong convictions about her use of historical information as regarded the Captain. The personal journals were not in public domain yet, but eventually would be. Then they would either confirm or contradict the records. It wasn't a question of if, only of when. But she needed them now to move forward with her writing.

Thankful she had divulged nothing about her recent findings on the land grant dating back to 1692 from King William III of England to Charles Gray, Madeline had hopes of being sponsored by a benefactor in London to further her research.

If she could convince *this* William to allow her access to his three-times-great-grandfather's journals, it could be the chapter leading to her doctoral degree. And that could make her career. She could almost envision the next volume—the one expanded on from Europe— becoming her dissertation.

"I object to it altogether." His stoic face still betrayed no emotion.

Moments of silence passed between them before she understood he would make no further statement until she responded. "Why?" she asked simply, unable to think of a more eloquent question in the heat of his stare.

He responded with an unemotional detachment which would have denied his interest at all, if it had not been for the words themselves. "What could possibly interest you about my family? What business is it of yours to snoop in our records? What is it you hope to gain?"

Laughter from outside wafted up on the spring breeze through the open window—silly, happy voices—defying the chill of the room she found herself in.

"Your ancestor was unconventional in his means of obtaining wealth and doing business, shunning the accepted practices of the day."

"Some people maintain he was a traitor. What if you find proof of that?"

Madeline didn't want to answer. Integrity would compel her to report her findings, as incriminating to the man as they might be. She was aware this would not be the appropriate response to convince the current William Gray to grant his permission. "What do you think?"

"I think you are trying to skirt the question by asking another of me." Both eyebrows lifted in unison with the dropping of his chin. "And I think you are getting a bit old for chasing college degrees."

She grimaced, sucking in a deep breath, and once again balling her fingers inward toward her palms. The road she traversed had been a rather curvy and unfortunate series of twists and turns setting her on a difficult path. She felt certain he knew of it and intended to make her uncomfortable with the innuendo he cleverly laid before her.

"Are we ever too mature to learn, Mr. Gray?"

A lopsided half-smile turned up the edge of his lip on one side. "Perhaps; perhaps not. Intention is what truly matters."

Madeline met his gaze with as much steel in her own as she could muster. "Then, may I ask, what is your intention for this meeting?"

William Gray tilted his head and lowered his eyelids. A full minute of silence passed between them before he glanced up again. A change seemed to have occurred in him. His eyes now sparkled where they had just been stormy.

"We both have something we need and can't seem

to get our hands on. Perhaps we can reach an amicable agreement." Leaning across the desk, he shortened the distance between them.

Madeline couldn't imagine what he might need of her. William Gray was a wealthy man. She was simply a photographer who received work in spurts and starts between college classes. Her recent gig at Jenkins Jewelers, photographing pieces of estate jewelry, had been the most profitable in a while. "I can't give you final say on the thesis. I'm sorry if that is what you are implying, but—"

"No, that isn't what I need."

"What then?"

"I understand you are quite the talented photographer, and I find I am in need of one."

"There are a number of photographers in our area…" She felt her brows furrowing. What could be so difficult to work with that he had trouble getting his hands on a good one?

"But none I trust, who are willing to return. I require someone with enough time to capture what I want in film, while granting silence about the assignment."

Pulling back from him, she thought about the implication of his statement. He must want something obscene photographed. Perhaps he had a weird fetish, or worse. A chill enveloped the room as a sinister pall fell between them. "I won't sacrifice my morals to get into the journals. I'm sorry if I wasted your time." Madeline started to rise.

He began to laugh, and it sounded a bit more genuine than his previous attempt. "Oh no. Please stay seated. It's nothing like that."

"Then why would other photographers refuse you?"

"Others haven't been presented the offer."

"So why me?" It made no sense. William Gray could have gotten the best photographers in all of South Carolina at a moment's notice, unless something was amiss.

"The subject is delicate. I must have your sworn silence in order to even mention what it is I want photographed." He hit a key on the computer's keyboard and the attached printer sprang to life, spitting out a document. "This assures you will not divulge the nature of my request." He pointed to the line requiring her signature.

Lifting it with shaky hands, Madeline read every sparse word before she would even dare agree to its terms. "And if I sign this, you will agree to allow me access to the journals?"

"Yes, of course."

"Then add that to the contract, and we'll both sign."

Hastily typing a few lines, he printed out a new contract with the request she had made, and scribbled his name across the bottom. She read it again, and signed as well. "So what is it you want photographed?"

"Captain William Gray." He grinned from ear to ear as he said the name.

"That's impossible. He's dead—"

"But not gone. At least, not from these grounds. He'll show up and I want you here when he does."

"How will we know when he is going to show up?"

William Gray talked on, ignoring her question. "Here's my proposition. You stay here, as my guest, upon the very grounds you seem so curious about. When he shows up, you'll capture his image for me."

He poked the desk with his forefinger. Leaving the finger planted there suggested he needed to hold it down to prevent its levitation. "In the meantime, you can photograph the ball and all of my lovely guests enjoying themselves. Only those pictures I approve will be sent out to the newspapers. Understand?"

Stunned, Madeline feared it was she who might suddenly float off the floor. Of all the things he could have said, of all the requests he could have made, her staying here was the last she saw coming. "I didn't come prepared to stay. And I'm not sure I should," she mumbled.

"Then leave with the tour group, and return when you are ready. Otherwise, you will have to make do with the already-public information on Captain Gray."

"But a ghost? What makes you think there even is a ghost for me to capture in a picture?"

He pointed to the document she had just signed. "Everything we have said, or will say past the signing of this contract, is strictly confidential, and not to be repeated."

She nodded.

"He is haunting me. He is haunting this house."

William Gray got up and walked over to the window, staring out at something she couldn't quite identify. His gaze seemed otherworldly—neither up, nor down, nor out really, but into a vortex of a memory, or a vision.

"He always makes an appearance at the ball. He ruins photographs. If you were unaware, no photographer has ever handled the ball twice. I refuse it. Their collective shadows and fog belong to me and cannot be made whole enough to get a full rendering."

"Are you sure it's him? Maybe it's another spirit, an evil one. Is it dangerous?" Madeline knew the legends about ghosts in and around the area. She had grown up with tales of them sprinkled, as easily as salt on their ubiquitous watermelon, throughout locals' conversations.

The thought of facing one seemed ominous. Fear crept up her spine and hooked a long indelicate finger around her midsection, making her cringe.

His words were icy. "It's him. I can feel it."

"What does he want?"

"I don't know. Look at it this way; maybe you can talk to him in person. He completely takes over my body. He doesn't talk *to* me, but *through* me."

"I see." She slowly rose and turned to face the door. "How long do I have to consider this offer?"

"I expect a yes or no answer before the tour departs—say in about fifteen minutes."

On cue, the voice of the tour director wafted upward as she warned the sightseers should collect their belongings and prepare to exit.

"That isn't much time," she protested. Madeline thought this guy might be a little crazy.

"I don't have time to spare. The ball is scarcely around the corner, and I need a photographer. You need access to the journals which might put your name on the academic map."

"How long would the stay be for?"

"As long as it takes."

Madeline swallowed hard, knowing no real choice existed, but felt trapped. She either had to accept his terms and make plans to stay for an undetermined amount of time, in the house she secretly desired spending a few nights in, or walk away from her project permanently. *Is there really a choice?*

If she refused to stay, she would have to come up with another thesis. She had spent every spare minute on Captain Gray. Madeline stared at the stubborn William Gray, now glaring at her with arms crossed over his chest.

A slight upturn at the corners of his mouth made him appear to enjoy the turmoil he was putting her through way too much. She wouldn't call it a smile though. It more closely resembled a smirk.

The ancient mariner's clock, ticking in the background, filled her with foreboding. Every second brought her nearer the decision determining her next phase in life. She set her jaw and turned her back toward him for a moment as she gathered her courage.

When she spun around to face him, she stared him square in the eye. "Your answer is *no* then. I need a definitive period of time. I can't accept such open terms."

He inhaled sharply. "Twelve weeks should do it, if that is definitive enough for you?"

"Three months?" Her voice went up at least two octaves. "Have you lost your mind? I can't stay out here for three months!"

"How long are you willing to stay? Most writers' residencies are twelve weeks or longer, but if—"

"Four weeks," she declared, thinking it barely enough time to finish here and still comb through the journals by graduation in May.

"Eight," he countered.

She bit her lip. "Six, and not one more day."

"Six it is, beginning the day of the Azalea Ball." Their eyes locked, connecting for a brief moment. His icy blue orbs twinkled with a flash of merriment.

"Bring something appropriate to wear to the ball." The features in his face softened, slackening from their tightly-clenched position. Sitting down, he scribbled on a piece of paper, slid it into an envelope—which he sealed before handing it to her—and rose again, taking her gently by the arm and indicating the stairs. "Until then."

She nodded, glancing at the fine linen stationary envelope bearing a "G" crest. Her thumb caressed the embossment, feeling its bulge against the heavy weight of the paper. The envelope declared her the official ball photographer.

Madeline couldn't remember how she got back down the stairs, or out the door. Her mind raced faster than the tour van back to the congested area outside of the low country estates. She needed to pack, find something suitable to wear, and get someone to water her plants. But of all the details requiring her attention, the one gaining the largest portion of it was what she would wear, and where she might find something suitable on her limited budget.

Something else stabbed at her conscience. What was going to happen when she failed, as she was sure to do, to capture the ghost of Captain Gray?

Renee Canter Johnson

Chapter 3

Mrs. Jenkins squealed with excitement about the unexpected invitation extended to Madeline to Pine Island. "He might wish to sell some of the Grays' jewelry. I've heard it's magnificent. You will tell him about my store, won't you dear?"

"Yes, yes of course." Madeline's mind wasn't on jewelry, not even the new pieces she was hurriedly photographing.

"There's rumored to be more than a piece or two of rare vintage in the secret vaults of that antebellum house."

"I'm sure," she replied, still thinking about the strange conversation she'd had with the present-day William Gray.

"You must impress upon him the current market for estate jewelry and the trustworthiness of your employer in bringing the best prices for such items, in the event he ever wants or needs to part with any of it."

"Of course I will, Mrs. Jenkins," Madeline assured the older lady. She paused, her mouth partially open trying to form words. "I…you…I mean…"

"Whatever it is, say it straight out," Mrs. Jenkins advised.

"I was wondering about something. It isn't important. But…"

Mrs. Jenkins stood tall, hands on her hips. "Out

with it."

"Do you believe in ghosts?"

"Ghosts?" She appeared lost for a minute. Undoubtedly, it was the last thing she was expecting to hear Madeline say.

And why shouldn't she be shocked? They were talking about the upcoming stay at Pine Island and jewelry and William Gray. Madeline's mind seemed to be the only space where all of those things meandered together, but had now taken a random path.

It actually even surprised Madeline to hear the word *ghost* tumble out of her own mouth. She'd have to be careful, or she'd find herself in violation of the agreement she had signed. William Gray now dictated any disclosure of the story of the haunting of Pine Island, yet she needed some feedback on the subject.

"Yeah, like the ones rumored to haunt the *USS Harvest Moon* site at the bottom of the bay."

Mrs. Jenkins lost her expression of expectation. In its place a stern and serious countenance glazed her features. "I come from the sturdy stock of Gullahs from the Charleston area. We have a long history of living with our dead and bringing them with us throughout our journeys in this world."

"Gullahs? Aren't those the basket weavers down on Market Street?"

"They are much more than that, Madeline. They might sell baskets on the street side, but if you know what to ask for, you can get a small cloth sack of specially blended herbs accompanied by the proper words to chant to send away unhappy spirits, or thwart an evil eye, or make warts disappear." Her dark eyes glistened in her cinnamon face. The curly locks surrounding her now-sunken cheeks had long been tinged with gray.

"Have you ever bought such a sack?"

"Buy? No. Sell? Quite a few."

"You? No way." Madeline laughed at the thought. She finished with the ruby necklace and slipped it back into the glass-protected case.

"Oh yes. When I was a girl, I used to accompany my grandmother to the market. She would sit and weave sweetgrass into baskets while calling out in Gullah language to the folks she recognized. Occasionally she would sing out a bit differently, and I knew the code. I would grab a tiny lidded basket from the back storage and slip a sack of the special powder or herbs inside, along with a written chant or other specific instructions to accompany the contents. Then I would tie a black ribbon around it and present it to the customer." Her face softened with the memory and she seemed a hundred years away.

"And would it work? Did the customers ever come back and say it did or didn't have the desired effect?"

"If they weren't satisfied, she'd call to me to do the same again, only then I would hold my hand over it and say a few words in Gullah—a mixture of languages from the Caribbean, French, and English—as she had taught me. Either it worked then, or they simply didn't want to return and embarrass a child."

"What would you say?"

"It's been a long time. But gramma said I had the touch of the 'voodoo priestesses.' What a thing to tell a child!" The sound of her guffawing rang out through the store.

"You don't happen to know a spell to locate

evening gowns for broke, middle-aged college students moonlighting as photographers do you?"

Mrs. Jenkins whispered a few things in a secret language and then motioned for Madeline to follow her through the storage room and into the back of the store. A series of closets lined the wall, and in one of them, hanging on padded wooden hangers in natural fiber bags, gowns of distinction waited. "I wore each of these beauties myself some thirty—maybe forty—years ago, but never to the Grays' Azalea Ball at Pine Island..."

Her words faded. *Did she forget what she meant to say next?* Madeline wondered.

Then they returned to her, after a pregnant pause, as she revealed another ball gown. "But they should have been because they were—and are—divine." She tossed aside the drab overwrapping and dangled a sparkly long shift.

"Vintage perfection," Madeline cooed. Mrs. Jenkins' assortment sprang to life as their protective dreary covers slipped away revealing a kaleidoscope of silks, chiffons, sequins, and laces. "But do you think I can wear any of them?"

"Honey, I wasn't always this thin," the older lady said. "I used to be curvy and vivacious, just like you."

She meant it as a compliment, though Madeline knew today's woman couldn't be considered fashionable unless a size two or smaller. Her size ten body—often a twelve, though she refused to buy a fourteen even when she should have—made her feel pudgy on most days, and quite large on the others.

Mrs. Jenkins insisted. "Go, try them on."

The fit surprised Madeline. She couldn't have chosen better in a shop for couture. Most of them skimmed her perfectly, seeming to be sewn for her figure.

"Take more than one," Mrs. Jenkins advised. "Since you don't know how long you will be there, you can't know how many you will have occasion to require."

Madeline shook her head, pushing the proffered gowns back into the direction of their owner. "Oh, but what if something happens to one of them? I couldn't take more than one, Mrs. Jenkins; really I couldn't."

But her mentor insisted and would settle for nothing less than a full endowment of her frocks upon Madeline. "If I can't go to the ball, at least my dresses can. Besides, do you think I'll ever wear these again?"

It was decided.

Chapter 4

William watched from his office window as the vans filled with caterers, decorators, florists, and their wares all rounded the final curve onto his property. Rented crystal, silver, china, and numerous serving platters and warming trays were now being carried up to the entrance.

He could have used his own, the family heirlooms with the giant 'G' crest in the center. But so much of it had been lost to Hurricane Hugo he feared losing even another single piece during a party.

Scribbling onto a legal pad, he added *pictures of family china* to his list of things to have Madeline Waters photograph while she was staying at Pine Island. *It will give her something to do while she waits for...*

Rubbing his eyes, he wondered if she would really show up. Perhaps his request had been too odd, too strange. Who made such demands?

William continued to stare down the driveway. He didn't know what kind of car she might be arriving in, but he wanted to see her the minute she did.

This was how he had watched all of his guests arrive. At least, it was since the unexplainable incident of nearly a decade ago. Maybe he was losing his mind and...

No, he wasn't going crazy. Most of the time he was

completely normal and in possession of a sharp memory. But around the wrong people—or was it the right people? It was impossible to tell which triggered an episode—he seemed to morph into the Captain himself.

He had been told stories of his sudden flashes of anger. Apparently he had pushed one guest and denied him access. William confessed to having had too much to drink before the guests arrived, when in fact he had consumed nothing but coffee and water up to then. It had taken two therapists to assure him he wasn't losing his mind.

And though he had told no one of his suspicions, he knew it was the ghost of Pine Island entering his body and making him act at its will. How could he prove it? And unless he did, how could he rid the house of its presence?

Instinctively he knew Madeline Waters held the answer. Not only was she a photographer, but she had a deep curiosity about the long-deceased mariner whose legacy he'd been bequeathed. She *was* the key to unlocking this mystery. He felt it in his bones.

William began to pace again. What if she changed her mind? If she hadn't decided against it, where was she? He watched every flicker, every strike of sun on metal, from his window-side perch, each failing to produce the one person he hoped to see more than anyone else.

****

Madeline Waters packed up her car and headed onto the lonely stretch of swampland and forest sandwiched between the city and Pine Island. The estate's gates, standing open, relieved her of the necessity to be buzzed in. She pulled all the way up to the front, where she had seen the last van stopping for unloading, and cut the engine.

A young man ran at her, waving his arms. "You can't park here. This is solely for staff use."

"I am part of the staff tonight." She flashed her invitation labeled *photographer* at him. "If you'll help me, it won't take long for me to unpack my things."

"How much help can one require to unload a camera?" He paused, and stared at her for a moment. "When you've finished, pull this heap around to the gravel lot." He pointed to the side of the house and disappeared.

How rude! He could have helped me, she thought as she dragged the various mismatched luggage containing enough garments, beauty treatments—wishing any of them worked—camera and lenses, laptop, and the long garment bag housing Mrs. Jenkins' dresses, from her trunk. After parking her car in the specified lot, she walked back to find all of her belongings missing.

In a moment of panic, she ran around the side of the house, thinking she might have gotten confused as to which entrance she had left them. But on calmer examination, she realized only one faced the driveway. Someone had moved her things. Yes, that had to be it.

She raced back to the door to find the older lady she had met on her first trip out to Pine Island there. "Ms. Waters?"

"Yes, hello," she managed, though already in a sweat from the running around and the sudden panic.

"Follow me. Mr. Gray has left instructions for you to be taken immediately to your room, where you can get acclimated and unpacked before this evening's events."

"My luggage," she turned and pointed to the spot where she had last seen the missing pieces.

"Your luggage is waiting for you there," she said coolly. Suspicious eyes suggested she couldn't imagine why Madeline would think otherwise.

"Of course." She let out the constricting breath she had been holding since realizing her things were not where they'd been left. "We haven't been officially introduced. I'm Madeline."

"I remember, and I'm Mrs. Farthing," the woman said. "I've been with the Grays most of my adult life."

Her comment sounded territorial. *Had she meant it as a warning?*

Mrs. Farthing turned and mounted the stairs— winding round and round. A light source beamed downward from high above.

Madeline fell into step behind her, climbing upward through the center of the house.

"I hope you won't mind the climb," the woman said. "Your room is on the fourth floor, just beneath the cupola." She exited the staircase and walked along a hallway. There she opened a door and motioned for Madeline to enter.

"I'm afraid you won't get much in the way of service today. Everyone is busy preparing for this evening's event. But you should find whatever you need and if you can't, someone in the kitchen should be able to assist. I really must get back there myself and oversee the preparations." The woman started to retreat.

"Mrs. Farthing?" Madeline called out to her.

She had already taken a few steps toward the stairs

and with a huff, doubled back.

"Wait, please. I was hoping to see Mr. Gray. Do you know where I might find him? I have a few things to go over with him before the party."

"You won't be seeing Mr. Gray today. He never shows until his party is well under way, well, not since…" She looked off into the same space Madeline had seen William Gray staring into during her initial visit. "Never mind. Mr. Gray hired you for your expertise. I'm sure you'll know what to do."

Mrs. Farthing shut the door firmly behind her and disappeared too quickly for additional questions to be asked. But her comments made Madeline more curious. What had she meant by "*not since?*" Not since what? What had happened to dissuade William Gray from manning the door at his own party?

And why had he hired her? Expertise? She had no expertise in *live* photography. Sure she had captured images of people at parties, but not for official documentation. If one wasn't framed exactly right, it hadn't mattered. Why had he chosen her for this project? Had another photographer been scheduled and backed out at the last minute with unforeseen reasons?

It seemed odd to her to be awarded such a prestigious venue when she wasn't particularly well-known in the photography world. The thoughts ran rampantly through her mind as she settled her belongings into the armoires and dresser drawers. When she finished unpacking, she climbed to the top of the cupola to capture the view.

Madeline's body tingled with excitement as her eyes scanned across the water onto an endless blue horizon on one side and a dappled green forest on the other. It could have been 1810. No other buildings or structures of any kind obstructed the infinite landscape. Most likely all that she surveyed comprised the original plot of land she now stood atop—perched in its crown like a jewel dangling in a queen's tiara.

The undulating water in her line of vision made her sway. Madeline imagined the feeling might be similar to boarding a ship—anchored firmly in the dock, yet buoyant enough to shift and give. The fantasy was easier to maintain the further out she gazed.

She could almost picture herself bobbing in a boat in the distance, glancing back at this spot and seeing herself here, waving up to the double. Lifting a hand, she waved back. "*I'm here,*" she whispered, feeling the rush of a breeze against the back of her hand.

Turning to capture the cooling wind on her face, she saw instead a great spiral of dust or sand. It spun in front of her, whipped by an invisible zephyr, until it became almost opaque.

Was it fog? she wondered. Stretching out her palm toward the gust, it surged forward to meet her quivering fingertips. Without stopping at the solid wall of her skin and bones, it billowed through her body, making her heart flutter and her flesh dance—the strangest sensation she could ever remember having.

For a moment she was frozen to the floor, too shocked to think or react. Static electricity crackled the hairs on her arms. Her breath changed from smooth inhalations to frenzied pants. This wasn't an ordinary occurrence. It was something strange and supernatural.

Her mind suddenly kicked into gear, unlocking the grip fear had temporarily imposed on her. Instinct-driven, she fled to the safety of the floors below with the teams of workers doing sound checks and polishing silver.

Madeline sought William Gray, to no avail. He had either gone to town, or to sea, but was definitely not on the immediate grounds, unless sealed in behind one of the closed doors on the upper floors. Someone slid a tray of champagne glasses into her hands, with a sneer and a comment about making herself useful.

She meant to protest but found herself ignored by the others now engrossed in different tasks. Madeline did as directed and delivered the glasses to the center hall where a large fountain was being cleaned and decorated in preparation for the magnums of champagne that would flow through it. The inner workings of preparing for such an event amazed her, along with the knowledge she would be attending it, even if only as the photographer.

She snapped a few pictures of the comings and goings of trays on legs. Or so they appeared, as the heads of those to whom the legs belonged were lost behind the tall goblets, decanters, and platters of stacked ham or vegetables resting on the giant serving dishes.

The hubbub wound down along with the clock. As the sun raced west, Madeline attacked the climbing of the stairs to make herself presentable for the evening. When she returned to the center hall and massive ballroom, the transformation had been completed, with none of the stresses or clatter of frenzied activity.

Elegance and grace defied the agitation of its creation. It seemed wholly different in the evening than in the light of day. The ambiance was complete, with the last vase in place, music emanating from the orchestra on the balcony ledge, softly accented pink bulbs overhead, and candles flickering behind glass. Guests had begun arriving and a soft buzz of conversation rose up from small gatherings.

Trying to be inconspicuous, Madeline snapped the arrivals of the bright-eyed and well-heeled guests—the intimate pairs and trios lost in their whispers. She scanned the crowd for a glimpse of William Gray, anticipating he would be there to greet his guests in spite of what Mrs. Farthing had said. But he was nowhere to be seen, a fact that didn't appear to bother the others who were amusing themselves without their host.

Madeline walked around the interior in what she considered to be the prettiest of her borrowed gowns, an off-white Halston column. Plain and simple, not unlike herself, the cap sleeves hid enough of her upper arms to make them appear thinner. With her hair up and wearing the bronze heels she had purchased, she thought she looked the best she ever had.

A firm grip on her shoulder caused her to spin around. "Did you misunderstand the meaning of unobtrusive?" her host asked. His sudden appearance was accompanied by thinly veiled hostility in his voice.

She met his eyes. They had lost the twinkle she recalled from the end of their previous meeting. Now they were prismatic pools, steaming with intensity.

"Did you want me to hide in the cellar and use a telescoping lens," she asked through clenched teeth.

His shoulders raced upward toward his ears as his chest heaved. "Of course not, but neither did I expect you to point *that* thing up into the faces of my guests." He gestured to her camera with one hand and waved toward the growing crowd with the other before stalking off.

Shaking from his rudeness and feeling even more out of place, she quickly scanned for a friendly face. Finding none—at least none appearing to desire conversation with her—she turned her back to the throng of partiers and focused on the architecture of the ballroom.

Amazing thick molding defined every niche, doorway, window, floorboard, and ceiling. After capturing the beauty with both her eyes and camera lens, she ran her hand along a piece of it, feeling the etched carvings bump against her palm.

"It's early nineteenth century woodwork," a familiar voice said from behind her.

She didn't need to turn around to know it belonged to William Gray. "Hand carved, of course?" she said.

"Absolutely. Everything within these walls is of artisan quality." By the sound of subtle pride in his voice, he might have been the artist who had created the lovely pieces. Having regained his equanimity from their previous encounter, he was now almost pleasant and attractive. Perhaps he'd had an attack of sudden contrition.

Madeline could feel his presence behind her. He was standing close, so close he had only to whisper to have her hear what he was saying. She flushed with warmth, feeling the rush of hot blood to her face and a bead of sweat to her forehead, becoming speechless.

"Why don't we step out onto the terrace? We can talk better there."

She nodded, following his lead through the crowd and out into the cooler night air. The beautiful evening offered low humidity—a rarity in the area—and stars twinkled overhead. Chuckling, she realized it wouldn't have surprised her to learn William Gray had hired someone to hang them in the sky for the sole purpose of his party.

Music wafted up from the moon garden, a swath of white blossoms reflecting the light. "Care to dance?" He offered his hand in an apparent apology.

Madeline accepted. Did she imagine the sharp intake of his breath as he clasped his fingers around her palm? Or was it her own inhalation getting caught in her throat?

Her heart fluttered. Her eyes snapped quickly upward, finding his to be sparkling like aquamarine stones from the jewelry store. They had lost their previous coldness and his face had softened its tense expression.

"You are quite lovely tonight," he whispered, as they waltzed among the flowers.

She supposed she could understand how this version of William Gray could lure women into his net. If a person could believe the rumors, he hauled them back to the house until they failed to satisfy his short attention span. She hadn't seen the appealing side of him until now.

"And you are rather dashing yourself."

In a voice both soulful and wistful, he responded. "Dashing is a fine way to think of a sea captain."

His answer surprised her, having not shown up in any of her research. "Oh, I didn't realize you captained a ship."

"What do you mean?" he snapped, suddenly turning sullen again. "I do no such thing." He stopped abruptly and dropped his hands. He couldn't have been more brusque had she turned into radioactive waste. Mumbling to himself, he stalked off.

Madeline shook her head, trying to resolve the two different sides of William Gray. He seemed as pleasant as they came, until he wasn't; as charming as a storybook hero, until he turned into the villain; complimentary one moment, insulting the next.

She gave William Gray time to put a little distance between them before returning to the ballroom. All of the doors had been left open to allow a cross breeze to cool the house. It was such a lovely evening, she would have liked to stay on the terrace, but duty called.

There had been little discussion as to how many snapshots of the guests he desired, or what was either on or off limits. He had made it very clear he desired no up-close photography. With this singular request in mind, she kept a subtle distance between herself and her subjects, capturing them in action without their knowledge.

She'd caught a waltzing duo, her head back, the silken gown draping at an angle from her bent knees. There was the shot of two couples sharing a laugh, and another pair clinking glasses together in a toast. She snapped three men out on the terrace with cigars. A picture of the wait staff, in black and white, almost captured the effect that they all wore soft shoes, so they made no discernible sounds as they refilled platters of chicken and shrimp. She was sure the photo of the champagne fountain, with its bubbling cascade of golden liquid, backlit by the lights in the structure would be remarkable.

She wanted to capture a shot of William Gray, one

he would be proud of. He appeared to be avoiding her, though. Making her way back to the outer edge of the ballroom, Madeline simply observed the wealthiest of the Georgetown enclave of Millionaire's Row mingling with Charleston's elite. Old southern money mixed with the newest dollars to be found in the eastern part of the country. They had a swagger she didn't possess and a sense of belonging she would never have.

Two women had the nerve to actually laugh about her gown within earshot. "Can you believe someone would wear *that* outdated thing?" one asked.

"Talk about taking vintage to a whole new level," the other sneered. Apparently they did not see her beside the green wall of palms—acting as sentinels to the open doors—or did not care if they had.

Madeline's face flushed hot again. She had thought she looked nice in the vintage gown. *Who am I kidding?*

She lowered her camera, refusing to capture a picture of the haughty women. Leaving them out of the press should exact a little revenge. *How could anyone stand to be a part of such snobbery?*

Yet, William Gray seemed to be enjoying his guests. The sound of his laughter directed her to him. He was chuckling, head back, at the tales of one of his guests. *Of course he would find them entertaining,* she thought, *he's as arrogant as the rest of them.*

Frustrated and feeling as lonely as she ever had in her life, she ducked from behind the fronds and dashed out to the terrace. The table in the center of the outdoor living space was decorated with a spray of white peonies. Gardenias filled terra cotta pots. The pots, appearing to be as timeworn as the house, were covered in a patina only age and moss spores could achieve.

A wrought iron serving cart sat in a corner of the terrace. Crystal flutes, stems up and bowls down on a white linen cloth, sat in military formation next to an ice-filled silver bucket with three champagne bottles nestled in the chilly container.

After capturing a picture of the elegant outdoor table, Madeline headed down the path to the beach. She swiped the heeled shoes from her feet as soon as she cleared the dunes where sand spurs were less prone to pierce through her sensitive skin.

Waves crashed against the shore, making foamy lines of white across the dark water. Madeline turned from the beach to look back at the house awash in moonglow, glittering in artificial lighting. It made a lovely snapshot, though it filled her with emptiness as she realized how fake it all really was. She dreaded telling Mrs. Jenkins that although her dress had made it to the ball, it was about as welcome as Madeline was.

A chill passed through her, carrying the sensation she was no longer alone. She turned left and right, but saw no one or nothing save a white mist of sea spray. Her mind was playing tricks on her, turning the mist into the shape of a body walking atop the ocean waves. Although she attempted to capture the image, it didn't show in her viewfinder. Only the waves rolling ashore were visible.

She watched for a moment more, before deciding she'd had enough for one night. Slipping silently back into the Gray Estate ballroom, she could have been a spirit herself, wandering around unseen. Nobody spoke to her or even acknowledged her presence with a nod.

Apparently they were used to being the subjects of

a camera lens and were unaffected by its presence. Madeline strolled out to the front of the house, waiting silently for the crowd to start dispersing, in order to capture their departure.

Her chest thumped with agitation. Was it due to the rude guests, the unfamiliar surroundings, or the unpredictable behavior of William Gray? Not likely, she reasoned, as her attention span slipped away from the exiting crowd. Scrolling backward through the frames, she couldn't resist looking once more for the odd shape of a figure atop the water.

Chapter 5

William lingered in bed the following morning. It was his favorite day of the year, the day *after* the loathsome party. He had only a few moments of no discernible memory, and only for brief amounts of time this year.

One jarring memory was with his houseguest, Madeline Waters. He had been talking to one of his best friends and the next thing he knew, he was waltzing in the moon garden with the photographer. She was responding to something he had said, something along the lines of him being a sea captain. What in the world had he said to her?

He couldn't remember. William didn't even know how they had come to be dancing alone on the terrace.

He probably should try to see her today, make gentle conversation while waiting to see if she mentioned anything strange. She might bolt, if things had been too intense.

But he was tired and lethargic. Turning over, he hit the remote that lowered the room-darkening shades and lulled him back to dream land.

****

Madeline took breakfast in the sunny kitchen, dining alone. Coffee was at the ready on a server, along with freshly squeezed orange juice and a steamer full of grits and shrimp. Another housed soft biscuits and a third offered scrambled eggs. Small crystal bowls of strawberry jam and blackberry preserves resided at both ends of the serving table. A thick slab of softened butter rested beneath a dome and a bee-hive shaped ewer drizzled honey from its spout the instant she tipped it over.

She ate slowly, hoping to see William Gray. The pictures from the party had already been uploaded onto her computer and she was organizing them into files labeled for the different areas they represented; preparations, arrivals, decorations, activities, departures.

A few guests, still in their party apparel, straggled in, disheveled and bleary-eyed. Apparently they had stayed over after having a bit too much to drink. They nodded at her but made no attempt at conversation.

Mrs. Farthing returned to remove the items from the serving table. Madeline knew this was her signal to move along. Scooping up her laptop, she retreated to her room where she stayed for another hour before the urge to get moving set in.

Apparently, William Gray wasn't in a hurry to speak with her. Grabbing her camera, she set off for the path leading to the beach. It seemed different in the brilliant white light of day than it had in the romantic star-lit night. She stood at the spot she had visited the previous evening, suspecting she had been rather fanciful.

Of course waves churned white froth and foamy crests. It didn't mean it was the body of a ghost coming for her. It was all the talk about Gullah legends from Mrs. Jenkins, coupled with William Gray's assertion of sometimes being possessed by the spirit of his long-dead ancestor that had her imagination working overtime. She hadn't found one picture in the lot with a ghostly image fogging the corner.

William Gray was either laughing his head off at her gullible nature, or he was suffering a mental collapse. Possibly, both things were going on simultaneously.

Madeline jogged back up the path, determined to explore the grounds. If she intruded on some private space, surely the recluse would turn up to dispel her of her notions of becoming too intimately acquainted with her new home for the next six weeks.

****

William stretched before throwing on some jogging pants and a T-shirt. He felt better after putting the party behind him and getting some much-needed sleep. The house was hopping once again by the time he descended the stairs.

"Anything to eat?" he asked Mrs. Farthing. She was busy polishing the tops of the mahogany tables. Although she wasn't assigned cleaning duties, as her job was purely to oversee the staff now, she always stayed busy.

"You missed breakfast. And it was your favorite, too." She didn't lift her head from its angled position as she scrubbed with the micro-fiber cloths until the serving table shone as it must have when brand new.

"Shrimp and grits? Please say you saved some for me."

"Of course I did. Covered plate on the second shelf of the fridge."

He pulled the plate out and made a few sounds of appreciation. "You know you're the best, right?" he called out to her.

"Yeah, yeah. Put it in the form of a raise," she teased back with him, the way she had for more years than he could count.

"I don't suppose you've seen the house guest?" He knew Doris Farthing didn't miss anything. If Madeline Waters was up and moving about, she would know.

"Which one?" She ceased the endless polishing and turned toward him, hands perched on her hips. "Seems we've had a rather steady stream of people seeking coffee, toast, and headache medicine this morning."

"There's always a few who fail to read the request about furnishing a designated driver."

"Good thing you allow them to spend the night here. Otherwise, the causeway would be littered with people stuck in the soft marshes alongside the road."

"I wouldn't want anyone to get hurt or injure someone else. Don't need a tragedy on my conscience."

The sound of someone closing one of the entryway doors echoed through the house.

"Could that be the person you're searching for?" Doris jerked her head toward the sound as she stowed the cleaning liquid beneath the sink.

"Might be." He leaned forward to peep through the glass doors. They had been thrown open the night before, making the entire space part of one huge ballroom.

"Hello," he called out. "Ms. Waters?"

The sound of her footsteps coming toward them resounded clearly.

She appeared a bit disheveled and wind-whipped, her curls sticking out in various directions. "Good...afternoon," she said, checking her watch.

"Been out enjoying the pretty weather?"

"Yes, actually I have. But not before compiling your pictures from last evening. Would you care to look them over? I can be back with my laptop in only a minute or two."

"Not today. We'll have plenty of time for that later." He assumed she would have several with the ubiquitous trail of smoke and vapor, and he had no desire to discuss the implications in front of anyone else.

"Well then, I was wondering if you would mind if I take rubbings of the stones in the cemetery."

"A rubbing?"

"Yes, you know, where you rub a pencil over a piece of paper to transfer the etching onto it." She made a quick back and forth motion with her hand.

"Oh, a rubbing…" Where was his mind? Of course he knew what a rubbing was. "All of the stones, or one in particular?" His family cemetery was a mixture of ancient thick concrete slabs over shallow graves, laying behind one of the low brick walls, and a more modern mausoleum for the future family members to find their everlasting peace.

Madeline blushed, the color instantly making her look younger. "I noticed a lone grave lying outside of the confined area. It had a most compelling epitaph."

"Ah…" William wiped his mouth and leaned back in the chair. "So you found Magdalene Gray."

She pulled out a chair and joined him at the table. He noticed her dirt-embedded fingernails. Apparently self-conscious, she tugged them inward toward her palms. "Guess I got a little overeager pulling the ivy away from the stone so I could photograph the inscription. But I'd love to have a rubbing." Madeline turned the viewfinder toward him, showing the poem inscribed on the stone.

"Magdalene Gray, thy light is naught,
amidst thy wandering souls,
thee searcheth what is fore'er lost,
and thy bell mournfully tolls."

He read it aloud, not needing the words before him in order to recite it by rote memory.

"Impressive," she said. "Is it who I think it is? Is this the grave of Captain William Gray's wife?"

"Yes, the one and only."

"I read she died under mysterious circumstances. One rumor suspected the Captain may have killed her after returning from a long voyage and finding her with a neighbor's son."

"I suppose we'll never know." The suggestion his ancestor may have committed murder irritated William.

"Would you walk with me to the site while I get the rubbing? I'd love to discuss a few things with you."

He hesitated, though only for a moment. This Waters woman probably wanted to inform him of the strange shadows in her pictures. There might be a few decent enough to forward to the newspapers. He never allowed them to send their own photographers.

"All right. But we need to be quick about it." He retrieved a piece of paper and a pencil from the kitchen desk and they walked quietly to the single lonely space, away from all the other stones and markers, in the graveyard.

"Why is she out here all alone? He didn't remarry. Or at least by my research, he didn't."

William shrugged. "Maybe he simply changed his

mind later about where to put the cemetery."

Madeline rested her hand against the stone. "It's warm," she said.

"Probably absorbs the heat from the sun," he explained.

"What sun?"

It was true. There was very little sun in the small corner where ivy, a shade-loving plant, had rooted and thrived. It was now carpeting the entire space beneath their feet.

****

William was unmistakably dubious. He didn't seem to share her opinion of the shade being too omnipresent in April for much sun to get through, at least enough to warm the stone. She had only just freed it from its leafy vine covering.

Madeline turned back toward the stone. A wisp of steam rose from its slightly pointed apex and wafted gently toward her. *Steam? Maybe in July, but definitely not in April,* she reasoned.

She backed away from it, keeping her eye on the strange phenomenon resembling a ribbon of smoke or steam or fog. She couldn't decide which most accurately described it.

William seemed to be unaffected by the anomaly, squatting by the stone to take the rubbing for her. She wasn't even certain he had seen the odd wisp.

It floated right past him, coming close to her face. The chill it left in its wake ruled out steam and smoke. It had to be latter of the three, she decided. It had to be fog.

Yet, it was the only bit to be found. *One streamer of fog? Was that even possible?*

A long, cold finger wrapped around Madeline's cheek. Her heart palpitated in an uneven rhythm, drumming an odd cadence in her chest and causing sweat to bead along her forehead. She was frozen to the ground, unable to make her feet move as the strange wisp made chilly contact.

It moved along her arm and touched her hand as she watched it slipping through her flesh, entering on one side and exiting on the other. A scream formed. It built, silently, and remained without sound, her entire vocal system shutting down.

And then it was gone. It didn't float away; it simply faded to nothing right in front of her. With its disappearance went her inability to move. Madeline shot toward the house, running as swiftly as her feet could carry her.

William was on her heels, calling her name. She was sure of it. She heard the sounds of her name. "Madeline, Madeline wait."

She couldn't stop. On a mission to put as much space and ground between her and the mirage as possible, she nearly ran over Mrs. Farthing.

The older woman was taking a giant bowl of vegetable trimmings and coffee grounds from the kitchen to the composter for the gardener. "Good grief," she yelled, yanking the bowl into her chest as one might cuddle a football. "Watch where you're going. Slow down; how about it?"

"Sorry," Madeline called over her shoulder.

She could hear the woman grumbling about her soiled shirt right before she shouted after her. "You can be thankful it is near the end of my shift!"

"Madeline, stop," William called. "What

happened? What is wrong?"

She stopped at the stairs trying to catch her breath. She was being silly. There had to be some logical explanation.

William caught up with her. "What the devil happened to you? Did you get stung by a bee or something?"

"You didn't see it? You didn't see the vapor, or the fog or mist, or whatever the devil it was rising up from the stone?"

"No. I didn't see anything. I was trying to capture this rubbing for you." He held it out to her, confusion on his face. "Let's get you a sip of water. You can tell me about it."

Madeline did her best to explain, in human words, the inhuman experience she had seen and felt. She half-expected him to guffaw and tell her she was crazy.

William listened with rapt attention. He nodded and absorbed the details—the sensation of cold, the finger of fear, the ability of the smoke to waft throughout her body—giving her no sign of disbelief. And then he grinned.

It infuriated her. How dare he amuse himself at her expense? "I wasn't trying to be funny," she snapped.

"No, I didn't think so," he assured her. "It's just…" He paused for a moment. "Do you have any idea how long I have waited for another human being to experience some of the same things as I? Can you see how this is the first time in years I have felt less than a bit crazy?"

"Well, if it is validation you are seeking, consider it received. That was the spookiest thing I've ever encountered." She turned away from him and started up the steps.

William followed. "Let me accompany you," he whispered. "You seem shaken."

She glanced backward. "Who wouldn't be?"

He matched her pace, slowly ascending the stairs floor by floor, until reaching the one beneath the cupola.

Madeline turned to continue toward her room and he touched her arm.

"Come with me to the cupola."

She hesitated, recalling the previous day's scary venture into the bird's nest of the house. But William was with her this time, and she had her camera.

The cupola was the largest of its kind she had ever seen, topping the four story architectural marvel the way the centerpiece of a magnificent wedding cake might crown its top layer.

In fact, the house reminded her of a wedding cake with its tall center made wide at the bottom with the porches, balconies feathering off the remaining three stories in graduated widths, narrowing as they reached the uppermost floor, the decorative cupola perched atop the meringue-colored structure as delicately as piped white icing.

From this vantage point, she could see further than the eye from ground level could discern. The edges of the horizon became an impressionist painting of swirls and melting colors. The azaleas were starting to develop brown tips, slightly past their prime, but still blazing the verdant landscape with dots of amazing pinks and reds and even bright oranges. From her top-of-the-world view, they resembled balls of color in a sea of green.

She walked around the cupola, gazing in the opposite direction, lifting a hand over her eyes to shield the reflecting sunlight, while looking out across the water. It shimmered in the bright rays, making it as dazzling as the cumulative diamonds in Mrs. Jenkins' showcase.

"What a spot." Madeline imagined witnessing a storm blowing in or a sailboat slicing through the full palette of blue. Lost in the vision of sunlight, water, and green expanses, the sudden whisper of breath on her neck took her by surprise.

Startled, she jumped and looked behind her, expecting to see William there. But he had his back to her, facing north. Her imagination suddenly appeared to be running away with her. *It's because of the incident in the cemetery,* she assured herself.

She exhaled the breath she had been holding since feeling the puff of something mistaken for another person. It met with the wind, assuring her she had only felt a slight breeze, a puff of air off the water. She brushed off the circumstance but started for the stairs anyway.

"I think I've had enough for one day..." Before she finished her sentence it dawned on her the sea was perfectly calm. Not a single ripple danced across the liquid surface. So why was a whirlwind blowing, like a small tornado, in only a corner of the cupola?

She wanted to flee, to follow her instinct to get out of this place teaming with its unnatural phenomena. But her curiosity got the better of her.

Unable to turn away from the spiraling breeze right before her eyes, she watched as the figure of a man formed. Two detachments split from the sides of the spiral forming arms. The top pinched together and bubbled out a head. The creature—formed from air and wind and seawater—stretched out his hands and reached for her.

Madeline wasn't sure which came first; the screaming or the running. She took the stairs two at a time, retreating to her room and bolting the door.

The sound of William's furious knocking reverberated inside of it. "Madeline, let me in."

"Go away," she ordered. "I've had enough."

"I need to talk to you. He seems more interested in you than me right now."

"No. Go away." Her fear was subsiding, leaving a vacuum seeking to be full once again. For a brief instant she felt empty and listless before a strange roiling and boiling and gurgling began to fester and stew, just as a pot of soup on an antiquated wood stove might. What filled her void was anger.

"Madeline please…"

"No. What do you want? What do you expect from me? How can I accomplish the task you desire when I can't even think in its presence?" She flung the forgotten camera from around her neck onto the bed. She could have easily snapped the picture and been done with William Gray and his spooky house.

"I'm sorry. I shouldn't have asked this of you." The knocking ceased, and the sound of William's footsteps retreating was all she could hear. And then there was nothing.

Chapter 6

Madeline didn't venture out of her room again until late in the day. She wanted to brush the events in the cupola off as being her imagination. Yet she knew she would never be able to. William had been with her. He had seen. He had warned her of it before she had even accepted the job.

Now she had to gather her courage and face the spirit, camera firmly in hand. Her stomach churned at the realization of what had to be done. She needed more courage than had ever been asked of her.

No, she thought, *that isn't true.* How much bravery had it taken to raise her son alone? How much had been required when her very young husband—still older than her by two years—decided he didn't want to be part of her life or their son's?

And how much courage had she mustered to return to college, after Jacob had grown up and left home? She leaned against the door and recalled the day in the briefest flash of her mind. Leaving Jacob, her nearly constant companion after the quick divorce, to his dorm mates had been agonizing. She had vowed not to cry, and hadn't until she reached the nearby restaurant where she sobbed so forlornly over a glass of wine the waitress had been frightened.

Madeline summoned her strength, calling it forth from the events of her life that had forged it within her.

She calmed herself now and steadied her camera, checking to make sure the belligerent toss onto the bed coverings hadn't knocked loose her settings. Then she hung it by the strap around her neck.

With a flashlight gripped firmly in hand, she unlatched the door and crept into the quiet hall. Each footstep took determination to proceed further. Both hands held the railing, nearly pulling herself upward.

A swirl of brilliant fuchsia painted the sky. Its glow illuminated the heavily-windowed cupola and spilled over onto the stairs. Halfway up, she spotted the lantern hanging from the tip-top of the center of the cupola. She focused on it, trying not to think of ghosts or William or fog or scary unexplainable wisps of mist with the ability to pierce through her flesh without leaving a mark.

Madeline stepped up onto the landing and marveled at its girth. The massive four-sided lamp must have been used as a beacon. She suspected it burned gas or oil. The rope attached to it coiled around a bulbous handle near the top of the wall. And next to the handle, also anchored to the wall, was an antique tin box—long and narrow—with a lid that appeared to lift and lower.

She had noticed, but hadn't checked out, a similar one beside the fireplace in her room and another larger one beside the fireplace in the dining room. While Madeline didn't consider herself an expert on antiques, it would have been impossible to be a history major and not learn a few things about period items.

Surely those lovely boxes were intended to hold matches. She tried the lid when she reached the section of wall where it hung. It wouldn't budge; probably rusted shut in the humidity and salty air. Madeline glanced around, absorbing the view.

It would be a spectacular sunset, one she intended to capture whether or not the strange phenomenon appeared. She turned on her camera and snapped a few experimental shots. Everything seemed to be working as it should, the images in the viewfinder being exactly as she expected.

The sky appeared touchable and alive, the first time Madeline had thought of it as not being perfectly firm in its position. Practically undulating, it quivered and raced toward dusk, the sun a ball of blazing charcoal. It dropped behind a cloud and lines of white split it into half-moon shapes.

The sky changed continuously, a perpetually fresh backdrop. It turned a dozen shades of gold mixed with orange by the lowering glow of the sun's descent beyond the horizon. She busily snapped the shutter in rapid succession, getting each change as it occurred, forgetting her fears.

"Twilight," Madeline whispered aloud, delighting in the indigo sky. Had she ever seen a night so deeply blue? It wasn't dark and it wasn't light, but a perfect mix of them, cobalt and ink.

A soft breeze wafted upward, warm and billowy. It brought with it a piece of Spanish moss. Quivering, in the form of an old man's beard, it floated across the cupola, bouncing on lips which could have been speaking to her. The mesmerizing feathery gray lace of the live oaks diffused whatever was left of her thinking mind.

In the absence of pure thought, the form of William Gray appeared as a shape from a projector, piercing the shadowy boundary of the earth's hold. He had grown stronger, this apparition, and stood clearly visible to her now.

"Magdalene," he whispered. Reaching for her, his hands slipped effortlessly through her body. "My Magdalene."

Even the words felt chilly, carpeting her body with a spray of goosebumps. She shook her head and reached for the camera, grabbing hold of a space of cold air instead.

He was there, against her body. She tried to maintain a physical connection, but her hands could not hold onto the rarified air forming his shape. Walking straight into her, the solid form of her body presented no barrier to him. He continued; past the frayed knit sweater and cotton blouse, past the layer of dermis and epidermis, past her ribs, and straight inside her chest.

At first, a strange frostiness spread throughout her abdomen as if she had swallowed a tray of ice cubes and they were sending their iciness from the inside out. And then the sensation warmed, growing steamy and bathing her in affection. She was too mesmerized to immediately fear what was happening. Feeling him inside of her chest, his great love overwhelmed her with emotion. Then he backed away, taking all of the sensations with him, leaving her empty and cold.

He stood before her for only a moment, a man in a wavy outline of powder and smoke. Fading to little more than that first fist of Spanish moss drifting in on the breeze, she realized it was the ghost of a man.

Without the great emotional bath inside of her to squelch the urge to fear, she began to shake, unable to hold her camera steady. The apparition moved forward once again. Madeline was too frightened to make a sound. The scream she wanted to make was there. It was trying to get out, but was trapped behind her suddenly swollen tongue and constricted throat. The man turned back into moss, twirling and spinning, until it finally disappeared into a thread of smoke.

Madeline stood rooted to the spot, unable to move. Darkness had all but devoured the remaining filaments of light. Somewhere deep inside of her, the strength to leave the cupola took over. Her hands trembled as she reached for the flashlight she'd had the foresight to bring with her. She fumbled with the switch, turned it on, and ran for the stairs. Fear grew with every shadowy shape formed along the walls in the tunnel of light emanating for only a few feet in front of her. Darkness remained behind and on both sides of the circle of battery-charged glow.

Bolting the bedroom door behind her once again, she sank against it. Her skin hadn't stopped crawling. It still tingled from the mysterious encounter. She had definitely experienced a ghost. Although she doubted locked doors would discourage the efforts of a nether world spirit who could enter through her chest, she felt better knowing the effort to throw a deadbolt had been put into action.

Sitting alone, reliving every detail of the uncanny meeting, a knock at the door sent her into another screaming fit.

"It is the butler, Ms. Waters. Mr. Gray is extending an invitation to you for dinner tonight—one hour from now in the private dining room."

Madeline, rousing from her fear-induced fit, offered apologies as she scrambled to unbolt the door.

"I'm sorry. I was dreaming, I suppose, and you startled me. Of course I'd love to share dinner with Mr. Gray."

"Very well then," the attendant turned to leave.

"But where is the private dining room?" She had only seen the huge dining room for official dinners.

"Right off the study, ma'am," he snarled.

Chapter 7

In spite of having invited her to dinner, William Gray seemed surprised when she entered the dining room. "Can I help you with something?" He sat the book he had been flipping through down. It landed with a thud against the wood of the table.

"I'm here as you requested—for dinner—your butler delivered the invitation to me about an hour ago."

"My butler?" He wore the curious expression of someone listening to a foreign language tape and being totally confused as to the meaning of the words being spoken.

"Tall man, white jacket, same curious expression as the one on your face right now." Madeline didn't know *what* was wrong with William Gray. She suspected he had taken up drinking, though he didn't appear to be drunk enough to forget invitations he had extended within the past hour. Perhaps he had hoped she would refuse his offer. "If you've changed your mind, I can come back later. I don't mind dining alone."

His shook his head and held up a hand. "Of course not. If I invited you to dinner, then you must stay."

Madeline had to bite her lip to keep from snarling at him. Her nerves were still a bit frayed, and she felt ready to snap at any minute. *"If"* he *invited her to dinner?* What kind of twisted thing was that to say? If he hadn't extended the invitation through his own employee, why would she be sitting here across from him?

For a moment she wondered if the butler had set them up, but he hadn't seemed particularly pleased about the whole idea either. So she said nothing, her default during times of self-protection.

William Gray didn't say much either, so the meal progressed in near silence.

What the conversation lacked, the food made up for. Delicious crispy rounds of fried green tomatoes, warm spinach salad, grilled local shrimp, pecan pie, and a peppery pinot grigio—tasting equally fantastic with the salad and the shrimp—rounded out the meal. In between bites and sips the few spoken words were awkward and forced.

"Is the meal satisfying to you?" he asked, his eyes darting from hers to the opposite corner of the room.

"Yes, quite." Due to a sudden attack of nerves, she wiped her mouth with the linen napkin more times than should have been necessary. He must have had a reason for inviting her to dine with him.

"Good," he responded and then quite a long time passed before either spoke again. "Shrimp is my favorite," he finally added.

She nodded, recalling the large serving dish of the marine crustaceans atop the grits at breakfast. Madeline waited for him to instigate the real topic of conversation—the ghost at Pine Island. But nothing of consequence was brought up. Nothing was mentioned about her research, or his family, or the reason a spirit might want to scare them away.

"Would you care for more wine?" He lifted the

bottle and poised it above her near-empty glass.

"Yes, please." She had already downed her first glass, although in small but frequent sips, and feared it would go to her head. But it was something to occupy her hands in between morsels of food, not to mention the diffusing effect it had on the fright she had experienced in the cupola.

William poured expertly, flicking his wrist with a graceful motion, avoiding any drips as he lifted it away. He refilled his own with the same ease. The butler rapped, with his knuckles, against the door jamb before entering, clearing his throat to announce his presence.

"Would either of you care for coffee?"

"None for me, thanks," William answered, "but maybe Ms. Waters…" He gestured toward her.

"No, thank you." She folded her napkin and placed it on the table. "The meal was wonderful though, the food delightful."

"I'll tell the cook," the servant replied, with no semblance of emotion. He began gathering dishes and placing them on the tray.

"You may leave the wine and our glasses," William instructed.

The man nodded, took the tray to the dumbwaiter, and buzzed it down.

Madeline wondered if she was supposed to ask questions of her host, if he was waiting for her to initiate the topic. She paused for a moment, giving the butler time to meet the tray in the kitchen, thus ensuring he wasn't poised outside their door.

"Mr. Gray…" she began.

His head jerked upward. He looked calmer than he had been before. Perhaps he, too, had been under stress and the wine and food had sated him.

"Let's take a walk, shall we?" He abruptly stood, interrupting her thoughts.

"Yes, of course."

He stepped aside so she might precede him out into the hall and along the staircase. In the great foyer, he lunged forward and opened the door ahead of her, smiling and nodding with old-fashioned gallantry.

Madeline inhaled the soft spring air made fragrant by the presence of hyacinths, and lilacs, and something else—jasmine, or maybe gardenia.

She started to ask, but then he leaned in toward her.

"You are lovely tonight," he whispered, "but then, you always are." His hand brushed her face as he moved a wayward strand of hair from her forehead. His eyes turned to warm pools of intensity and she felt trapped by them, unable to look away. "Magdalene," he called her, as he leaned closer in.

The memory of the ghost who had frightened her caused her to pull away from him.

A hand shot to his mouth as William's expression changed from sensual to confused, and then to irate. The anger flared—a spark on dry leaves—lapping the flame onto whatever lay in its wake. William pushed her from him and turned on his heels, leaving her in the garden, baffled as she watched him retreat to the house.

"Wait," she called after him.

It was no use. He didn't look back. When she followed after him, all she heard was a slam of an upstairs door.

Madeline took her still half-full glass of wine and retreated to her room on the upper story of the house, wondering what was wrong with her host.

Chapter 8

Madeline awoke to a headache and the realization she was no better off than she had been the night before. William Gray seemed to adore her one minute and despise her in the next. Did she simply imagine he was about to kiss her the previous evening in the garden? Had she misheard her name when he called it? Surely he didn't think her name was Magdalene—the same name as Captain William Gray's wife?

Something was definitely afoot in this old manse of a house, and she was expected to get to the bottom of it. Now more than ever the place called to her for attention and discovery. And if it was as unique as she expected it to be, she would have a better thesis than even she had bargained for.

Seeking coffee and headache medicine, she padded to the kitchen in her robe. Finding William Gray, fully dressed and spectacularly suave, came as an unexpected surprise.

"Good morning," he offered in a chipper tone that nearly angered her.

"Did you stay behind today to grant me a personal tour of the house and grounds?"

"Sorry, no. I have a business meeting and then a hot date. Don't wait up for me." He folded his paper back together and leapt from the bar, unfazed by her glare at him.

"I'll be out here all alone?" She tried to keep anger and frustration—mixed with a bit of fear—out of her voice, but heard her tone and knew she had failed.

"You're a big girl. I'm sure you can handle it." His flippant answer annoyed her further, pushing her patience beyond the level that a normal person could be expected to remain calm. Had he meant "big girl" as an insult to her size, or age? Either way, it would be hard to be seen as a compliment.

"Your ghost isn't showing up in my pictures. How do I photograph a spirit?"

"That's for you to figure out. Aren't you supposed to be in a graduate program?"

He drank his last drops of coffee and slammed the cup down on the countertop. "And if you run out of things to occupy your time, you can always photograph some of the family heirlooms throughout the house, such as the china."

William turned and bolted from the room in long strides leaving her to fume in his wake.

What the hell? She downed a cup of coffee and three pain relievers before dressing and taking it upon herself to wander around the grounds.

The fresh spring—fragrant with morning moisture on the blossoms—returned her senses to her. She had apparently misunderstood the evasive Mr. Gray's willingness to assist her with the project. Contemplating the knowledge he didn't wish to be inconvenienced by her, she found herself back onto the path that circled the house and led off to the beach.

Somehow, she had the distinct feeling she wasn't alone. A puff of breath, soft butterfly-strokes along her arm, the flutter of her heart, a twinkle of merriment as though someone had said something clever, all pointed to a mysterious stranger walking beside her—who simply wasn't there. Yet she sensed someone. How odd.

She shook off the feeling, determined to enjoy the brilliant day, a mid-April wonder of warmth and glistening water. Just beyond the wave break shells beckoned, and she rolled up her Capris. Madeline removed her shoes, balancing her camera inside one, and ventured out into the shallow water. It was still cool from the chilly nights and short days.

It was a treat to be on the island alone, even if the house itself was a bit spooky. She couldn't afford such luxurious surroundings on her budget. Most days at the beach were reached by public access and shared with a throng of other people.

Having this stretch of shore to herself made her smile. She waded around in the shallow pools of water, searching for seashells. It had always been her favorite beachside thing to do, Jacob's too. When he was small, they had spent entire days seeking the best ones.

A large glass bowl of various shells the two of them had collected over the years still graced her dining room table. Lettered olives had been his best-loved treasures. Madeline snatched a couple of them from the sand now, and carried them back to her shoes. Running her thumb along the brown zigzagged markings, she thought they did indeed resemble writing.

Maybe I'll find a sand dollar or a starfish. She walked back to the water's edge. Broken bits of these prizes were all she had been able to find on the heavily trodden public beaches. But here, on this private stretch, it could be possible.

She was staging a photo shoot of seashells in her mind as her eyes scanned for interesting ones. Snatching a rounded clam shell, a few elongated pointed augers, and a pair of angel wings, she added them to her growing collection.

If only I could find one unexpected trophy to add to the center. She rolled her Capris up a bit higher and stepped out further into the water. Making her way slowly through the sand's indentions and the incoming waves, the water soaked her legs and splashed onto her as the waves crashed closer and closer together. She tried to strike a balance between paying attention to the waves and to the hidden treasures buried on the ocean floor.

Each undertow carried away a bit of the sandy covering, exposing pieces of shell. Between the wave breaks, she snatched up a whelk, saw a pulsating mass sticking out from it, and threw it back into the sea. With a living creature inside, it was off-limits for harvest.

She looked up in time to dodge a crashing wall of water, the swift jerky motion sending her off-center. After regaining her balance, she scanned the ocean floor once more and spotted the large curled edge of a conch shell. Madeline's heart leapt. *A conch shell*! A rare treat indeed.

It teased her, more of its form being uncovered as the sand was carried away by the receding water. In her mind she was already telling Jacob about the find, imagining the excitement in his voiced responses.

Madeline ignored the bite of the water as it soaked her thighs, although she gasped involuntarily and her teeth chattered. Too close to the conch to stop, she reached down for it. A wave broke before her, knocking her down as the sand disappeared under her feet. She bubbled and gurgled beneath the cold fist of spiraling water, unsure which way was up or down. The tug toward the ocean depths clutched her as soundly as if the very sea witch herself had tangled her up in a net.

Damn!

Her head banged something. What should have been a sharp intake of breath turned out to be water sucked into her lungs. It burned and choked. Panic ensued. She thrashed in the water as a fish against line. *What a bad way to die,* she thought, assuming she might not even be found. She had told no one of her plans to go walking on the beach.

Madeline had a brief flash of her life, and those who had been important to her. She was a child on the beach with her parents, next on her college campus with the man she would marry and divorce, then back on the beach with her young son, and finally leaving Jacob at his own dormitory when he left home for college.

Then her parents were back—only this time they wore white robes and were bathed in golden light. A great sense of peace consumed her. She stopped thrashing and floated to the bottom of the sea, imagining the faces of those she loved and hadn't seen in so long she had forgotten how much she ached for them. They held out their arms to her and she felt herself struggling to rise, shedding her body as one sheds a stubbornly clinging overcoat.

Another outline appeared just as she was finding the ease of slipping out of the heavy body beneath her. The shadowy shape of William Gray knocked into her, pushing her back into the physical housing of flesh and bone. She was then shoved up and above the swirling water and onto the sand. He blew through her with such force the water in her lungs flew out of her mouth and nose in a coughing fit.

"Oh no! No, Magdalene, you cannot leave me again. I have waited for your return for far too long to lose you now." The voice, the same as the one in the cupola, belonged to the ghost of Pine Island, the spirit of the original William Gray.

But that wasn't possible. It was delirium—had to be. They say you see things from the other side before you die. This must be part of her hallucination, the one containing her parents. There was no other explanation.

Madeline could not deny the feeling of love and longing enveloping her as she lay on the sand with no visible savior in sight. Yet tangible emotions were so strong they left her on the verge of tears.

Fingertips, light as the brush of a butterfly wing, stroked her face. Warmth spread throughout her body in a radiating fashion from her heart. She closed her eyes and languished in the sun. Immense love washed through her, and Madeline was certain she had never felt as adored before. In a moment of satiety, she opened her eyes to see the clear blue ones—though a watered-down version, chalk drawing instead of oil painting on canvas—of William Gray staring back at her.

He smiled at her. "You can see me, can't you?" he whispered.

"And why would I not be able to?" she asked.

"Because I've been dead for more than a century."

Chapter 9

Madeline's sudden realization it was the elder William Gray instead of the younger brought a gasp from her throat, He disappeared from view. She began to shake uncontrollably, barely managing to rise from the beach. She wound her way back to the house and then collapsed in her room.

"Here, drink this," a man's voice encouraged. One hand lifted her head from the pillow.

She opened her eyes and, startled at the sight of the eerie blue ones staring back at her, jumped backward.

"Are you…are you…?" she sputtered, frightened.

"I am no illusion if that is what you are asking."

He tilted the glass toward her lips, and fiery warm liquid raced down her throat. She swallowed and blinked. The solid form of the man in front of her was evidence of his presence. Yet she couldn't resist touching his hand to be sure her own wouldn't slide through his. It rested squarely on sun-tanned flesh and tendons made sinewy by work and work outs.

"And why would you suspect I believed you to be an illusion?"

"You've seen him, haven't you Madeline? And more than a wisp or a trail of fog. You've *experienced* the spirit of Pine Island."

The knowing smile on William's sure and certain face left her unable to deny the truth. "Yes. How did you know?"

He held up a faded photograph of the original William Gray and his bride, Magdalene Brannock. "You have many similar physical characteristics of the first woman of Pine Island. She knew this place but a few short years before death claimed her. When I heard you were collecting data on Pine Island and the Grays of the ancient estate, well, it stood to reason you might have a connection. If not, I'd at least have someone out here to photograph his presence."

"That's ridiculous." She sat up in the bed and swigged a little of the brandy, glancing briefly at the image. The sepia-toned picture was too old and blurry to offer much detail.

"Is it?" William's brows lifted, forcing crinkles upward along his forehead.

"I'm simply a woman working on a thesis about the history of Winyah Bay, and Captain William Gray is part of that history. His success proves the fallacy that it is essential in young economies to use indentured servitude. Trade and progress were entirely possible without it."

She fanned her hand out to punctuate her absolute certainty that ghosts and spirits could not cross through time and space "This is all coincidental." Though she had never felt less certain about anything in her life.

"There are no such things as coincidental meetings." He leaned in closer, studying her face.

"Then why would I be here, if not by chance? What purpose would I serve? He might appear in other people's work, but he's not showing up in mine." Madeline pointed to her camera, although she knew she hadn't really given herself a fair chance at collecting his image. Every time the spirit came near her, she quivered and shook, and forgot about the assignment. Had she remembered, she was too nervous to get a clear shot.

"There are some who believe Magdalene was murdered by her husband, the first William Gray. They say he returned unexpectedly from a voyage and found her in the arms of another. Then there's another rumor of an ancient Native American tribal burial ground supposedly right underneath us, cursing whoever dares to build upon it and desecrate their holy place. Another story of the ancients involves the Spanish moss and how, to fuel its appetite, it devours the most beautiful creatures. I have personally witnessed bats fly into its beard never to be seen again. And we can't rule out the witchcraft of the time—voodoo brought to the American shore by the slaves."

"Oh you can't possibly believe in voodoo and witchcraft," Madeline scoffed, although the memory of Mrs. Jenkins' stories about the Gullahs flashed before her. She shook her head, trying to erase the recollection. "Besides, there weren't any slaves at Pine Island."

"Not at Pine Island—but there were plenty in the area. And I absolutely believe those who believe in a power create one. Perhaps the strength is in the belief rather than the craft. I'm betting you didn't believe in ghosts either, before coming to Pine Island."

"Even if I were to concede you are correct in the possible existence of a ghost here, what is it you want from me, besides a picture?"

He started to interrupt and she held up a hand. "No, don't say it. Don't mention the contract and the pictures I agreed to take. We both know you want more than a snapshot."

William Gray met her knowing stare. A sly smile formed along his lips. "You are a clever woman. I'll give you that."

"'Clever woman' is much better than 'big girl.' Just so you know." She gave him her best glower. "So out with it. What do you really want from me?"

"I want you to find out what happened to the first Mrs. Gray of Pine Island. With the elder William Gray's help, perhaps the mystery can be put to bed so his soul can also rest. Then maybe I can get some peace and quiet, and move on with my life."

"What does any of this have to do with you?"

"It is a strange bond we have. I can feel his unrest, his deep abiding love for Magdalene, and the sorrow he bore and still carries, even beyond death. I can have no peace until he does. Of this much I am sure."

William turned away from Madeline. His back heaved with long pulls of deep breaths. As she started to speak, he spun around, puffing out an exhalation. "My future happiness lies in your ability to help me put the past behind us, once and for all. If you will help me, I will give you free and unlimited access to whatever information you want to know about the Grays and the private inner book room beyond the walls of my library. You can roam the house at will; see any of its rooms, even the hidden ones. And you can add them to your thesis."

"Hidden rooms, ghosts, voodoo?" Madeline shook her head. It was too much to take in. "You expect me to believe in these strange things?"

"Of course. American Gothic, in the colonial south, at its best!"

His laughter lit his eyes like the prismatic pools she had once seen at Yellowstone. *The clearer the eye, the more smoldering inner workings and the deeper the heat,* she thought. He could be trouble. She was certain of it. But he appeared to be telling the truth, and her curiosity rendered it too difficult to back away from the request. Of course, that had been what he hoped for, and what he achieved.

"Think about it."

"I will," she said.

"That's all I ask. If at any time it gets too intense for you, I'll pull the plug and move on. I just don't think I can be at peace, take a bride, and continue the Gray lineage at Pine Island if this isn't laid to rest along with the corpse of the woman with your similar name on her headstone, in the graveyard."

He closed the door behind him and Madeline collapsed in a dazed and confused state of wonderment. What in the hell had she volunteered for?

Chapter 10

Madeline awoke with a start. Rising up in the bed, she glanced around the room for signs of the mysterious Captain Gray. Now that his presence had been verified, there was no way to talk herself out of believing the wily sea captain had been coming to call on her specifically. Every sound, be it a tree limb scraping the window pane or the wind in the leaves, made her jump to the conclusion that the veritable haunt, who had rescued her from the sea, was returning for her. She could not make out his form in the room at present and gave up the notion he waited by her side.

Having quickly lost her fear of him, she found herself anticipating their next meeting with renewed curiosity. Was it the way he touched her, the excitement of communicating with a spirit from another life, or merely curiosity about what he might tell her about the history of Pine Island and the mysterious death of the woman he claimed to have loved so dearly?

She had hoped to see him again before her appointment with William on Saturday. He had "some loose ends to settle," he had said, and then he would be available to spend the rest of the day showing her the private libraries and something of the secretive workings of the house.

If she could spend some time with the Captain—as she had come to refer to the ghost—she might have something interesting to share with William. For some reason his impression of her efforts mattered.

In her dreams, he didn't appear as a spirit, but as a fully-formed man who bore the combined effect of the two William Grays. He could touch her without slicing through her body, solid form against solid form.

She wanted to discuss this with William, but didn't know quite how to approach him with her desire to make physical contact with a spirit. Perhaps it had taken all of the Captain's other-worldly strength to pull her from the ocean's grip, leaving him unable to get back. Who do you ask such things of? A psychic? A priest?

She giggled as she imagined the shocked expression on Father Washburn's face right before he would call the nuns to escort her to the hospital for a brain scan. No, she didn't think he was ready to face the prospect of the dead returning to life.

The long-awaited Saturday arrived with no sign of William. He had stayed out all night, apparently with one of his many lady friends, if the whispers of the housekeeper to the gardener could be believed.

They weren't used to having another set of ears within hearing distance of their private conversations, and Madeline had tried to keep a low-enough profile to ensure they wouldn't. She wanted to learn all she could about the comings and goings of William before they realized she was under foot.

Perhaps they saw things too. Maybe they had even seen the Captain from time to time. Staff could be too loyal to share confidences about their employer, or eager to gossip; one never knew which. However, they would need to trust her before she could count on any confidences from them.

Chapter 11

William Gray shook his head, trying to clear it of the cobwebs that fogged his thoughts from time to time. His memory often failed him, and his inability to recall some things alarmed him. Then there were the bizarre sensations he sometimes experienced. He shuddered at the thought of the way they suddenly came over him.

Lately, the brain fog had worsened. He couldn't remember a lot of things associated with Madeline Waters, the woman who had chosen his ancestors as some philanthropic/historic project for a thesis. Still, he intuited something lurking in the past that held the original William Gray to this realm.

He had grown up hearing stories about ghosts and haunted areas of the south, but what he had personally witnessed left the deepest impression on him—the milky visions of a sea captain, the peculiar, shadowy appearances of someone else in the room with him, the odd sensations, the breath of an invisible being in his ear.

It had made him determined to discover what caused this apparition, even if it meant allowing this strange woman to roam about the grounds sniffing out clues in the same way a bloodhound would. He simply had to put this spirit to rest before he could be happy himself.

If no ghost existed, if he was not seeing and

hearing the trapped soul of someone unable to move on to the afterlife by letting go of the things of this earth, then he was emphatically crazy. The thought angered him, scared him, and lent itself to a sense of urgency demanding acknowledgement.

His entire future might lay in the hands of the hour-glass shaped woman who unnerved him by digging up clues into his ancestors' pasts. Nonetheless, he also felt strangely attracted to her, though not always. It was unsettling when she appeared places he had no memory of inviting her to—such as dancing on the terrace, having dinner in his private dining room.

Was he losing his mind? An uncle, on his mother's side of the family, had committed suicide after having hallucinations and hearing strange voices. Uncle Henry had left a note explaining how he had to make the voices stop.

William guessed jumping out of the window of a twenty-story building had accomplished that. He was hardly ready for something equally as drastic without first trying every other means—conventional or not—he could arrange.

He wondered about bringing in a psychic or a clairvoyant and hadn't ruled it out. The only thing stopping him, so far, was the realization that once it hit the local papers he had brought in such a person, the word would spread quicker than wildfire in his gossipy little corner of the south.

His reputation would be damaged, unless, of course, he did it in the name of research for someone else. Someone such as the graduate program student seeking all kinds of answers. He still didn't quite understand what caused Madeline Waters to be so interested in his ancestors. And was her resemblance to the house's first Mrs. Gray uncanny? Odd.

Many of his peers believed having a ghost haunting their grounds made for great publicity. There were guided tours through many historic southern cities specializing in *ghosts*. For a cut of the proceeds, privately owned antebellum mansions often lent themselves to such ventures, supplying the stories of the identity of the spirit and their supposed reason for haunting.

One such story existed about an upriver plantation house where a century ago a curious young wife had watched her husband place what she suspected to be a love letter atop of a highboy chest of drawers. After he went out to inspect the grounds, she slipped into the room. She couldn't reach the top of the bureau, so pulling a drawer partially open, she used it as a step ladder to reach the top. Just as she pulled the letter down, with her added weight, the whole bureau fell forward, crushing her to death before she could even read the contents of the letter. She was said to still be searching for the letter, unable to rest until it is found and its contents revealed.

The south was full of these sad stories, like the one about the arranged marriage between two cousins—first cousins no less—sometimes practiced in antebellum days to ensure all of the property stayed within the family. Their union produced only one living child, though many late-term miscarriages were evidenced by two rows of stones in the family cemetery marking the couple's infants.

Some accused the house servants of placing curses on the young mother so they wouldn't have to care for another baby. Some said the father killed them because of deformities, while others believed the family cat had sucked the life out of the babies soon after they were born. Whatever the reason for their untimely deaths, the sound of the infants wailing audibly, after midnight, was purportedly because the babies had been put to bed without their supper and cried for it every night .

Witchcraft, voodoo, evil cats, spoiled owners, mistreated servants—all were suspects. Weaving stories around strange and unbelievable events made them easier to accept than the more apparent truth that life was harsh. Pain and suffering were equal-opportunity offenders, and animal sounds often mimicked crying babies.

William knew this all too well from hunting the bobcat frequently seen tearing into a friend's chicken coup. Once cornered, its cries were so similar to a baby he had been too confounded to be able to kill the thing. Managing to get it into a cage, he had taken it to the swamps where it must have been much happier as it hadn't bothered making the long trek back.

Warf rats, thick at the harbor where the shrimping boats docked, also made crying sounds. He'd seen some as large as cats. So William accepted every ghost story probably have a logical explanation.

But there was one thing no amount of logic could reason away. What in the world could explain the type of physical contact this spirit seemed to make with him, merging within his own body sometimes as effortless as a part of his anatomy? Although he hadn't told anyone about this—except Madeline—he could feel the immediate chill, followed by warmth as it overtook him. Most often he forgot what happened for a little while, as he made strange invitations and felt oddly attracted to people he didn't even know, like this Madeline. It was even worse with her.

He seemed possessed at times—a feeling too strange to contemplate, but the way he felt, nonetheless. He didn't know what he might do under the power of this spirit. What if it was an evil spirit and not really that of his ancestor? What if it somehow made him break the law? What if he couldn't get away from the possessor and lost himself forever? He didn't know which scenario he feared the most. None of them were appealing.

He would clearly have to get to the bottom of this hallucination, or possession, or whatever it was, and remedy the situation. The only intuition he had about a solution lay in finding out what had killed the Captain's wife, Magdalene, and returning him to the other world with a clean conscience.

Now that Madeline had seen the Captain for herself, she should be more receptive to the challenge.

Chapter 12

Madeline searched through the Gray Estate's extensive library at a hare's pace. She'd been at it for two days, intending to peruse every book in the off chance a clue or a golden nugget of information lay hidden between unlikely pages. Some of them were so fragile they were kept behind glass. She was required to wear cotton gloves while handling those.

Flattened flowers and foliage of various kinds were still pressed between the pages of some, except now they were in cellophane sleeves, their browned shadowy shapes staining the pages on either side an indication of where they had originally been stored. It gave her search an air of importance and romanticism.

But she didn't find a connection to the Grays in anything other than sentimental notes and lineage. She also didn't see any records of the income and expenditures of the household from any time frame. Judging by her knowledge of most antebellum homes, this practice had been ubiquitous. Maybe the sea captain disliked record-keeping and thumbed his nose at attempts to hold him accountable for his imports and exports. If so, he had passed his contempt down to his children and grandchildren.

Something touched her shoulder. Madeline screamed and jumped backward away from the thing making contact. Her reflexes brought a hand to her head against the spot she had hit on the beach. Turning from a knot to a touchy and tender gray-green reminder of nearly drowning, it was an understandable reason for her to be jumpy.

"It's only me. Sorry," a familiar voice assured her, as William tried to settle her down. "I didn't mean to startle you."

She turned and locked onto ghostly blue eyes. "Host or ghost?" she asked.

"Former, I'm afraid. I have a feeling I'd be more welcome as the latter."

Madeline sized him up, watching for signs that would make it more apparent in the future which she was dealing with; man or apparition. Initially, it had been much easier, but the Captain's spirit seemed to be gaining strength and the ability to hold together better.

What had started out as a mere wisp of smoke had now formed an energy field strong enough to be completely visible. When he slipped through her body, she now felt more in the way of emotion than shock and fear.

When he used William's body, as she came to think of it, he made his descendant irresistible. She guessed that would be the best way to discern whom she was dealing with.

She peered into the face of the person known as "William" in both worlds. "Yes, I can tell by the worried expression and the knitted brow, you are William and not the Captain."

He let go of her after steadying her sway and jerked his chin up. "So the charming side of me will forever be thought of as *possession by a spirit*?"

She had no desire to banter with him, may as well

be straightforward. "How else would I know it?"

His jaw clenched. She braced for a quick change in attitude, expecting an attack of insults or barbs.

As it approached from behind William's back, she saw the apparition then. "Uh…William…" She pointed, but he failed to understand.

"I'm not trying anything, if that's why you're giving me—"

The words she wanted to say wouldn't form into a coherent sentence. "No…no…behind—"

"Behind in your work? Yes, I understand. I won't bother you…"

He wasn't listening. Couldn't he tell by the expression on her face? It was too late. She could only watch as the Captain's ghost floated across the floor and merged into the man standing inches from her.

William's only reaction was a sharp intake of breath before his whole demeanor changed. "How are you this day?" he asked, his hand reaching upward to caress her hair. The spirit was talking, forming sentences and touching her through his future relative.

Mesmerized, and shocked, by what she had just witnessed, she failed to react the way she might have assumed she would if such a thing were to happen in front of her. "I'm fine. I'm okay, really."

"I have missed you much. The years have been torturous, angry seas of time, Magdalene. Now you are here, and I can finally touch you as I have longed to do." His eyes locked onto hers, and she couldn't look away.

Madeline's hand disappeared in his large palm before being encircled by the long sinewy fingers burning into the very places they settled on. His other hand took her by the waist as he pulled her into his chest.

"Oh yes," he whispered. His breathing quickened as he pressed against her.

She felt her body responding in ways it hadn't for a while. When he lowered his head toward hers, her lips parted of their own accord. Madeline couldn't have stopped him if she had wanted to, but she didn't want to.

Being held gently, though firmly, while waiting for lips promising something she hadn't identified yet, was similar to being suspended mid-air on a Ferris wheel. Butterflies danced in her stomach and sensations from the spot at her waist where his hand urged her forward, caused her to lean toward him, breathless and anxious. She closed her eyes.

A long moment passed while she waited to feel his cheek against hers, his lips parting hers. Every part of her body—inner and outer—tingled with anticipation.

His touch deepened, tightening on her flesh. But instead of the kiss she expected, she received a push backward. Her eyes flew open, and she looked up in time to see William's facial expressions change.

"Get out," he yelled. Then he stalked out of the library.

Madeline stood for a while, her back to the bookshelves, watching the door. *What the hell just happened?* she asked herself about a dozen times.

She knew the answer, she simply couldn't accept it. Hadn't she seen the spirit of Captain William Gray merge into the body of the current William Gray? Hadn't she had her suspicions verified he was the one who had saved her at the beach? Hadn't she felt his passion for her in the lightness of his touch as he caressed her hand?

But then he yelled, "Get out." Or did the current William regain control of his senses in a moment of strength? How would she know who she was dealing with?

It was too much, too intense, and time to leave.

She'd either abandon the project or make the most of what she already had. She certainly couldn't take this story back to campus and present it as an intelligent piece of academic study. Racing up the stairs, Madeline was breathless by the time she reached her room. But she didn't dare stop.

Grabbing her luggage, she emptied the contents of the wardrobe into it.

Chapter 13

"What are you doing?" William asked, with surprise in his voice. He must have followed her up the stairs and now stood just inside the door watching her pack.

"Getting out, as you demanded." She barely glanced upward at him as she emptied another drawer into the luggage piece.

"No...I...didn't mean you."

"Well there were only the two of us in the library. I don't suppose you were addressing the books."

He carried the soft cotton sweaters back to the drawer she had emptied. "Please, listen to me."

"You've got about one minute to convince me you were talking to someone besides me." She folded her arms across her chest.

"I think you know who else was in the library. And you are the only other person who I know has witnessed the overtaking of my body by his ethereal spirit. You hold the life line—*my* life line." His eyes searched hers for understanding and pleaded for help. What he had only been able to assume, she had witnessed as the truth.

"How am I supposed to know when you are talking to me or when you are talking to him? Or when he is talking to me?" She sat down on the bed, ending the tug of war with the same drawer of sweaters they had been battling over.

William sat down beside her, looking as lost as she felt. "I still believe the answer lies in his wife's early death. And now you've opened up this investigation into the history of this place and of the captain himself. That seems to have further provoked him."

"But how?" She searched his face for the answer.

"He is making himself apparent to you, allowing you to see him. He is growing stronger every day. I can feel him more powerfully than ever before. There is an energy here he is emitting. For whatever reason, I feel he wants you to be able to see him. Maybe, there is something he wants to tell you."

"Tell *me*?"

"What do I say when he has control of me? Has he spoken to you when he appears at other times? Can you hear his voice?"

The questions poured out of him faster than she could think of answers. "Slow down," she urged, holding her hands up in the universally accepted gesture of easing up. "Do you think your mood swings, forgetfulness, and bad attitude are all attributed to this so-called *possession*?"

"As crazy as it sounds, yes!"

Madeline took a deep breath and replayed the last few days in her mind. William started to speak, but she held a hand up in front of him.

Understanding the gesture, he clamped his lips together and sat on the bed.

For what seemed an hour, but was most likely in the neighborhood of a few terribly stretched minutes, she pondered. "Do you think it was his idea, instead of yours, for me to be here?" She gave him what she hoped was a threatening stare. "And if I feel your answer is anything less than one hundred percent honest I will not engage in even one more moment's conversation with you."

She could tell that William wasn't used to anyone being so direct with him. For an instant—taken aback—he appeared as shocked as he might had she slapped him across the face instead of issuing the verbal assault.

He made eye contact when he spoke, assuring her of his honesty. "Initially, maybe. Perhaps it was a combination of what I thought and what he placed into my head. This is where it all gets a bit tricky for me. I don't remember everything, so I can't be sure."

"So, if I tell you what has been said, and what has transpired from my perspective, you will accept it as truth and not berate me for things you don't recall saying?"

"What does either of us have to gain by being less than truthful now?"

She nodded agreement.

He rose and extended his hand. "Come with me; I think we need a little something on our stomachs before we get started."

She laid her hand into his, and though it was the same hand she had held earlier, when sensations had spread throughout her body as quick as a virus, this feeling was different.

William had a strong, masculine grip. But it wasn't the same as when the spirit of his forefather poured out through his fingertips into her flesh. Madeline wondered if she should tell him about the way the Captain made her feel, but decided against it, at least for the moment.

He led the way to the kitchen and plopped a tray down on the black granite countertop. Then he began to fish condiments from jars—pickled okra, roasted red peppers, grainy mustard, garlic-stuffed olives the size of plums—and placed them onto a multi-tiered serving dish. William shuffled through the refrigerator and added cheese, salami, and crab dip to another platter. A hearty loaf of crusty bread, tossed atop a cutting board along with a serrated knife, waited to be sliced.

He opened a smaller black refrigerator which turned out to be a wine cooler. His head bobbed up and down, searching for the perfect wine. Reaching in, he snagged a bottle before snapping the door shut. With deftness, he produced a small corkscrew. After scoring the seal, he wound the tool into the cork, placed the edge against the bottle, and pulled the cork from the wine bottle.

"You've obviously done this before," she said.

"I've even toyed with the idea of producing my own wine." He smiled when he said it, something she rarely saw him do—smile genuinely.

"So what's stopping you?"

He set two glasses in front of her and partially filled each one. With his palm against the granite, the stem of the glass caught between two fingers, he swirled the liquid. He took the second goblet and did the same.

Madeline was awestruck, convinced at any moment they would both be wearing the contents of the wineglass as the fluid raced up to the edge in flying momentum. Yet, he didn't spill a drop.

"If I know ahead of time which wine I'll be drinking, I open it, decant it, and let it have a little time to breathe. Otherwise, a good swirl aerates, and the same effect is accomplished."

He offered a glass to her and caught her staring at the contents. Some of it still clung to the edges, making long striations back into the contents of the bowl. He pointed to them. "It's got good legs."

"Good legs?" She continued to watch the thick wine in the glass before her.

"It's the mark of a good wine. Its body will allow for a slow descent back into the bottom. That's commonly called 'legs.' If you swirl a wine and the empty half of the glass goes clear immediately, it's too thin and poor quality."

"So what you're saying is you are a leg man," she teased. Madeline was happy for the shared carefree banter replacing the tense mouse trap of conversation about visitors from another dimension inhabiting the space—and bodies—they possessed.

He chuckled. "I guess you could say as much. Here, taste."

He brought his own glass of wine toward his face and stuck his nose into its bowl, inhaling the scent.

She followed his example.

"Taste by taking just a small sip and sucking in a breath of air over the top of it as it sits in your mouth."

She gave him a quizzical expression.

"Like this." He showed her the method for getting every note of the wine into the olfactory system.

She tried to follow his lead, but sucked the liquid down her windpipe and nearly choked. When she stopped coughing, he suggested trying it again but she refused. "No, either I'm drinking it, or I'm sniffing it, but apparently I didn't get the gene allowing me to do both simultaneously."

He laughed. "Maybe you're right. Just enjoy it."

Madeline took a sip, one that managed not to go down the wrong way. "Mmm, nice," she said.

"I think you can do better than just 'nice,'" he encouraged. "What do you taste? Try to tease out the different notes."

"Blackberry," she said right away, "And a little cherry."

"What else? And it doesn't have to be a food. Inhale the aromas again."

"Something smoky?"

"So you get the tobacco? Good. Now go even deeper. See if you can get leather."

"I never considered wine this way before." She was a little amazed at what could happen in a glass of fermented grape juice.

"That's the beauty of wine-making. You take something simple—the unpretentious grape—and let time and conditions turn it into something else entirely. Amazing, really." He turned the glass around in his hand, watching the liquid cling to the sides as he tilted it first one way, then the other.

Madeline observed the way he seemed to caress the wine glass, describing its contents as earnestly as he might a medieval treasure. He looked as comfortable as he might if he walked right out of Pine Island and into a winery. She doubted he'd even notice the transition.

"You didn't answer my question," she continued. "What's stopping you from making wine? You seem to have a passion for it."

"You did ask me that; didn't you? Well, for starters, I don't have a vineyard."

"But you have all of this land. Can't you plant one?"

"Not here. It's too far south and east. The only grape with the ability to survive our southern climate is the muscadine, and although some vintners are doing good things with wine made from it, I personally don't care for it."

"But I've bought wine from southern wineries. There were grapes planted outside of them. I'm pretty sure of it." She searched her memory for the right recollections of her visits to pick up a bottle or two as a gift.

"I'd be willing to bet everything I have they were muscadine vines planted for show. The wine produced was likely made from imported grapes. You simply won't find a pinot noir or a chardonnay southeast of the frost line."

"Why not?"

"Umm, they need to struggle. If conditions are too ideal they don't put their roots down very deeply. Then they can't survive when the first problem arises."

"Like humans?" She raised an eyebrow.

"So, you see why I'm so fascinated with it?"

Madeline thought of all of the people she had known who had everything handed to them. Without respect for work, their typical characteristics were diametrically opposed to those who had to struggle— even inside of their own family's company—for their upkeep. Undoubtedly, those who had slogged through conflicts had developed the most insight and the deepest degree of empathy and compassion. They knew how to appreciate the simple luxuries.

But how did this relate to William Gray? His

lifestyle wasn't too shabby. It didn't seem to reflect any degree of strife to maintain. "So what's your story with striving to develop roots?" She caught the surprise in his eyes when she posed the question.

"You may be the first person to have ever asked me that." He took a couple of plates from the cupboard and obtained a handful of silver from the display case of antique coin silver. It had a soft matte hue and striations of tarnish. William ran his hand down the front of the glass and became silent.

Madeline slathered some of the crab dip onto a crust of bread. "Mmm, this is really good." She hoped to deflect the bit of tension she sensed when she asked the question about his challenges. She still couldn't figure him out. He seemed ready to share bits of himself one minute and absolutely compelled not to the next. How could she ever deal with that?

"I get it from a deli on the downtown boardwalk. Do you ever shop along there?"

Madeline listened to him chatter on about the offerings to be had from the quaint shops in historic Georgetown. He busied himself with tiny details of serving dishes and utensils that were probably less than interesting to him, but more about preventing the inevitable topic from being addressed.

She knew she would have to intervene in order to assure they wouldn't still be sitting at the table long after dark. She waited until he seemed to run out of steam, something she found amusing given his previous penchant for saying next to nothing. But eventually, even his jittery procrastination wore him down.

"I appreciate this little get-better-acquainted party you've spread out for me, but I think we both know I'm not here to discuss crab dip and the shops along the boardwalk." She sipped her wine casually, but her eyes held steady with his. He needed to know she didn't intend to be distracted more than she already had been.

"Yes,"—he sat down opposite her—"we do. I need to know what you have seen and heard. Have you unearthed anything about the Grays I should know about?"

Madeline almost regretted homing him in. Now she had to decide how much to tell him. Should she admit the strange attraction she felt? *No. Definitely not,* she decided.

"Is it that bad?" Head bent, staring into the wine, he could have been seeking the answer in its contents.

"It's not bad. It's merely…different." She turned away, afraid to meet his eyes.

"Tell me."

Whether due to the wine's influence or the intensity of the man she faced, Madeline revealed her research—the land grant, the suspected Spanish treasure, the pirate ships—but said nothing about the apparition.

William didn't interrupt her. Taking it all in so seamlessly, he appeared to not be hearing these things for the very first time. Surely he would be more surprised if he had been in the dark about the actions of his ancestor.

"You knew this?" she asked.

"Not all of it, but most of it," he confessed.

"If you knew it, then why did you ask me about it?"

"As I said—not all of it. You haven't said anything about the sightings of the Captain's spirit you have witnessed, or the things he has said to you."

Madeline gulped her wine. "He calls me Magdalene. I think he is mistaking me for her."

William appeared to be sizing up the woman sitting in his kitchen. "You do resemble her a bit."

Madeline stopped swallowing and stared at him. Was he under the influence of the Captain? "How would you know unless there is a better picture of her than the one you showed me?"

"It's more of a painting really."

"Will you show me?" Relieved to know it was still the younger William in her presence, she sat her glass down with a *thunk*, sloshing wine onto the countertop.

"Of course." He wiped the spill with a nonchalant swipe of a cloth. "This way." He pointed to the stairs, and she climbed ahead of him up one flight.

William motioned skyward again, and she climbed up another floor. Beneath the room she had been staying in was a suite—the master suite where Captain William Gray had brought his young wife.

Chapter 14

William produced a long skeleton-style key and ran it through the keyhole of the antique door latch with the oblong handle set parallel to the floor. It seemed to be a bit tetchy as he listened to the tumblers connect with the teeth of the key, but he made the necessary alignments and twisted the knob. The door creaked, the hinges moaned. They had apparently been resting for a very long time. Stale air greeted them, dust flying up in the disturbance.

"Welcome to the master suite of every couple who lived at Pine Island." His jaw clenched, and though his words said *welcome* his tone suggested something else entirely.

"Why is this room closed off?" Madeline inquired.

"The last couple it was prepared for never even spent the first night here." His jaw clenched again.

"Did something bad happen?" Madeline envisioned an accident or illness. She tried to recall the family tree she had copied from the historical society and could think of no sibling for William.

"Yes, something bad happened." His spine stiffened and he jerked erect; his eyes scanned the room, as a hawk searching a field for a mouse might.

She didn't want to ask directly but sensed these two events were inexplicably tied to each other. "Could it have something to do with the appearance of the

Captain?"

"It's unlikely." William continued to scan the room, suddenly turning a frame face down with a snap against the bed stand.

Madeline jumped, startled at the sound.

"Sorry," he said. "Something I didn't want to be reminded of." He walked to a different corner of the room.

Madeline's curiosity played on her nerves. She ached to know what was underneath the back of the frame he had slammed against the table. But she hesitated, fearing to lose his favor or to be labeled "nosy."

"Ah-ha," he said, reaching the back corner and uncovering a large oil painting.

Madeline had just reached for the overturned frame, but jerked her hand away as he turned toward her.

He motioned for her. "Come, it's over here."

Madeline reluctantly walked away from the memory he apparently wished to forget and toward William and the portrait of the first Mrs. Gray of Pine Island. She could even see a resemblance to herself; meaning it was probably more than a little slight. Most often people rarely see the resemblance of themselves in others, even when the masses find it to be uncanny.

She could have easily been convinced it was a trick portrait—such as those taken at fair and tourist sites in costumes slit down the back and draped over the modern day poser, along with a hat and a wig. Magdalene had a slender neck and a slimmer face than she, but the nose, the chin, eyes, mouth, all resembled hers.

Shivering, she recalled the uneasy feeling her mother referred to as "someone walking over your grave."

William pointed to the portrait. "The hair is radically different, of course, and she was younger and more petite than you, but the resemblance is definitely there."

Madeline continued to tremble. She caught a glimpse of herself standing beside William, in the mirror over the bureau, and could almost be convinced they were both the reincarnations of Captain William and his Magdalene.

Putting his arm around her shoulders, William rubbed her briskly with his hand, warming her and stopping the shivering. "Come on; let me get you out of this stale air." He guided her back across the floor to the open door.

With a backward glance at the carved fourposter bed and the overturned picture, Madeline ached to know more. Why the secrecy? Why was the largest bedroom in the house drowning in dust and cobwebs?

William closed the door and twisted the key in the lock. It seemed that shutting the room off again made it mentally cease to exist and allowed his every emotion to be contained once again.

She watched the key drop into his pocket, desiring it more than she could have imagined. Madeline knew she would seek that key so she could be alone in the master suite with the portrait of herself…and the memory William wished not to be reminded of.

****

"Don't you find it odd?" Madeline asked when they were back downstairs with a considerable amount of good wine downed.

"What?" Haunted by the images in the master suite, discussing them had been too intense immediately afterward.

William and she had spent the past half an hour, or so, loosely exchanging conversation of no consequence. "That I resemble her, and you resemble him. And now there's this whole ghostly apparition and…" Her words trailed off as her mind ran ahead in the direction neither wished to follow.

"Yes," he replied simply, "thus my request that you stay here for a while."

"I wonder what *he* wants."

"Probably just to feel love again." William crossed to her side, rubbing her arm once again, only this time, with more feeling. He reached beneath her chin and lifted her face to his, lowering his own toward her.

The backs of his fingertips brushed against her throat, gently stroking her collarbone and the line of her neck from chin to chest. His cheek brushed hers seductively.

Under the influence of hurriedly downed wine, she didn't question. Glancing upward into his smoldering eyes, she accepted the super-heated kisses that left him in moans and her desiring more.

Hearing the sounds emanating from William as their lips touched fueled longings Madeline hadn't expected. With ardor, she matched his appetite, searching the soft recesses beyond the straight row of pearly teeth. Her chest was heaving as he released the connection, pulling back only long enough to rake ravenous eyes down the length of her body.

"Come," he demanded, and she followed in his

wake. Leading the way back up the stairs, all the way to the master suite, he paused only long enough to fish the key out.

Assuming he had decided to share the surreptitious photo in the frame, she attempted to check her emotions. Maybe there was something in the room he felt she needed to know after all. Her mind had ceded control to her libido, and the sudden frenzy made her nervous.

William must have consumed more wine than either of them realized, or perhaps it had just gone to his head. Kissing her the way he had, looking at her with such lust, couldn't have happened otherwise.

Moving past the threshold side-by-side, he took the key and locked them in behind the closed door of the shrine to coupledom. "I don't want to lose you again," he whispered.

Being the object of his sudden thirsty attention made Madeline weak. Feeling her knees wobble as pent-up yearnings blazed a trail throughout her body, she was helpless to stave them off.

It felt good to experience the urges of her youth. In the years since her husband had left her at eighteen, pregnant and desperately in love, she had not allowed another man to touch her, kiss her.

Madeline had vowed never to give another man the upper hand over her life. She had raised Jacob alone without any means of support from anyone, struggling with college and odd jobs and daycare and her son's asthma and childhood illnesses. There had been no time for another man in her life.

Eventually, she gave up on everything, except being the best mother she could be. She'd accepted she would finish her life without the degree she desired, or the love of a man.

Now she was so hungry for physical love, the spell of its magic left her unable to reason or to think past the act of it. He wanted her and she wanted him. They were both racing toward forty. He may have already arrived.

Finding her voice through the heart-pounding onslaught of raw passion, she asked, "Lose me again?"

He tugged her bottom lip with his teeth and gripped her firmly by both arms before pulling his body from hers. The shape of William's twin, the apparition of the Captain, peeled from his body and hovered between them for only a moment before swirling into her, giving her satiety as she had never before experienced.

The sudden explosion of his spirit within her touched her heart and mind. It swirled throughout her body, along every nerve ending, warming her blood. It couldn't have raced hotter through her veins if it had first passed through a radiator. It built its own brand of steam.

Her heart thundered wildly, and the sound of its push of blood through her head swelled in her ears. Madeline's breath became shallow and fast as her center of pleasure bloomed. She shook with an inner explosion before collapsing with a spasm into William's arms.

"I love you forever," the Captain whispered. He exited her body and then from sight.

William suddenly pulled her close. "I don't know whether to run from this house, or call an exorcist," he said, with a tremble in his voice.

Madeline seemed to be having an out-of-body experience. The phantasm had taken turns occupying their bodies and their minds. She didn't even know what to call what she had just experienced. It was pleasurable, comforting, and yet frightening and alarming. She feared she might be losing her mind. Had William not witnessed it, she wondered if she would have believed it really occurred.

Pulling her to the door, he tried to turn the handle, obviously unaware he had locked it from the inside while possessed by the spirit of the Captain.

Madeline, shaking, said nothing. She simply pointed to his pocket.

He patted the outer fabric, retrieved the key inside, and once they were safely outside the door, locked it up again.

They didn't speak until they were back in the dining room, downing more of the wine.

"What the hell…?" She dropped it, not knowing what to finish asking, yet certain he understood the question she was trying to formulate.

He shook his head and wiped at the bead of sweat popping out along his hairline. "This thing is more intense than I imagined. Do you want to leave?"

She stared at him, carefully assessing the now-pale version of the tanned and confidant man she had not cared very much for since being summoned to this house. "I don't think it would matter. He would follow me. There is definitely something he wants from both of us. I think we have to see it through."

"Are you sure? It's okay if you don't stay. I'm not even sure I want to follow this strange occurrence to its conclusion, much less bring someone else along."

"I don't think we have a choice."

He shrugged his shoulders. "So where do we start?

Do we need to get a psychic or a medium to talk to him?"

She laughed. "He already talks to me. Why would we need to pull someone else into the middle of this?"

He sipped and nodded. "That's right. What was I thinking?" He hit his forehead with the flat palm of his hand.

"I don't think either of us knows the first thing to do about these unearthly occurrences, but we can figure it out. Clearly, this is connected to the death of the Captain's wife. We need to find out everything we can about her and the circumstances under which she died. We may also want to try to find out more about his lifestyle."

He observed her as though she had grown an extra head. "How can you be so reasonable? How can you treat this as purely a mystery to try and figure out? I'm losing my mind and you seem calm and collected."

"Don't be fooled by appearances."

"You're not the one who is being possessed by him. You aren't saying and doing things you have no control over and then barely, if at all, remembering." William paced the floor.

Madeline knew he was talking about kissing her earlier, and touching her in a pleasing way. "I understand what you are saying, and I do not hold you responsible for the things he has you doing. Okay?"

He nodded. "I just don't want to give you any false impressions that I am—"

She shot him a warning look. "You don't have to finish. I know you are about as attracted to me as I am to you. Neither of us chose this path, it has chosen us. So don't think I'm laboring under the misapprehension you feel a connection to me or desire me in any way. Do we understand each other?" Her face warmed from the spike of humiliation mixed with the wine.

"I simply can't remember what I say and do when he...when I...when..." He rubbed his face with both hands. "Try to imagine you say things you don't have control over, and then can't remember. I don't know what I've said to you. Try to imagine losing consciousness and when it returns you are fondling someone whom you shouldn't. I don't know all of the places you may have felt my touch, and yet it wasn't me doing the caressing."

The heat rose in her face, the blaze of embarrassment engorging her flesh. "I understand. You do not desire me. You really don't have to keep pointing it out. If the Captain is using your body to say and do things he cannot in spirit form, then I fully understand it is him, and not you. I release you from any personal responsibility, if that is what you're getting at."

William stopped pacing and leaned over the counter, placing his hands together in front of her. "I saw what happened upstairs. I know your body received pleasure from whatever interlude we had. These hands were all over you. My hands! Can you really tell me you can look at them and not remember the moment upstairs when you shook with longing?"

Her face grew even hotter. She feared she might explode with the rising vitriol collecting in the space between her ears. "Those hands did not bring pleasure to me. It was the moment when the Captain merged into my body and showered me from the inside with something more than sexual energy. I felt his love and the deep longing for the woman that was taken from him after only a short time. He's letting me know how much he loved her, and that he didn't kill her."

William's fingers flexed with tension. His eyes grew round, flitting back and forth. It was clear to Madeline he detested what was happening.

"Don't worry, William. I won't mistake any of it as coming from you." She leapt from her seat and made for the door, with William at her heels.

"Madeline, come back. I didn't mean to offend you."

Making for the beach, she needed time to think. *How dare he be so presumptive?* At the same time, he had a point—though she would never let him know it. She did have trouble gazing into his eyes and knowing the last time it was in the throes of passion. She saw his hands and imagined them in places they hadn't been before. Could she continue this venture without falling in love with him? He resembled the Captain so much.

"Good evening," a confident voice said. She had been so lost in her own thoughts she hadn't noticed William's approach. He was still pale from the ghostly encounter.

"What are you doing? Why did you follow me?" She heard the anger in her voice but couldn't take the irritated edge from its tone.

"I am worried danger may find you."

"I don't know why that would be of concern to you" She hugged her knees to her chest and buried her head against them.

Madeline felt the gentle touch of his hand against her hair, a soft caress along her neck.

"Why do you hurt me with these words?"

Tingles ran the length of her spine and she resisted the urge to run. This was not William. It was the specter of the Captain. "I thought you were *him*."

"Aye, and now?" His whispers were simultaneously warm and cold—warm to the inside, cold to the outside.

"You are the spirit of Captain William, his long-deceased ancestor." She didn't look up. Perhaps it would be easier to communicate if she didn't have to see him resembling his infuriating future grandson.

"That is true. Yet you are not frightened by me." He continued to bathe her in the emotions of love, all he could give without aid of a more physical body.

"No, I do not fear you now. But I do want to know why you are still here. Shouldn't you have moved on to the next life?"

Madeline watched him then, growing paler with each touch. The waves crashed against the shoreline and sent sprays of salt water into the air. It was a few moments before he spoke again. She feared she had caused offense, and he might not.

"Our legacy is all we truly possess. Mine has been pirated by those who envied me in my own lifetime, and beyond. I want the truth to surface. If William continues to be a bachelor, this place I built, as no other of her time, will pass into hands which do not care about truth. I may become the greatest exploitation of the era."

She could hear the agony of his words through the thin façade of his appearance. "This pain has held you here for all of these years?"

"'Tis true. And then I saw you holding ledgers about me in the town building housing such items now."

"The historical society. But surely others have held these books over time."

"But not with your intent."

"You can read intention?"

"You cannot?"

"I guess it's a skill that has been lost to us. No, I cannot."

"I see her in you." He cupped her chin in his gossamer palm. "Even the twitch of your cheek. She's inside of you."

His feathery fingers stroked her face, and the intense emotion of love filled her up once again. She heard the sound of another's footsteps approaching but couldn't pull herself away. The Captain was pouring his feelings into her heart and mind. She was only the receptacle, receiving them without question. Undoubtedly he must have been a good, honest man.

"Madeline…Madeline…? Oh there you are!"

The Captain seized the opportunity to caress his beloved by sliding into William's body. He embraced her before she could protest, kissing her forehead and the bridge of her nose.

"He hates it when you do that." She stared into William's eyes, sensing the emotions were those of the Captain.

"When I do what?" he asked, with the innocence of a child.

"When you jump into his body and use it to caress me. He isn't fond of, nor does he desire me."

"Then he is a fool. But I think you may be wrong." He sat down on the sand beside her, pulling her into the crevice between his chest and arm. "This feels perfect to both of us."

She looked up into the sky-colored pair of eyes and escaped outside of herself. Whatever control she may have possessed on another day, was clearly missing on this one.

Captain William leaned in, and she let him, accepting the kisses he dropped, feeling desires spring to life again. He removed his shirt and spread it on the sand behind her, then gently laid her backward upon it before covering her mouth with his.

She could taste the wine they had just consumed in the house. She knew she should insist he not use another's body for things that person didn't want to do. Yet, she craved him, as no other, and knew he could never fulfill her in ghostly form.

William had used so many women for his own pleasure, what difference did it make if the Captain used him to please her? This was what she told herself in order to accept his passion, and meet it with her own.

Madeline ran her hands along his back, feeling the chiseled muscles there. She gasped as he opened her blouse and trailed his long fingers along her cleavage. One hand fumbled with the buttons on her pants and she helped him release the top one and pulled the tab on the zipper.

"Oh Magdalene." His hand slid downward, into the space below her naval.

"I'm not Magdalene." She pushed up with her elbows against the sand. Although her body ached for his touch, and she still throbbed where his fingertips had been, she couldn't stand thinking he was only using her body with another woman in his mind.

Her words were enough to break the spell attaching

him to William, and he floated out over the tops of the waves.

"What the hell!" William exclaimed. He realized where he was and what he had been about to do.

"Don't get excited. I know it wasn't you who was about to make love to me." With that correction, she began to right her clothing.

He crouched over her, incensed by the knowledge. "You knew it wasn't me, yet you were going to let him make love to you, using my body!"

His eyes scanned the scene, missing nothing. She saw them pause over her opened blouse and undone pants.

His hands raced down his bare chest and quickly refastened his pants.

"I stopped it, okay?" She continued to button her clothing, though her hands shook uncontrollably.

"You don't have permission to use my body!" he yelled at her.

"Oh yeah! Now suddenly you are so righteous. What about all of the bodies you have used. Huh? And for the record, I am not *using your body*—he is. So if you are unhappy about the sight of your precious hands on my less-than-ideal body, talk to *him*!"

Scooting backward, she pushed herself up, grabbed her shoes, and took off down the beach.

"I can't talk to him," he shouted after her. "He only talks to you."

She turned to level one observation at him. "Maybe he would, if you weren't such an asshole." Taking off at a jog before he could reply was Madeline's way of letting him know she didn't care what he had to say.

But she was beginning to care about the Captain,

for some unexplainable reason. Perhaps because they had both raised a son alone. Maybe it was that society scorned them. She had not been deaf to the remarks made about her when she wound up pregnant in her first year at college.

Or maybe it was their decisions to live loveless lives. She didn't know of any other women in the Captain's, and there had certainly been no other men in hers. It could have been what made her vulnerable to him.

She longed for him, God help her. How strongly he ignited the flames of desire within her. And although she felt it was wrong for the Captain to use William's body to touch her, how else would he ever make love to her? If she had to sacrifice a little morality to feel for a brief moment what others did all of the time, what difference did it make?

It wasn't as if William were a virgin, or married, or even in a relationship, for crying out loud. He gave it out to anyone within touching distance. Well, not anyone. That was what made his violent reaction to touching her so upsetting.

A canal split the land just in front of her. Regrettably, she would have to turn and go back. She didn't want to have to face William and his disgust at being used.

Perhaps she should shelve the whole project and find something else to do her thesis on. But even if she did, she had become too enraptured by the Captain to pull out. Now, she wanted to help him. She felt she owed him that.

Even if William demanded she not use the paper for her dissertation, she needed to give the Captain whatever would allow him to rest in peace. She gasped, realizing doing so would mean losing him. Yet, he was already gone and had been for more than a century-and-a-half.

Chapter 15

William wasn't on the beach when Madeline reached the path, nor at the house when she returned to it. Most likely he had gone out for the evening, and she would be alone to think.

She ran a bath. Soaking beneath a layer of bubbles, she tried to make sense of what was happening but failed to do so. After drying her hair, she crawled into bed. It had been a trying day. Perhaps sleep would help.

The sound of a woman's laughter interrupted her dreams. A door slammed and voices wafted upward. William had company—a female. She heard them saying. "shh" to one another, and then the sound of footsteps on the stairs.

He was taking her to his room. *Asshole*, Madeline thought again, and covered her head with a pillow. They were two floors down so, once they left the open staircase, thankfully the sound died.

The last thing she needed to do was listen to William make love to a woman he actually desired. And she definitely didn't need to hear the young bimbo he'd brought home in the throes of passion. She tried to return to her own dreams.

Loud voices woke her again. William and his guest appeared to be arguing. A door slammed, footsteps stomped down the stairs. More voices raised in anger, then another door slamming.

Madeline giggled in spite of herself. Apparently William wasn't any better with the women he desired than he was with the ones he didn't.

Heavy footsteps rang out on the stairs, a single pair. She assumed he was going back to his room. But they kept climbing all the way to her door. A knock reverberated and then he announced, "Madeline, make yourself decent. I'm coming in."

She barely had time to switch on the table lamp before he barged through the door wearing only pajama bottoms and a huge frown.

Sitting up; she was glad she had made the decision to bring pajamas instead of the over-sized T-shirt she normally wore to bed. "What is the matter with you? What are you doing in my room in the middle of the night?"

"You call him up here. Right now. Get him here!" He pointed with a finger to the space in front of him.

"Have you lost your mind? What on earth are you talking about? Get who here?" She was still half asleep, and he was apparently incoherent.

"The apparition. The Captain. Whatever it is you call him. Get him here now," he demanded.

"He isn't a puppy. I can't whistle and expect him to appear. What's the matter with you?"

"What have you been saying to him? Have you put him up to something?"

He was clearly angry, but she didn't have a clue as to why. "Listen, why don't you calm down and try to tell me what it is you are so unhappy about?" She motioned to the chair beside the bedstand, and he walked over to it. Swinging her legs over the edge of the bed, she sat facing him.

"I know it's him," he said, jaw jerking.

"What's him? Why don't you tell me what this is about?"

"You know how he possesses me into making love to you against my will?"

She felt the heat of anger sting her fully awake. "For the record, we have never actually made love. So you can get that off your conscience, if it's bothering you."

"Not the point." He waved his hands back and forth and shook his head. "Now, he is possessing me into *not* making love to the women I intend to!"

Madeline laughed in spite of herself. "You want to blame a little erectile dysfunction on a ghost?" She knew she was hitting below the belt—in more ways than one—but felt redemption in the saying of the words. He had hurt her feelings in so many ways, it seemed justified.

"Very funny. Ha-ha-ha." Sarcasm dripped from his voice.

"I'm serious. What makes you think this particular incident has something to do with him?" She tried not to snicker when she spoke, and was glad for the half light of the lamp illuminating his face more than her own. "You've never had trouble maintaining an erection before?"

He blushed and his mouth twisted into a sneer. "Not that it's any of your business, but only on rare occasions if I've had too much to drink."

"Listen, I'm not the one beating on your bedroom door demanding explanations. I couldn't care less about your sexual performance, or lack thereof. But you did have a lot to drink today, and most likely had more tonight. Don't blame the Captain for your own actions, and I won't blame you for his."

A shadow of embarrassment crept across his face. "If I could only remember."

"Remember what?"

"Anything. I was about to make love to her, and the next thing I knew she was angry, and I wasn't working, if you know what I mean."

"Again, probably too much alcohol. Did the Captain say anything to you?"

"No, but he doesn't talk to me. You're the one he communicates with." He clearly wanted this episode to be the fault of the apparition.

"Listen"—she had calmed down enough to realize he was teetering on the edge of insanity—"if he were here in this room, my bedroom, you only in bottoms and me in very little, don't you think he would have already shown up?"

"Maybe he needs a little incitement." With that he lunged for her.

"Stop, William, stop. You've lost your mind." She struggled to free herself from his grip.

"Why? If he can use me at his will, why can't I use him at mine?"

A great force of wind blew William off her and onto the floor. The apparition stood between them. Madeline could feel his anger radiating through the atmosphere as formidably as electrical currents running through a stream of water.

"Captain," she whispered.

"Yes my love. Are you hurt?"

"No, and I don't think he really meant to harm me."

"Be that as it may; you tell him if he ever touches you again, without your consent, I will hang him from the cupola. Even if he is my heir."

"But Captain—" she protested.

"Tell him!" he roared.

She repeated the words as directed.

William slunk out into the hall and back down the stairs.

Madeline stared at the shape standing protectively in front of her.

He crossed to her and breathed into her hair, ruffling it as his words washed over her. "Know I am here for you. Sleep well. We will be together again soon."

The light extinguished itself, and she pulled the covers over herself. The Captain's words echoed in her head as she proceeded to have a wonderful night's sleep. No one had ever been there for her before. Not ever. Maybe she didn't want him to be redeemed. That would make him go away.

Chapter 16

William wished the scene in Madeline's bedroom would disappear from his memory. He had acted horribly and to say he was ashamed was too benign. Mortified would come closer to the truth. The ghost of Pine Island was driving him crazy and making him resort to things he would have never considered before.

The following morning, waiting for the sounds of her footsteps on the stairs, he tried to make amends. "Good morning," he called out cheerfully.

"I'm surprised to see you up so early," she said with a note of sarcasm. "I figured you'd be in bed nursing a sore head."

"Sore pride is more like it. Listen, Madeline, about last night—"

Madeline held up a hand. "No. I don't want to hear anything about it; no explanations, no excuses. It's done."

"But…" He did need to apologize and to explain. If only he knew how.

"You'd had too much to drink. Leave it at that."

"But—"

"No buts. I've been thinking. We're not progressing fast enough. You need to be more involved. I want to see every document you can produce."

"Actually, I've already mustered a few." He handed her a stack of copied documents.

Accompanying them were typed explanations of the nearly-illegible handwritten notes.

"Have you read these?" She flipped through the pages.

"Yeah. It seems the Captain was a Union sympathizer. It makes him seem patriotic now, but would have been considered highly traitorous to his neighbors and to the south back then."

"And he'd already thumbed his nose at their methods of farming with slaves."

He recalled their discussion about the Captain's insistence on building his dream house without the use of slavery, and making a good living without tilling soil. "Yet he prospered. That probably drove many of them nuts."

William was so thankful to have something to discuss besides his horrible behavior. He handed her a cup of coffee and cracked a few eggs into a bowl.

"You're making breakfast?" Surprise tinged Madeline's voice.

"I've given the help a vacation. I didn't know what else might happen, and I thought it would be best if they weren't privy to the apparition and our digging around for the reason he can't cross over." He beat the eggs and opened the oven door, releasing the heavenly smell of bacon.

"You're cooking bacon in the oven?"

"Wait 'til you taste it. It keeps its shape and doesn't splatter over the stove top—a little trick I learned watching the cook."

"Impressive!" She smiled and turned her attention back to the documents. "So it was rumored the Captain was supplying the Union army?"

"Looks like." William poured the eggs into a skillet laced with melted butter.

"But didn't Georgetown get taken over by the Yankees pretty early on?"

He nodded.

"So if they had this seaport, why would they need the Captain and his vessel?"

"Maybe it was a *you wash my hands and I'll wash yours* kind of deal." He shrugged. "Perhaps they let him make his own runs while picking up useful items for them."

"If so, many of his neighbors would have lost sons due to his gains."

"Exactly. They even accused him of piracy himself."

"Which document has those details?" She flipped through them.

"He was accused of possessing French gold, the kind that disappeared on *Le Concorde* when Blackbeard acquisitioned it for himself."

She grimaced, confused. "I thought Blackbeard's ship was *Queen Anne's Revenge*."

"He renamed *Le Concorde*; even forced some of the help to stay on the ship and assist him."

"But it ran aground a hundred years before the Captain sailed these waters."

"Yes, but it was never found." William dished up the eggs and pushed the toaster lever down as he retrieved the perfectly crisp bacon from the oven. Then he refilled their coffee cups, poured two glasses of juice, and buttered the toast as soon as it popped up.

"Thank you," she said, as the food was set before her.

"It's the least I could do after last night."

She raised her hand and flicked it back and forth. "That's behind us. We have much more important things to focus on." She bit into the bacon and forkful of eggs. "Like this wonderful breakfast!"

He smiled at having pleased her, and for her gracious acceptance of his apology. Women, in his experience, typically used any offense as an excuse to torture him. He had never known one to be so forgiving.

Of course, Madeline wasn't emotionally invested in him. The only connection they had was the Captain, and the only time she longed for his touch was when he wasn't even aware they were in contact. He didn't have to make false assumptions she was attracted to him.

"If you keep reading, you'll find where he was caught with some of the old coins in his possession. He said he was given them in exchange for other goods—cloth, glassware, spices, rum—things not readily available during the Civil War."

"And the French also traded with the West Indies. It was plausible he might have gotten them when he went to the Indies. He would have been smart not to accept too much in the way of Confederate Dollars."

"Another point probably angering the rest of the community, who were knee-deep in Confederate debt."

"So any one of his neighbors might have had reason to confront his wife, while he was absent, and murder her. Then they could have set him up for it," she concluded. "My feeling, from the Captain, leaves me with no doubt as to his innocence in the death of his beloved Magdalene."

"Would seem so. Has he mentioned anything to

you about this?"

"No. Mostly he talks about how much he loved her. I remind him of her." Madeline stared at him, her questioning expression begging an answer as to what she should do about it.

"Come with me today. You haven't been off the island since arriving. I think another look around the historical societies' papers might produce a fresh clue."

They rinsed their dishes, stacked them in the washer, and headed for town along the forest road.

Chapter 17

William and Madeline, in his car, swung into a parking lot across from the Kaminski House which shared a walkway with the Historical Society. William slid another skeleton key, from the car's console, into his pocket.

Inside, they were ushered through a set of sliding doors into a chamber Madeline previously had no idea existed. Set into the wall was a vault with a wooden paneled front that could have been an ordinary door.

The president of the society, Carol Lewis, took out a key similar to the one William held. Together, with a set of synchronized turns, keys rolling the tumblers, the door released. After a few creaks and moans, it opened up to reveal an interior the size of a walk-in closet any woman would be proud of.

But these weren't shelves meant for boots and coats. They were for books and leather journals and important papers all about the history of Georgetown. It felt as significant as the Smithsonian to Madeline and was equally so to the long-term residents of this genteel city.

William went straight to a locked box inside the vault and produced another key—much more modern than the knobby skeleton ones. He turned the key, pulled open the drawer, and spun around.

Madeline caught the expression on William's face.

Something was wrong, terribly wrong.

"Carol," he yelled.

She had made to leave but turned back at the sound of her name.

"Come back in here now," he demanded.

"Yes?" the tall stocky lady answered.

"The Captain's journals are not in their normal place. Have you moved them?" He pointed to the drawer Madeline could see was empty.

"Why, no, of course not." She appeared equally stricken and joined him in staring downward into nothing but clean space.

William's voice rose even slightly higher, indicating growing concern. "Then why are they not here?"

"Who would have access? Only you have the key to this drawer and only other members, with personal rare belongings, have skeleton keys to the main door. My key alone will not open it."

"Perhaps it is in a different drawer." He tried the other drawers he held a key to and then turned back to Carol. "Send out requests for all key holders to meet us at the Society's front hall at their earliest convenience."

Her face blazed red before fading to ashen gray. "I'll get right on it, Mr. Gray."

William's jaw jerked. In a dazed frenzy, he paced from side to side, digging at every book and in each tiny nook. "How could this happen?" he mumbled.

Madeline wanted to ask the question foremost on her mind but knew it was best to wait for him to volunteer the information about the obvious problem. Besides, he might find what he was seeking and all would be okay.

Suddenly he glanced up at her. "They are missing," he said. "The Captain's journals are all missing."

"But who…why…how…?" she stuttered and spat. Her mind spun with the few possibilities. She had just witnessed the complicated method of opening the secret room door and then the vault. It seemed unlikely most people would know this even existed. She had spent several days in the facility and had missed it completely. "Who even knew about them, and why would they want them?"

He ran a hand through his hair. "That certainly seems to be the million dollar question now, doesn't it?"

"What was in them someone else might need?"

He shook his head. "I've attempted to read them periodically, but it is time-consuming." Reaching for another leather-bound tome above her head, he flipped it open and shoved it under her nose. "Can you tell me what this says?"

Madeline looked at the ancient scribbles, half old-English and the other half loops of letters and misspelled words—or not—she couldn't really tell as the writing was faded, old, and scripted in a way which wasn't currently utilized. "I'd need a little time to go over it."

"Exactly. This is what the script in the journals resembles, nearly unintelligible to me. I've been meaning to get an expert in to help me decipher them, but considered it would be a great pastime for old age."

"So you think someone took them for their age alone? Otherwise, it would have to be someone who specializes in reading pre-Civil War script that found out about these journals, managed to break in here, and took them?" It all seemed a bit convoluted for belief.

Carol returned saying she had contacted all but one of the other vault drawer holders. Ray was on an extended trip aboard a sailboat. The rest could meet with William at noon the following day. Possibly they could weed out the need for Ray's participation. It was settled. William escorted Carol and Madeline out, with the understanding he would return the next day.

The drive back to Pine Island was quiet. William appeared to be doing some serious thinking and Madeline didn't want to interfere with his thoughts.

She gazed out the window at swamp marshes, and snowy egrets, and cypress knees, and an occasional pair of eyes bobbing at water's edge—the alligator's giveaway trait. She tried to focus on the kind of patience needed to be that reptile, waiting for the right snack to unsuspectingly come along.

"When he returns to you, you must ask him about this," William suddenly said.

"What do you mean?" She knew the answer before uttering the question.

"The next time you see him, and you will see him again, you must ask him what was in the journals and why anyone would want them? Then tell him to go hang out at the Historical Society and find out who took his important life's worth of notes." He kept staring straight ahead as he issued the demands she must make on the spirit of the Captain.

"We don't really talk very much."

"You do now." He said this in a manner suggesting his mere proclamation would make it so.

She nodded, and returned to thinking about the alligator—only this time she felt like the prey.

Chapter 18

The Captain didn't show up that night. Perhaps he sensed her desire for him to appear and rebelled.

William seemed most unhappy about it the next morning at breakfast. "Perhaps I need to make out with you in order to convince him to make an appearance around here." He said this with a bite in his voice making it sound akin to the most despicable thing he could imagine doing.

Madeline slammed her coffee mug onto the table top. "Well, I would hate for you to have to stoop to something as low as that."

"I didn't mean it derogatorily. Only as...hell...I don't know what I meant." He paced and slammed his own mug down, sloshing coffee out onto the table's surface. "Sorry. I didn't get much sleep."

"Unfortunately you did not inherit his penchant for charm and tact, did you?"

"Well, you stirred all of this up. You know that, right?" He had turned again. He was like that. One minute he appeared one way, the next something else entirely.

"You really do have a split personality, you know *that*—right?" She jumped out of the seat and headed out the door.

"Hey, where are you going? You know I didn't mean anything..." His voice trailed off as the door slammed behind her.

Clouds loomed overhead, a thick gray blanket promising a nice rain. The sea grass lining the path whispered to her as she passed, its feathery tips dancing to the wind. When she arrived at the coast, roiling waves greeted her.

The tide was in, and it was aggressive. Salt water spray splattered Madeline's clothing and hair as she walked along the stretch of sand made smaller by the usurping waves. Terns ran at the retreating water and then scurried back. Sand crabs sidestepped to the safety of shore rocks.

Wind tousled her hair back and forth in front of her face, whipping it like wet ropes onto her cheeks. She tried pushing it back, but it escaped and blew back at her eyes.

"Over here," a familiar voice said. The soft touch of fingertips tugged at her as she turned to see the Captain smiling at her. In the grayness of the morning, he appeared brighter than ever.

She smiled, happy to see him, and followed him into the safety of a rocky alcove that shut out the wind and the noise of the churning sea.

"You are more lifelike today," she noted.

"I feel more alive than I have in many years. I think I am gaining strength."

"Will you stay and talk with me awhile?"

"You no longer fear me?" His fingertips brushed her cheek and she instinctively knew there was nothing to fear from him.

"Why would I fear the one who rescued me from the sea, pushed away an aggressive grandson, and touched me with such love I cannot deny it?"

"Even if that person is in spirit form only?"

"I know. It sounds strange, even to me, as I say it. But you've had every opportunity to cause harm and have not. And at each point I have needed you, you have been right there. I am grateful really."

"So I have grown on you?" He grinned at her in a mischievous way.

"I didn't know apparitions could be so teasing," she replied with a grin.

"You may also not have previously been aware of the immense pleasure one could offer." The grin deepened.

She laughed, recalling the sensations in the upper room of the house. "You are a rascal, you know that, right? Even in death—which I can't believe I am saying—you are a flirtatious rascal!"

"What is this 'rascal'? Is it good?" He kept trying to hold her hand but could only brush against it.

"Yeah, I guess." She had relaxed enough to blush and enjoy his company.

"Yeah?"

"It means yes. Sorry. I forget sometimes you are not from here, exactly."

"You said you wanted to talk to me. I am here. Talk. But I must warn you, I will want something in return."

"What do you want?"

"I want to spend the night in your arms. I want to feel you pressed against me. I want to show you my love in all of its forms."

"You can't even hold my hand, what makes you think you can make love to me or hold me?"

"I can, and I will." He grinned again. "I just need

the permission of my stubborn great-great-great-grandson to use his body. He keeps tossing me out. I find it a bit rude actually. He does live in my house."

"I don't think he desires me the same way you do."

"He is a fool, then, and should vacate the premises at once. I can arrange it. Would you desire for me to do so?"

Madeline got the distinct feeling he would enjoy tossing his last remaining heir out onto his rear. But it didn't seem like the right thing to do. "Perhaps he could be persuaded. There is something he wants and something I need from you."

The Captain leaned backward, at least the shape of him shifted. "I am only too willing to oblige your needs. His we can discuss later."

He encircled her with a halo of his shape. She didn't know how else to describe it. He appeared to turn into vapor and then pour himself into the area around her. She closed her eyes and felt so peaceful she doubted she would ever have another bad day. It was the most comforted and cheerful she had felt in her life.

"I could get used to this," she muttered as she searched his eyes and found a type of love waiting for her there she couldn't remember ever feeling before.

"Supply me with the consent of William to inhabit his body for one entire night, and I will give him whatever he wishes. Tell him this."

She tried to warn him William didn't share his ancestor's desire for her. "He'll never hear of it. He doesn't find me attractive. Also, he hates it when you pass through him."

"And you? How do you feel when I pass through you?"

"I feel sublime peace and happiness—at least now I do. At first it was a little frightening."

"I will never do anything to hurt you. I did never do anything to hurt you before, and I will not now, my lovely Magdalene."

Oh no, she thought, *he still thinks I'm Magdalene.* Well, what difference did it make? "Madeline, not Magdalene. And yes, I believe you would never hurt me."

"Then go back to him, Magdalene Madeline, and tell him I want his body for one entire night and day, sundown to sundown. If he agrees, I will grant him with all of the information he requests."

"If he doesn't?"

"I tell him nothing."

"Can you at least tell me where…?" The words slipped away, as he had disappeared.

"Captain? Are you there?" She looked left and right, but could see no sign of him. In the distance a voice called out her name. She stepped out of the shelter and saw William walking toward her, calling for her. She answered, and he ran to meet her.

"Thank God, I was so worried." Without thought, he embraced her.

Though it felt warm and nice and concerned, it didn't spark the same sensations as the Captain's powerful ones. "He was here," she said.

William released her, pushing her back from him with his arms stretched out in front of him. He couldn't hide his excitement. "Did you talk to him? Did you ask about the journals? Did you ask about the society's members? Does he know anything?"

"Yes, and no," she hedged.

"Which part 'yes' and which part 'no'?"

"Come on. Let's walk back to the house and talk about this."

"Yeah, those clouds are ominous."

****

They hurried from the beach to the house. Its shape was the same from the beach path as it appeared from the inlet, forest road, or field. All four sides gabled exactly the same way, matching entrances welcomed visitors to a proper view of the house regardless of their means of transportation.

With the enormous amount of curiosity pressing upon him, as well as the threat of the rain, William's steps were long and caused Madeline to jog to keep up with him. Large drops began to fall and plop onto them as they neared the entrance. He grabbed two towels from the bath nearest that side of the house and returned to the place she was planted.

He couldn't keep the anxiousness from his voice as he rubbed his head with the thick terry towel. "Listen, it's almost eleven. I'm supposed to meet the others at the Historical Society at noon. That doesn't give me long to change and get going. Give me the gist of what he had to say, and who he thinks it might be?"

"We didn't get to that." She wrapped the towel around her midsection.

"So what exactly did you 'get to'?"

"He doesn't want to discuss anything until you agree to something." Her voice quivered.

He could tell he was not going to approve of the demands. "What?" He felt his forehead crinkling, his brows knitting together, and he tried to force them into a more natural position. By the expression on her face, he wasn't being very successful. Or the request was worse than he had feared.

"He wants permission to use your body for one night and day." She blurted it out, without warning or an appropriate lead-up.

The sound of her words sent icicles along his spine. "Why? Why would he want to use my body?"

"To make love to me, I think." She enunciated each word, though with a fair amount of uncertainty.

William backed away and held up his hand. Surely she had misunderstood the request. Or he had misunderstood her. "Oh, no. No, no, and no!"

She stared at him.

"You're pulling my leg, right? Ha-ha. Funny. Now, tell me the truth."

She continued to glare at him, with a serious look on her face communicating the lack of a joke.

William dropped his shoulders and stuck his chin forward. "You're serious? He wants to use my body…to bed you?"

She nodded, silently agreeing.

"And you're okay with that?"

Madeline threw her arms out to the side. "I don't know. I didn't give it much thought. I assumed you would never agree, so it didn't seem to be something I'd need to consider."

He rubbed his forehead with both hands. "I tell you what. You stay here and contemplate this, while I go in to town. How do you know this ghost is who he says he is? How do you know he can be trusted? What if he uses my body to do things you don't want him to do? What if…?"

She took his hands, and he stopped the frantic

ramblings. "I do not doubt he is who he says he is. He looks exactly like you. He knows things about this place and the area. And I trust him. He saved me on the beach earlier. He pushed you away from me when he thought you were forcing yourself on me. I do not, and cannot, believe he means me any harm."

William slipped his hands from hers, using one to point accusingly at her. "I am going to leave you with that thought. You'd better be sure you are on board with whatever could go wrong. I am not at all sure I can go along with this insanity. Not having control of my own body? I don't think so!"

He grabbed an umbrella from the stand and headed off to the garage, pretending not to hear the remark she threw behind his back—about the noticeable improvement when he didn't have control.

Chapter 19

The rain pelted the car's windows long before William had time to get into town. He fumed the entire way, barely noticing how high the water was rising in the low areas of the road. It was utter nonsense, all of it. Even though he had seen and felt the force of this ghost, he couldn't give himself over to the notion it was totally real.

And as far as letting this apparition use his body, it was beyond belief such a thing could happen and that he would agree to it even if it could. It was true he had been the one requesting Madeline's assistance in putting this whole thing to rest—putting the Captain to rest. For all he knew, the haunting was the reason he wasn't married today.

The pain of Julia's memory still burned too deeply to recover from. If he was a little harsh, especially with women, perhaps these were acts of self-preservation. If he could get rid of this entity, this haunting spirit, maybe he could have enough peace to settle in to a life where his bride wouldn't think she was losing her mind, or he was losing his.

Now he almost resented Pine Island and the legacy he had to wear like an albatross. Nobody knew this, of course, but he wanted to plant the vineyard in his drawing and tend to it for however many vintages life saw fit to give him. And he couldn't do it here. Not unless he wanted to use a coastal vine, such as the great Mother Vine on Roanoke Island, the muscadine.

He wasn't fond of muscadine grapes, nor the wine made from them. No, he enjoyed chardonnay and pinot noir—subtle wines that enhanced the flavor of the foods they was paired with—not the oversweet, flowery, musky, competitive sharpness of muscadine wine.

Everyone called him foolish. He had plenty of wealth, a lovely ancestral home on a private stretch of beach, and good health. Who wanted to listen to his complaints? But did it matter whether you were a poor man who couldn't afford to follow your dreams, or a rich man unable to pursue them, being shackled by fate?

The death of one's dreams prefaced the death of one's soul. At least that was how he felt. Maybe he should let the long-dead sea captain, whose seed he had sprung from, borrow him for a while. At least he might enjoy it. That annoying woman, Madeline, certainly seemed to enjoy the Captain. She'd given William no attention, but when the apparition appeared, she seemed totally enthralled.

He thought about her for the rest of the ride into town—the way she lit up for the Captain, the way she quivered in his arms, the feel of her touch. She wasn't like the typical woman he dated—supermodel good looks with big southern hair and swanky clothes—but she had appeal in her own way.

Perhaps it was her confidence. Or was it perversely her obvious lack of enjoying his presence except when she was responding to a deceased man's touch? She preferred the spirit of a dead man to him. *Did she know how insulting that was? Did she care,* he wondered?

The other members were waiting for him when he pulled up outside of the Historical Society. "Hurry up, a bad storm is headed this way."

He ran for the door, shed his wet overcoat, and produced the necessary keys, as did the others. But nothing unusual was to be found. The belongings of the others were safely tucked into their drawers, minus any of his.

"How could your journals go missing?" one asked.

"It makes me a little nervous," another agreed.

"Has the security service been down?"

Carol Lewis stood stoically, arms crossed over her chest, refusing to believe anything had gone wrong at her end. "I have experienced nothing out of the ordinary, gentlemen. Maybe you should count your keys again and verify someone hasn't helped themselves to something they ought not to have."

"You have been a little preoccupied lately," his life-long friend Alex Hamilton said to William. "Why don't you come to supper, and we can discuss it over a nice brandy."

William grimaced. He knew Alex was right but didn't want to admit it. "I'd love nothing more, but I have that damned woman staying out at Pine Island, and I don't think she should be left out there alone."

Carol's head jerked around at him. "The same one who was spending a lot of time in here asking all kinds of questions and doing her best to procure access to the journals?"

"Yes, actually."

"Well there you are," she purred in her best southern accent. "She probably got a little sticky-fingered when it came to your journals."

He dangled the key to the drawer in front of her. "Impossible. She didn't have this."

The oldest gentleman laughed. "I never knew a woman who couldn't get her hands on anything she wanted to badly enough. There's your answer, old boy."

"You don't think it could be in this one?" William jerked his head toward the one unopened drawer, the one belonging to the sailor out riding the high seas.

"Ray's been out on the water for quite some time now. I seriously doubt it."

"No, this woman friend of yours is the obvious culprit, ol' pal," said another.

Carol continued her speculation, "She told me she was determined to find out everything she could about the man who built his home on Pine Island."

William nodded, taking in their skepticism and knowing more than he could allow them to suspect. For a moment, he wondered what they would think of him if he started telling them about the ghostly apparition and its demands.

"Well, I guess I'd better get back out there before she makes off with the silver tea service," William said.

"Oh you'll never get back out there tonight," Alex said.

"Why not?"

"Haven't you been watching the weather? This is a fierce storm. It's already dropped several inches."

"Since it started this morning?"

"Easily. Come on down to my house. We can talk this over."

William felt panic rising, sweat forming on his brow. "But what about Madeline? I must get back out

135

there." He didn't know if she knew where to find flashlights and candles. She would probably be scared witless, should the power fail, with the ghost prowling around.

"You'll never make it. The water will probably go down by tomorrow evening. She'll be fine. Give her a call and explain where she can find the necessities."

"Yeah," said Carol, "I can think of far worse places to be caught in a storm than Pine Island. I believe it's withstood storms for more than a few generations."

"Almost two hundred years," William answered, feeling the pressure once again to be its keeper and protector.

"Well, then, I don't suppose one more night will make much difference."

He tried to phone Madeline using his cell phone, but the signal died. He grabbed the society's phone and managed to make a connection. He heard her say "Hello, Pine Island," followed by a lot of static.

William yelled into the receiver, "Madeline can you hear me? I can't get back. They say the road is under water until tomorrow. It happens sometimes. Madeline, Madeline—are you there?"

Nothing but silence followed the crinkling of static and sudden pop. He laid the receiver back in the cradle, feeling a sense of doom. His fate had been determined by the weather, something he didn't mind normally. But having her out there alone caused him no small amount of concern.

Carol said, "We'd better get going as well."

William followed his friend Alex to their cars and on to his house a couple of streets down.

On a nice day, they would have walked, feeling the

soft moist breezes through the shade of the trees, admiring the timeworn structures and the architecture specific to the area—sweeping porches to catch sea breezes, entrances in crazy places to avoid extra taxes, carved pineapples atop columns.

But in the drenching rain, it was all William could do to see the taillights of the car in front of him. He knew they had been right about his inability to get back to Pine Island.

What would Madeline think? She would be crazed with worry, and quite lonely.

Chapter 20

Madeline heard William call her name before the line went dead, but that was all. The rest she had to fill in for herself. Knowing the area, she could only imagine how fast the road into Pine Island flooded. The whole of it was barely above, and some parts of it were actually below, sea level.

The causeways and roads through the swamps and along the International Waterway were quick to cover over with water. He probably wasn't going to be able to make it back. Or he might try, and something awful could happen. She could either trust he was safe for the time being, or face a long night of worry. The former sounded better.

Her only problem was the darkness.

Storm clouds and walls of rainwater would douse the light of an ordinary afternoon, but this evening's darkness left her with dread. It would be sunrise before she could see anything again. Her room was up three flights of stairs, where the only flashlight she had was lying on her bed stand.

She blamed herself for not realizing the storm would be so ferocious. Normally she stayed abreast of the news and knew when storms were coming and how intense they were expected to be. Since arriving at Pine Island, she had been too absorbed in life itself to be interested in the details of the six o'clock news.

While waiting for William's return, she had disregarded the chance of losing power, of needing flashlights, candles, and a bottle of wine to drown her miseries in. Now it was too dark to go snooping about. She tried to remember every tabletop display and then realized even if she found a candle she had no match.

She did the only thing she could think of to do, the only thing that made her feel better in the heat of a crisis. She yelled, "Fuck," at the top of her voice. As she shouted the word she had been raised to believe was one not for the lips of proper southern girls, it released her pent-up anxiety. Madeline supposed it was going against traditional discreetness that made it feel cathartic.

A whistle sounded through the library, a long male whistle. "What language to come from such a lovely lady!"

Even in the darkness she saw him—the Captain—a silhouette now seeming as real as she was in the black of the room.

Both hands flew to her face in embarrassment. "Oh, I'm sorry. I didn't know you were here." Her cheeks grew hot with the realization he had heard her use *that* word.

"I'm always here," he answered, as he sidled up next to her.

"That's oddly comforting," she confessed. She wondered if he meant always in *all* of the rooms.

"Don't worry. I don't peek where I shouldn't. Even the dead have some manners."

Dropping her hands from her still-warm face, she asked the looming questions. "Why are you still here? I mean to say, what is holding you to this realm? Isn't there an afterlife waiting for you somewhere over the rainbow?"

"Not without properly tending to my reputation."

"I don't understand how you have remained here all of these years. Why hasn't someone else helped you? Why do you think I can?"

"You are the first person to really see me. Others have caught glimpses, but nothing sustained over any period of time. In fact, that is how I know you are the embodiment of Magdalene. You are drawn to Pine Island, are you not?"

"Well yes, but—"

"You favor her, *and* can see me. Such a combination spells out a previous connection."

"You mean others can't see you the way I do?"

"Nor have we been able to communicate with one another. Not in the true sense of the word."

Madeline would have preferred to continue talking about his spirit and its failure to move into the appropriate afterlife, but the encroaching darkness rattled her with more imminent questions. "Tell me something. Do you know where I can find a candle and a match, or a flashlight, down here on this floor?"

If he had been hanging around this place for some years, surely he knew where things were. "Or do you even know what a flashlight is?"

His tone changed, indicating a slight offense had been leveled. "Just because my mortal life occurred over a century ago, doesn't mean I have remained uninformed about things of the present life."

It occurred to Madeline she didn't take his feelings into consideration most of the time. She hadn't even considered endowing him with them.

Nor had she thought a ghostly apparition would still be learning and observing things connected to the seen world. If she had ever given spirits any reflection at all, it was as shadows stuck in a moment of time unique to them. To think, for those stuck between worlds, one would continue to grow mentally and emotionally was a concept new to her.

"I didn't mean...I know you speak as we do now...well..." It got worse. The more she tried to backtrack the more demeaning it sounded.

"Stop, please, before I am unable to hold myself together." He clamped transparent hands across his ears.

"What do you mean by that?"

"We are all energy fields. You have a house for your field of energy—the physical body. You do not have to think about your hand dangling from the end of your forearm, it is simply housed there. I, however, must constantly think when I am in physical form about holding it together or I de-materialize—another way to say the energy that is me dissipates into the atmosphere."

"I didn't know any of this."

"Most living people don't. What is the saying you have—lighten up on yourself?"

"Oh, speaking of lighting up, can you tell me where to find a candle?" she asked the apparition.

"Yes. On the table across the room from you there is a candle in a stand covered by a glass globe. But there are no matches in this room. You must go to the kitchen and search in the drawer by the telephone."

"Can you help me get there?" It was fine to know where to locate the matches and candles, but if she couldn't find the right drawer in the kitchen, scrambling about in the dark could be dangerous.

"Yes, I will lead you. Stay close." His form appeared before her and she followed it, staying as near the shape of the Captain as she could. They slowly traversed the distance to the kitchen, and she opened drawers until she found the right one. The box of matches made her feel instantly calmer. Once she had the hurricane lamp lit, with its tall, thick taper capable of lasting through several hours of darkness, she felt even better.

"Shall we return to the library, or retire to your bedroom?" the Captain asked.

"Let's go on upstairs while I have this light and your guidance." She feared he would disappear and was suddenly feeling grateful to have him beside her.

"I'll lead," he offered, although she had lit the candle and had a nice soft glow surrounding her.

He paused at the door; she assumed waiting for her to enter first. But even after she had crossed the threshold, he stayed in the hallway. "Aren't you coming in with me?"

"Since you asked me," he answered.

Madeline placed the candle on the bedstand and watched the apparition settle into the chair on the other side of it. Sitting on the edge of the bed, she stared at him. "I can't get over how much you and William resemble one another."

"Only in appearances, I am sorry to say."

"You are disappointed in him?"

"He is not a bad person. If he does not possess my strengths, then I must note he also does not possess my weaknesses. He could be a worse heir to this property, but he could do much better."

She saw the tilt of his head, a subtle movement, but one she now understood took effort and thought. "What would you want to see him do?"

"I cannot deny sailing a sea vessel would delight me. It was a passion of mine, as you may know."

"Tell me about your days on the sea," she encouraged, genuinely interested in his life.

"Aah, you may wish you had not asked it of me. It has been a long time since I had the chance to recount those many adventures."

"Please, tell me. I want to know all about it."

"Have you never experienced a sea voyage?" Surprise laced his voice.

"Not as you did; days upon days out on the ocean, at the mercy of the wind and the waves. I have only taken sailing day trips."

He glided to the edge of the bed and sat down beside her, though there was no shift in the mattress or even a crevice on the coverlet. "Oh, Magdalene—"

"I'm Madeline," she insisted. "Please call me Madeline."

"You are Magdalene inside," he whispered. He brushed her cheek with the feathery touch of his fingertips.

She felt herself softening, melting as his presence ignited desire within her. As strange as it sounded to even think such a thought, she wondered how it was possible to lust after a ghost. He touched her in ways no man ever had.

Maybe he was right. Maybe she did recognize him from some long ago time on this plane of earth that held more mysteries than it did concrete answers. "How can you be sure?" She took a deep breath and felt it catch in her throat as his hand merged into hers.

"This entire conversation would not have happened otherwise."

"Why not?"

"There has to be a connection to the spirit, or complete removal of the mind from the current realm, in order to sustain contact. Are there moments when glimpses of those who wander after death are seen by those living in their current time? Yes, absolutely. But the human brain is wired not to see things it cannot deal with in present time. So it engages and we go *poof*— gone—a mere mist or moving fog."

He continued to stroke her hand, and the energy from the contact danced atop her flesh as surely as static in a silk scarf. "Only those who can turn off their brains and listen with their spirits can see us—you call them ghost-whisperers or -hunters. Elsewise, the inner spirit of the body it is housed in must recognize the apparition. Then the inner self switches off the brain and allows the impossible to be made possible. You are not a seer or whisperer, are you?"

She shook her head.

"Go inward my love. Find Magdalene. Look into your heart and see if we are there."

Doing as he asked, she closed her eyes and the scent of salt water and sea marsh and spearmint filled her nostrils, followed by citrus, lemons, and pineapples.

"What is it?" he asked.

"I can smell things—things not in this room."

"What kind of things?"

"Salt water, sea marsh, spearmint, lemons and pineapples. And wait, there's something else, vanilla maybe, and spices—pepper?" She opened her eyes and looked at him, feeling a connection deeper than any she had ever known. "None of those are in this room. I can understand the salt water and sea marsh, but the rest?"

"We used to grow spearmint in the kitchen garden. Oh, how we loved a little spearmint tea out on the balcony while watching the distant waves crash against the shore. And when I returned from a voyage, there was always a treasure trove of goods for you—her—cloth, beads, glassware—but her favorites were lemons, pineapples, spices, and vanilla beans. Her spirit is in you, believe it or not. You are my Magdalene."

The shock of his words could barely match the jolt of his merging into her body once again, and the feeling he was welcome there. The agitation of being alone during the storm was over. She was not alone. She was reunited with her love, the once-great man who had built the house surrounding her. He could never harm her. She managed to push him aside, while holding him near.

"Okay, I believe you. I believe we have a connection. But if I am her, then I must have the knowledge of what happened to me—to her. Can we figure this out? And do you suppose there is a way to prove it all of these years later?"

"My reputation suffers either way," he said, thinning a bit.

"Don't go," she begged, watching him fade away. "No! Come back."

His shape evaporated. All that was left was a feeling he was still in the room somehow.

"I am always with you," he whispered.

It was the last she heard of him all evening.

****

Soft sunlight poured in through the windows, refracted by thousands of rain droplets gathered on the glass. Madeline glanced at the candle, now burned out in a puddle of wax encircling the bottom of the dish beneath the hurricane globe.

Memories of the previous evening came rushing back, bringing with them the realization that somehow, in some previous life, she had lived briefly in this house, on these grounds, as the wife of Captain William Gray. And she still loved him, even though he was only a spirit now, caught between two worlds.

People had often asked why she had chosen the Captain's saga to write about. She had a very intelligent answer and it was such that no one guessed the truth, not even herself. Now, she knew.

She had felt compelled to write about him. There was never another topic of interest in her mind. Even as a child she had been interested in the history of this house and its legacy of pirates and sea traders, the ways of the archaic south mixed with the Grays' obstinacy not to proliferate the business of bondage.

Madeline tried to recall the first time she had seen the historic house. Her dad had been watching a nest of eagles on the bay side, eyes glued to his rubber-rimmed binoculars. The water was unbelievably clear that day; she remembered it because of the strange glowing fish she could see beneath its depths.

While they bobbed in the bay, she had allowed her hand to dangle in the water, mentally calling the fish up to her. As if hearing her silent plea, the fish sprang to the surface, nibbling at her fingertips. For a moment, she nearly became the fish, could almost feel the coolness of the sea against her body.

When she looked up again, the house was gleaming. Every sparkle of sunshine seemed focused on it, highlighting it. She could only see the cupola and the top two floors, but the need to walk through Gray Estate had filled her so thoroughly that day she had never been able to release its grip.

She didn't choose to write about Pine Island and Captain William Gray. It had chosen her. But how could she explain such a thing to anybody? They'd never understand.

Coming back to the present, Madeline padded up to the cupola to look out over the landscape. The water was still pretty high. From her bird's eye view, she might have been on a barge afloat in a lake of water. If the waters didn't recede quickly, William would not make it home today either.

She smiled. Maybe then she would get a little more time with the Captain. Maybe he would visit her again and sit beside her bed and tell her stories—the ones he didn't get to last night. She wanted to see him again, now more than ever before.

Chapter 21

William shared coffee and pastries with Alex. It had been a restless night and his concern for his own guest, alone out on Pine Island, had made it nearly impossible to sleep. He had never known such worry before. He chalked it up to legal liability. After all, he couldn't be developing feelings for her. He had shelved all sentimentality a long time ago.

"Sorry William, it isn't promising for you to be able to cross to the island until at least tomorrow. Maybe the phones will get up and running though, so you can contact your guest."

"I can get a boat to take me out, maybe," he reasoned. William didn't care about his car right now. It was the need to return to Pine Island absorbing him.

"I doubt it. They're all tethered up until the water recedes a little. Besides, who is going to risk hitting a shoal or running aground? Don't worry; you can stay here as long as you need to."

William's mind raced. How could he not worry? His house was haunted by a spirit wishing to devour his guest. How could he explain that to anyone else?

****

Madeline didn't see the Captain for the entire morning, although she had called out to him and asked him to materialize. She busied herself searching about the house for additional candles, flashlights, batteries, and any food suitable for eating without adding heat. She wished for coffee more than anything else, but, strangely enough, craved pineapple and lemon.

Feeling crafty, as a spy scavenging through drawers she didn't have permission to rifle, she excused herself on the premise it was due to the unexpected emergency only. Otherwise she would not have dared such an intrusion. After all, she had been here for nearly two weeks and had not done anything so bold to date.

Her searches were proving fruitful. She not only found another flashlight, but additional batteries and a few more matches. Now she sought candles. Surely William had more than one in a house this size. She climbed up to the second story.

His study was the most obvious place for such items to be stored. Even in an emergency, it seemed off limits. She stood in the narrow entryway—intentionally built, during an era, to keep wide skirts out—and breathed. Had Magdalene not been admitted into this room? Was that why it felt as forbidding as a brick wall when she tried to enter without permission?

She had to enter now, if only to prove to herself she could. Whatever invisible barrier stood between her and the interior of this sacred space, needed to be removed. Stepping forward, her heart raced.

Madeline took another breath and walked to the window. She turned and assessed her position in the room. *Best to start in one corner and circle,* she reasoned, reaching first for one drawer, then a cabinet pull, followed by a canister.

Contraband Cuban cigars in a humidor, a revolver, another handgun resembling something the police would carry, receipts, old photographs—one of William with a beautiful blonde woman—two wedding rings, and finally a drawer with useful things—tape, matches, a few candles, emergency flares.

She should have stopped there. She knew it, yet couldn't. There were more drawers with secret stashes, and her curiosity blossomed as she slid each one open and peeped inside. The wide one in the center held drawings of a vineyard. In another were details about the varieties of grapes that made the best wines, and the growing conditions they preferred. For a moment, she stopped digging and contemplated William's dilemmas.

He had this entire family structure to run, yet his passion obviously lay in making wine and tending a vineyard. He shunned the possibility of a relationship with a woman lasting longer than a few nights at best, while holding onto a portrait of himself gazing wistfully at a beauty. She had never seen him smoke or even smelled a cigar in the house, although he kept a humidor full of priceless cigars. Did he flagellate himself by denying those things he wished most to possess?

Madeline shook her head and moved on. The next drawer refused to open. It wasn't locked but would only slide out a few inches before catching on something. She went back to the wide drawer, remembering the metal straight edge beneath the drawings. Using this tool on the stuck drawer, she slid it to the back and swiped at the object that was apparently sticking up and preventing the tray from opening.

It took several tries, but suddenly it broke loose and she yanked open the stubborn drawer. A stiff envelope, with crinkled and torn edges where it had been caught in the drawer's mechanism, popped into view. A key stuck out of the hole in the envelope, a skeleton key similar to the one William had used to open the master suite door the other night.

Too tantalizing to be refused, she raced up the stairs to the room she had previously entered with such awe. It seemed to be waiting for her, as she turned the key in the lock. She listened for the reaction as the handle squeaked free and the door tumbled open. Stepping back in time, Madeline walked to the bed and lifted the still face-down picture next to it.

William stared back at her with the same blonde woman she had seen in the photo downstairs. This room—a mausoleum for William's heart—had been made ready for him and a bride. Something happened, apparently scaring her away. He buried his heart here and never returned to claim it, locked away in a place left unaired and untended.

There was something strangely familiar to Madeline in the feel of the space. She crossed to the portrait of Magdalene and looked into the face resembling a thinner version of herself. "Why do we favor so much?" she asked the portrait of a woman unable to answer back.

"Because you are one and the same," a voice answered.

Startled, she jumped.

The Captain stood in the open doorway, larger than life.

"Oh, it's you." There was a smile in her voice that was obvious, even to her.

"Happy to see me?" He placed one arm on the door frame, leaning against it as he watched her cross toward him.

"I've never been happier to see anyone."

He returned the smile and tried to embrace her.

Though she couldn't feel the physical touch, emotional tenderness coursed throughout her body.

"If my grandson would allow me the use of his physical body, I could make love to you as you have never known before," he assured her.

"Then we simply must convince him," she replied. The very sight of him aroused her in every way. She wanted to kiss him, hold him in her arms, and take him into the sanctuary of her deepest places.

He glided into the master suite. "We had much happiness in this room, though it seems different now."

"What did it look like before?"

"See if you can conjure it?"

"How on earth would I do that?"

"Stop using your head and start using your heart."

He breathed against her neck and she felt him attempting to embrace her from behind.

"Do you remember when I used to slip up behind you and plant kisses on your sweet neck?"

"You adored the scent of vanilla," she replied without even thinking.

The Captain laughed. "You used to put it—"

"Along my shoulders! Oh my God! How would I know such a thing?" Madeline gasped at the realization she had a memory not her own.

"Because you were here with me in this room and I loved you in every way a man can love a woman. You enjoyed it then, and I believe you do now."

"Could you show me?" She wanted to know him in the way he alluded to, the all-consuming physical passion.

"Sadly no. Not without human form. But with William's permission…" He ceased talking and began to spin, a great whirlwind whipping the moth-eaten coverlets back from their sleepy rest. The message was clear. If William agreed, a night with the Captain was within her grasp.

Chapter 22

William and Alex drove to the local diner. It had its own generator, ready for power outages, and was packed with people seeking a little hot food and a good cup of coffee.

"Hey. Over there," said Alex. "It's Ray, the last of our private drawer holders."

They edged through the crowd and greeted their seafaring friend. "Didn't know you were back," Alex said.

"Yeah, just got in," he said, rising to shake hands with the two men.

"You made it in through the storm?" William asked.

"Actually I got in right before the storm hit." Ray pulled a napkin through his hand and fingered it, clearly nervous about something. "I'd offer you a seat, but there isn't likely to be one freed up for a while around here." He pointed to the growing throng of people surrounding them.

"Yeah, guess the owners had better enjoy this financial boon while the power is out," said Alex.

"Why don't we take our food over to the Historical Society's veranda? We still need to have a peek inside of your drawer," William said, unable to keep the taint of suspicion out of his voice.

"Well, I'm half-finished, so I could meet you over

there in twenty minutes, or so."

Something told William not to let Ray out of his sight. "If you don't mind, I'd rather wait on you. I've just ordered coffee and a sandwich, not too hard to eat standing up."

Ray couldn't have been out to sea yesterday if he was in town today. Obviously William's request had been ignored. He didn't know exactly what to make of it, but assumed it meant something significant.

"Actually, I have a few errands—"

"It won't take but a second. Or you could give us your key, and we can return it to you before you even finish eating."

"What's up guys? What's the sudden emergency requiring a peek into my vault?" Ray jerked his head, giving the impression he wasn't happy with their request to inspect his private belongings.

"We simply need to verify some things didn't get mixed up, that's all. It'll only take a minute," Alex said.

"If there's been trouble over there—"

"We can't know until we have a look inside of your drawer. We'll fill you in on the way over. Enjoy the rest of your meal."

William stepped to the room's corner, dragging Alex with him. "He sure is acting oddly, don't you think?"

"When has Ray not acted oddly?"

"Good point."

"Better call Carol to make sure she can get down here. Otherwise, one of us might have to go pick her up." Alex stepped out to make the call. He returned with the news he needed to go over to get her. As Carol lived just over five minutes away, they would meet him and Ray at the inner chamber.

William stepped over and gave Ray the unwelcome news. "I'm going over with you. Alex is going to get Carol. In the meantime, why don't you tell me about your latest voyage?"

Ray appeared uncomfortable but managed to spin a yarn about narrowly escaping a vessel belonging to a modern-day pirate. When they stepped outside, he suddenly remembered he had ridden in with a friend and didn't have his car.

"Well lucky for us, it isn't a long walk."

"In the rain?" Ray asked.

"It isn't raining now. In fact, promises to be a nice day." William kept thinking Ray was acting guilty of something. His eyes spanned the parking lot behind the diner, and he realized there was at least one reason to be suspicious.

He pulled Ray toward the back lot over protests they should keep moving straight ahead if they didn't want to be late for the meeting. William pointed to the red Mini Cooper with the Union Jack emblazoned on the roof. "Has someone else here in Georgetown gotten a car exactly like yours?"

"I would think a lot of people, actually," Ray hedged. "They're rather popular you know."

"With a personalized 'raystoy2' license plate?" William asked. The sign boldly tattooed the ownership to the man just caught up in his own web of lies and deceit.

"I…I must have forgotten," he said, turning to walk up the path again.

"If it's your car, then why don't we take it to the Historical Society?"

"Right." He obligingly turned back toward the lot and produced a fob. The lights blinked when he pushed the "unlock" button.

Instinct told William to keep a watchful eye on every detail inside the car. Looking for an excuse to open the inner storage compartments, he knocked a pair of sunglasses from the console into the seat. Then he opened the glove compartment in the guise of putting them in there for safekeeping.

Ray shoved it closed before William could have a good look inside. "Do you mind?" he asked. Giving William a dirty, frustrated stare, he held his hand out for the glasses, shoving them atop his head the minute they crossed his palm. "Permission to snoop through my car doesn't come automatically with that to inspect the vault."

William nodded.

Minutes later they were careening into a parking spot and headed for the inner chamber.

"Is there something particular we are searching for?" Ray asked.

"Captain Gray's journals. Apparently, they've been misplaced."

"Inside of my vault? How would that be possible?"

"How is it possible they are missing at all?" William's stare quieted him.

Ray huffed as he begrudgingly produced the key to unlock the vault. The first drawer opened and produced nothing aside from the items expected to be in the drawer. "It seems a total waste of my time, that's all,"

When the next drawer was opened, miraculously the journals appeared. They were simply lying on top of the other important documents belonging to him.

"Waste of time, huh?" William asked, eyeing him suspiciously.

"Who would do this?" Ray spread his arms out before him, acting truly innocent rather than being caught red-handed.

William's jaw clenched. "Apparently *you* would."

"Now gentlemen," Carol interrupted, stepping between them. "Let's think about this intelligently, shall we? How would your key get into his hands? There has to be some explanation, though I'm not sure what it might be."

Alex stepped forward. "I think another meeting of the vault holders must be called and this mind-boggler resolved, or else none of us will feel assured our precious family heirlooms are safe here."

"Well, you'd better make it quick. I'll be back out to sea as soon as the weather clears," Ray snapped.

William wasn't pulling punches with this guy. Ray's possession of Captain Gray's journals made him the most obvious culprit, as far as William was concerned. "How's right now? Otherwise we could call the police and have them issue a warrant to search your little car and forbid your leaving town again until this is solved."

Ray's face turned a shade between purple and red, nearly beet-like. He definitely appeared at risk of having an aneurysm at any minute. He marched toward William with his hands on hips and his chest bowed out. "Those are fighting words," he declared.

William didn't cower from a fight. Stout and muscular, he took staying in shape seriously. Though he had missed a few trips to the gym since Madeline had been staying at Pine Island, it hadn't been enough to cause any decrease in his muscularity. "Yeah, well, if I wasn't concerned about soiling some of these precious belongings with your blood, I would have already punched you right in the face."

Alex stepped in between them. "Stop it guys. You're both upset. There has to be a reasonable explanation, and we'll find it. Then the two of you are going to be sorry about these comments."

Ray turned toward him. "You'd better be right. I intend to sail out of here in a few days, and I don't plan on letting something as ridiculous as this clown's old diaries stand in my way. Has it occurred to any of you *I've* been violated as well? Someone I didn't authorize obviously has a key to my drawer. I suppose I need to take an inventory, too."

"Everybody, settle down," Carol said. "I'll call and arrange a meeting that includes the entire group. Perhaps we need to change the locks, or add another piece of security equipment. But whatever we need to do, I promise the solution will be expedient."

They all left seemingly disturbed about the breach in their sanctuary. William carried the journals out with him, thinking this might be a good time to let Madeline thumb through them. He didn't know who had been tampering with them, nor what it was they were searching for. Until he did, he thought it best they stay close to him.

Alex met him at the door. "May as well come on back to my house. The road is closed and power lines are down. It may be tomorrow before you can get home, just as we feared."

"Damn!" William kicked a rock and watched it plunk into a puddle of water.

"Am I such a bad host? I'll let you beat me at chess, and I won't suggest you eat Helena's cooking again."

William recalled the previous night and her attempt to have them eat tofu and couscous mixed with vegetables. "If you say anything else about your wife's cooking, she's going to kick you out, and I'll be hosting you at Pine Island."

"Go ahead and prepare a room for me after the road opens up. I'll probably be out there before you know it. But tonight maybe we need to plan on taking over the kitchen."

William laughed, but his insides churned and fluttered. He needed to get back to Pine Island, but there wasn't much he could do about it now.

Chapter 23

"You don't need his body," Madeline whispered to the Captain.

"Oh, yes I do," he replied.

"How…how…? Never mind. I don't think I want to know." She ached to ask a thousand questions but decided against it. They were together, and for the time being it was enough.

"You can ask me anything. You know this, do you not?"

She decided to change the subject. "Assuming I believe you, and accept I was Magdalene in a previous life, how did we meet? And how did we make love then? And how did I die?"

"Ah my darling, you are Magdalene. We have already established this, have we not?" He sighed, sounding tired of the endless convincing. "As for how we met, it was fate."

"Fate?"

"What brings you here now?" he asked. "And don't say it is for scholarly work. We both know something deeper has been knocking at your heart."

Madeline didn't even try to deny it. It had been an interest of hers since the day in the boat with her dad. The opportunity to follow it through, due to her required thesis, was only a means for discovering more. "If it is fate, what is my destiny?"

"Only you can answer that."

"And you are dodging my questions. Please continue your story about how we met."

The Captain brushed her cheek. "You always were cantankerous." He chuckled. "But I will oblige you."

She nestled against his shape, trying to feel more than just the sense of him. He found her eyes, and Madeline's heart shuddered. She couldn't have adored the apparition more if he were a real flesh-and-bone man. It occurred to her she even loved the sound of his voice and the tales he seemed to never run dry of. He would have been a force to be reckoned with in his day.

"I was building this house," he continued, "and sailed into Charleston Harbor for a load of supplies. As I passed by the houses on the water's edge, I saw a vision of beauty in a pea-green dress with this swath of auburn hair hanging in curls around her shoulders, gliding across the porch of a yellow house. There I was, a slice of white sails caught between the blue of the sky and the sea, staring at this rainbow of colored houses and the damsel in green."

The Captain took Madeline back to that long-ago day in a forgotten world of long gowns, social mores, and difficult means of travel. She could imagine everything he spoke of, pictured it in her mind, seeing it a second time, not anew. His voice carried her along. She was not a spectator, but a participant in his tale, feeling the constricting fabric of the gown and its undergarments.

"It seemed my ship sailed on, and I stayed transfixed to the vision before me. As I finished my purchases, the owner of the general store invited me to join him and his family for dinner at his home before beginning my return voyage to Pine Island. Imagine my surprise when I followed him to none other than the yellow house and sat down at a table with the beauty in the green dress. I could barely take my eyes off you...her...and later when I retired to the gentleman's study for brandy and cigars, her father broached the subject of wedding a daughter to me. The problem was, he wanted to wed me to the oldest daughter, which you...she...was not."

"I...she...had sisters?" Madeline imagined being the young southern belle who had stolen the captain's heart from a distance. He had told the story so thoroughly she could almost believe it was her in a bygone era.

"Aye, but they were not as fair as you." He didn't correct himself, and she didn't mind. "But he refused your hand in marriage to me. I announced I would wait until the older two were wed so you could be mine."

"What did I...she...say about that?"

"Try to remember it yourself," he encouraged. "Let your mind take you to the yellow house with the wraparound porch. See the sea wall and the palms." His voice was hypnotic. "Then imagine a great sailing ship cuts the horizon with its sheets of sails. You catch the first glimpse of the man destined to become your true love riding the wind across the water."

Madeline closed her eyes and tried to envision it. The smells were easier to recall than the sights for some reason. "I can smell oil, and some kind of varnish or shellac, and lemons...always lemons."

He laughed. "That very night you rolled a lemon between your palms, releasing its oils, then held it up to your perky nose to capture the scent. I whispered in your ear that as long as there was a lemon to be found, I would think of you and bring it back for your pleasure. You gave me a heart-melting smile, and I embraced you without thinking. Your father caught me giving you the hug and threw me out of the house. The neighbors talked, and it was considered imperative I marry you as soon as possible."

"You are a rascal, and a scoundrel. You ruined her reputation."

"Thankfully. I might never have won your hand otherwise."

Madeline listened to the joy of his recollection, sensing the antebellum traditions made it difficult for anyone to get to know the person they were about to be pledged to. "Tell me about the wedding."

His voice softened. "We married right here at Pine Island. It was the first party hosted here. The coast and the waterway were lined with sails, and the carriages rolled one after another along the lane from the forest. We pledged our vows, on the first day of summer, out on the porch facing the sea. The warm breezes carried the scent of my first love—the ocean—to the place where I was pledging my trough to my true love— you—Magdalene. It felt to me as if all three of us were marrying on that day."

"It was a morning wedding, wasn't it?" Somehow she sensed it. The soft light of morning before the broiling sun would have cooked the guests.

"See? You do remember. It was a morning wedding, and we circled the house throughout the course of the day. We moved from the sea porch to the side porch facing the garden for a barbecue. And then the ladies retired for a nap during the hottest part of the day, while we men talked horses and trading wares in the shade of the forest. In the evening, a more formal dinner was served. After the tables were cleared and the doors thrown open, the entire ground floor became a giant ballroom. The band played, up on the second floor hallway overlooking the ground floor, and we danced until dawn."

"When did we first make love?" Madeline couldn't believe she asked the Captain such a question. It had slipped out. But he barely seemed to notice.

"We were exhausted after the guests left, though some stayed the night. There was a huge breakfast the following morning. In the afternoon, when the house was quiet and we had retired for a siesta, I lay here beside you stroking your long hair and soft skin and counting my blessings. You looked so fragile and innocent I almost hated to spoil it. But then, you began to breathe heavily, and asked me to make you a woman. I was so taken with your willingness, beauty, and curiosity I almost cried. Then, as now, you make me the best I can be."

Tears stung Madeline's eyes. To be loved so by a man was more than she could even hope for. And for the first sexual experience to be handled with such tenderness made her sad for herself and every woman she knew. "I wish you had been my first," she said.

"Maybe I can be your last," he replied.

"Captain, I think I'm falling in love with you," Madeline confessed, feeling emotions she hadn't suspected she was even capable of anymore. They appeared out of the ether, tap-dancing around her heart and soul until becoming so firmly planted, she could not deny them.

"Of course you are. It is inevitable."

"But what will come of it?" She turned toward him—his shape glowing beside her.

"It will last, when all else has turned to dust. Love does not die with the body."

"So how did Magdalene's body die? What happened to her?"

He faded a bit, the warm glow dimming. "I hated leaving you…her. I never expected to feel so protective over another human. But the sea, a jealous mistress, called. It was what I did, who I was. I vowed to stay until she was carrying my child."

Madeline winced.

"I know it may sound odd to you in this century, but in that time it was considered polite to refrain from touching a woman during her heaviest part of expectancy. I knew I could never refrain if we were in the same house, so it stood to reason I should stay until she was getting heavy with my child."

"And then?"

"Then I should take a voyage, return with a means of making money, and have my wife and child waiting for me. She was young, barely seventeen. We made love every day—sometimes more than once."

Madeline knew they married the girls off young back in the 1800s. She was probably only sixteen when he had seen her on the porch. "How old were you then?"

"I was a bit older—in my third decade."

"You were in your thirties, and she was in her teens?" Madeline was shocked. She had ceased to think of herself as Magdalene, and apparently the Captain had as well. He now referred to her as a separate entity, finding the need to explain their traditions.

"Aye, but remember the day. Times were different. Men were expected to go out and gather experience so they would know how to treat their wives in the bedroom. They were expected to have some wealth, and a home to bring their bride to. And the brides were almost always virgins who had been protected from knowing too much about sex. That would be hard to do once they are out of their teens."

Madeline suddenly felt sorry for Magdalene and all the women in her day and age that had no hope of doing anything else. "They went from their parents' house to their husband's house, never knowing who they might have become."

"But they were treated better than fairy princesses. We honored and valued them, and did whatever they wanted to keep them happy. I would sail across a thousand oceans to bring her back one single smile." He had grown wistful. He didn't speak for a long time and Madeline feared he had left.

"Tell me more Captain."

"Are you sure you want to hear it?"

"Oh yes, I'm sorry I interrupted. I want to know everything." The light was changing outside. Though the day was aging, she didn't want to leave the comfort of the room she might have once shared, as the captain's wife. Madeline couldn't think of anything more important than staying in that room, under dusty covers, hearing tales of what may have been her previous life in another body.

"She conceived right away. It didn't seem to faze her though. She did everything she normally did, and we kept spending afternoons making love right here. I introduced her to all kinds of pleasures and ways of satisfaction, making her blush with happiness."

The Captain's voice changed, it cracked with sadness. "When she grew large with our baby, I left for the Indies. She had the servants to watch over her and keep her company. When I returned, things were different."

Madeline knew something had gone wrong while he was away. "What happened?"

"She labored too early. The midwife didn't get here in time. The baby died. Our firstborn died while I was away, and could do nothing to help."

She knew the times were different. Lots of babies died then. "But it wasn't your fault. What could you have done differently? How could you have saved it?"

"Yes it was my fault. Magdalene was young and small. I shouldn't have left her out here, in this desolate place, where she couldn't get the help she needed. I should have taken her back to her parents' house while I was away; insisted on it." The pain in his voice was still audible after all of the decades of passed time.

Madeline wanted to keep him talking and was afraid he would lose his ability to hold himself together if he became too distraught. "How was she when you returned?"

"She was a shipwreck—a sad, broken, depressed little creature with sunken eyes and a broken heart. I feared I had lost her forever."

Some time passed in silence. Madeline felt her own heart sink and the fingers of depression pulling her down into the depths of darkness.

She could sympathize. After all she hadn't been much older than Magdalene when she had her own child. And though her child had survived, the terrible marriage did not. That brought with it its own brand of worthlessness and grief.

Madeline turned toward him, and he was gone. "Captain? Captain are you there? Come back!" It was no use. The grief had pulled him away, the sad remembrances too much for him.

She fixed the bed back and went downstairs, locking the door behind her.

Chapter 24

"What do you mean the road won't be passable today?" William protested. The phone lines were still down and so were the power lines in many areas. Though Georgetown itself was now up and running, the outlying areas weren't as high a priority.

"You could probably take a boat now," Alex said. "Maybe Ray will take you home."

He was only joking, but an idea blossomed. "You're exactly right."

Alex couldn't hide the surprise in his voice. "You're going to ask Ray to take you out to Pine Island after you essentially called him a liar and a thief?"

"No of course not. But I can hire a boat to take me there now that the storm is over." The possibility of getting home seemed suddenly doable and William turned jovial. "Care to ride out with me?"

"I'm going grocery shopping. Another night of Helena's wheat protein, or whatever that stuff is called, might do me in." Alex rubbed his stomach in a manner suggesting he could be sick any minute.

"I hear ya! I've given my staff a vacation, but if you can eat bread, cheese, and salami, ride out to Pine Island."

"Nah. Thanks anyway."

William shook his hand, slapped him on the back, and thanked him for his generous hospitality. Their friendship went back a long way, and he was thankful for it, but he had to get home.

A long wide boardwalk ran parallel to the harbor, with lots of ramps running to the docks or to the harbor shops and cafes. William wheeled into the parking lot for the tour boats and raced to the ticket window. Not seeing anyone, he called out. Except for some feral cats trolling for food, he was alone.

The boats in the harbor were tethered securely, yet they bobbed as the water pulsated landward. "Hello, anybody down here?" he called out. He still saw no one to make the request of. "Anyone? Hello?"

A voice boomed behind him. "Sorry fella, but there will be no tours going out today. The water is still too high and the shelling wouldn't be good."

"Is that the only reason? What if I don't care about sea shells and merely want to get back to my house on Pine Island?" He raced forward, hand extended in making introductions.

"I don't know," the man identifying himself as Captain Rick scratched his chin. "I've suffered financial losses due to the storm, but it could be a lot worse if my boat gets tangled up in debris."

William knew the dangerous places likely to cause a boat to suffer damage. And although any place, after such a storm, could be hiding potentials hazards, it was less likely on the route they could take over to Pine Island. "You gotta go out some time, right? We don't need to take the course around the far tip where Lafayette sailed into the North Island, just up around the outlying side."

"Hmm, it could take us a while to get around the places I feel most concerned about."

William knew what the *concern* was. It was about dollars. "I'll pay you well—private charter for the day?"

"And if we can't make it?"

"We'll make it one direction or the other," William assured him. "Sailing is in my blood, as well."

"So you could help out if we got into a jam?"

"Aye, sir, I most definitely can," William assured him.

"Well, hop aboard my friend. Daylight is burning."

William remembered the journals. Knowing he couldn't leave them behind, he feared the possibility of getting them wet. "Do you have a waterproof container of some kind on board? I have some papers that need protection from the spray."

"Oh sure," Captain Rick said. "There's a sealed box in the back. I'll open it for you."

Torn between two emotions, William retrieved the journals from his car, wrapped them up in his jacket, and set them gingerly into the back hold of the boat. On one hand, he feared the ruin of the journals should something happen to the boat. On the other, it felt good and natural to have his ancestor's journals back aboard a floating ship, as if they belonged there. It was definitely more appropriate than being stuffed into a cubby hole in an airtight room of a town building.

"Books?" Captain Rick asked as he opened the hold and lowered the tied up bundle down inside.

"Journals of one of my ancestors. You might have heard of him—Captain William Gray?"

William saw the man's face brighten. "The original old salt of the sea? You bet! He's pretty legendary around these parts."

"Tell me what you've heard about him." He grabbed a rope and untied it, releasing the hold.

"Let's get this rig out of the harbor, and we can swap tales," Captain Rick said with a grin, showing how intrigued he suddenly was with his passenger.

Once they were solidly out of the harbor, he opened an underbelly cooler. Snatching a beer from the icy chest, he tossed it to William. "I don't usually drink on the boat, but I believe Captain Gray would be disappointed if we didn't share an ale in his honor."

William grinned. "Yeah, here's to his spirit!" They clinked cans and eased through the water.

"So do those journals tell his secret findings?" Rick asked.

"I don't think they're much more than accounts of the West Indies, what he found appealing there, and there's mention of people he met along his many voyages. One has a great deal of detail about building the house at Pine Island, but I've never found anything suggesting he had a secret stash of wealth."

"Ah, there go the rumors." Rick's sigh indicated his disappointment in the answer.

"What rumors have you heard?"

"Oh, some old sailors claimed their ancestors told them Captain Gray discovered the wreck of *Queen Anne's Revenge,* and plundered it well."

"No! Really?" William laughed. "How would it even have been possible without modern diving equipment?"

"Yeah, I sort of thought it sounded silly, but he was rumored to have been caught with some treasure from the ship. People love to spin yarns around legendary sea goats." He laughed into the wind. "They even said he had met a man who knew how to breathe under water. Imagine that in the eighteen hundreds?"

William laughed too. "Wonder what they'll say about us once we have been dead and gone for a century or more?"

"Probably won't even know we were here." Rick took a swig from his beer.

A flash of white in the top of a tree caught William's eye. He grabbed Rick's shoulder. "Over there," he pointed, "an eagle up in her nest!"

"No matter how old we get or how many wonders we see, nothing beats the simple beauty of God's universe, does it?" Rick and William marveled at the eagle, regal in her perch, eyes always searching.

"Wow," William said as they passed, leaving her to her duty.

With the absence of other sailing vessels, they had the water in Winyah Bay to themselves. Debris careened along the shoreline and occasionally bobbed near their boat. Rick expertly guided them through broken limbs, driftwood, and an assortment of crumbling floats, bottles, pieces of boarding, and nets.

At one point they had to kill the engine and cut away some netting and plastic to prevent it from being sucked into the motor. By the time they reached William's dock, he was concerned about Rick's ability to navigate back by himself.

The old seadog maintained confidence in his abilities and wouldn't hear of coming up to Pine Island for the night.

William tossed him enough cash to make him solvent for a few days, more than compensating for the loss of business due to the storm.

Captain Rick waved farewell to William walking along the dock with the carefully tied knot of journals cradled under his arm.

Chapter 25

Madeline watched the ocean from the sea-facing porch, so, of course, didn't see the boat making its way up Winyah Bay and to the dock on the other side of the house. She was lost in a thought, one taking her back to a time when the house was new and its owner a dashing man with a mistress—the sea.

She could feel the excitement of the young bride escaping her father's house and all his rules, as well as those of the era she lived in. Out here, with no close neighbors to see someone run around the house without a parasol, she could let her hair get tousled by the sea breeze and walk barefoot through the grass in the side yard. She could make love to her husband on the sand, or in the surf.

But all of those freedoms came with a price, including being too far out to get help in time to save her child. Madeline could feel the pain as surely as her own. Was it true that the soul of Magdalene resided within her own body? Or was it safe to assume every mother on the planet would suffer vicariously through the story the Captain had shared?

She hadn't even gotten to any of the stuff she was supposed to ask him. When he was with her, she wasn't thinking about the questions William wanted answers to, or capturing his image with her camera. She got caught up in the moments they were sharing.

Now as she sat staring out at the same view Magdalene would have been privy to, she ached to know more about her. What did she do all day? Who did she talk to with the Captain at sea? Did she have hobbies? Or was it enough for someone her young age to simply stroll on the beach, search for shells, and plan a nursery? If merely seventeen when wed, and they were married for five years when she died, then she only lived to twenty-two.

Twenty-two! Her heart sank for the brief light which had once shone so brightly as the vivacious Magdalene Gray. Her legacy was that she'd left a son behind and he fathered children who fathered children and so on until here she sat, as a guest of the last heir of Pine Island.

"What are you doing out here alone?"

The voice startled her and she jumped up, seeing the dark curls and soft eyes. She raced to him, falling in his arms, forgetting temporarily he couldn't return the embrace. "You're back! Thank God! I was getting worried."

Her concern seemed to catch him off guard. "Well yes, I'm sorry to have worried you," he answered softly, stroking her back.

Feeling the sturdy sensation of his hand along her spine, she realized her mistake. Pulling away, the show of emotion embarrassed her. "I'm sorry, I thought you…" She stopped short of saying what she wanted to say; that she had thought he was the Captain.

"You thought I was dead? Washed away by the rising water? Hit over the head with a power pole?" He seemed softer somehow. Perhaps the trial caused by the storm had rolled him around and softened his edges the way it did sea glass.

"Is that a smile?" she teased.

"I have a couple of wonderful surprises. I think we should find something to share a toast with. You haven't drunk all of the wine, have you?" His attitude intrigued her.

"Yeah? You found the journals?"

He lifted them up. "In Ray's vault, no less."

He opened the door and she stepped into the house. "Why? What's in there that would make him want them?"

They walked to the kitchen, and he grabbed a bottle of wine, opened it, and began to tell his long story. He'd discovered where the journals were, tried to call her, figured out how to get back to Pine Island, saw the eagle—he had to tell her about that—and the told of the rumors of Captain Gray pirating a sunken vessel rumored to be *Queen Anne's Revenge*.

His adventure mesmerized her, especially with the bit about the ship. "Blackbeard's ship?"

"Yes. He was captured in North Carolina after he ran his ship aground. It was never found. And the area around the Outer Banks, where it was supposed to be, certainly wouldn't be hard for someone to get to from here." He poured the wine into two glasses as he spoke, and handed one to her.

"No. But how could the Captain have gone diving? There was no scuba equipment back then." She left the glass of wine on the counter, knowing William would have a compulsion to swirl it.

"That's where a comment Captain Rick, the man who brought me home, made has me thinking it could be possible. He said it was rumored our Captain met a man who had some kind of invention allowing underwater breathing. If that's true, Captain Gray may have discovered the world's most famous pirate's ship and the wealth of treasure it was rumored to be carrying."

He swirled both glasses of wine and pushed one toward her. Holding his up, he declared, "Here's to Captain William Gray, my ancestor and your obsession."

She smiled and clinked glasses with him. The Captain was her obsession, never more so than now. "I don't think I've ever seen you this animated."

"I have to say, this is pretty exciting stuff." William sipped the wine while continuing to gaze into Madeline's eyes.

"Have you had a chance to read over any of the journals?"

"Not yet. But if we can each grab a pair of white cotton gloves, we can comb through them and search for more information. Have you ever gone diving?"

"No, never, not at sea anyway. But if you give me one of those journals, I'll dive into it head first." She almost salivated at getting her hands on the Captain's private notes.

"So in all of my excitement I almost forgot to ask…did you happen to catch a glimpse of the Captain while I was away?" He eyed her expectantly.

How could she tell him they had shared conversation in the very room he had expected to share with his own wife? "Yeah. He still wants to obtain permission to spend a night with me in your body. And he'll cooperate with any of your requests, if you agree."

He put his hands over his eyes appearing to shield

himself from the thought. "How can I agree to that? Do you want me to agree to it?"

"He won't hurt me. He won't hurt you. I am convinced of it."

Chapter 26

Madeline and William combed through the journals, much of them unintelligible due to age, misspellings or different spellings, and the handwriting in thick ink spread with a quill-style pen. And what they did understand was mostly the sort of thing men in that era wrote about—supplies, acquisitions, trade routes.

What had she thought she would find in a sea captain's journals, a diary-style confession of his great love for his wife? It was slow going.

"So what is it you think someone was searching for in these journals? Do you believe it was Ray? Or do you think his drawer was merely a safe place to store them?"

William glanced up. "How would someone other than Ray have access to his key?"

"Who had access to your key?" she countered.

They locked eyes and he shut the journal. "I don't know. I can't figure out how Ray would get his hands on my key, and the lock wasn't tampered with. So whoever it was had both mine and his keys."

"Could it be someone who works there? Doesn't someone have keys to all the drawers?"

"It's set up similar to a bank vault and our drawers are privately held. There is a security system, which shall soon also have a camera. I don't think anything is missing; they were just not in the right place. So that leads us right back to where we started—who was it and what were they looking for?"

"But what would be intriguing enough in here for someone to go to the extremes it would take to get into the vault?"

"You wanted to see them. Why don't you answer that question?" William walked over to the table and sipped his wine. His eyes held the same suspicions as the tenor of his voice had implied.

Madeline shut the journal she was looking through and joined him. "Let's take our wine out on the porch." She led the way to the sea porch as she had come to call the one facing the ocean. It felt the most soothing, due to the rhythmic tousle of the sea grass, the curves of the dunes juxtaposed against the rising and falling of the ocean waves, and the calls of the shore birds.

For a few moments, they both sat lost in their own thoughts. Finally she broke the silence. "I don't know what is in the journals. I wanted to read through them to learn about the Captain's life for academic purposes. At no time did it occur to me to break into the vault to gain access."

"I wasn't accusing you—"

She held up a hand, stopping him from further interruption. Although it would be understandable if he was suspicious of her hunger for the knowledge contained in the Captain's journals, that's not her slant. "Human nature is such there must be a payoff, of some kind, to take such a risk. And normally it is monetary. So I'm guessing someone believes there is a treasure the Captain left behind whose location is disclosed in one of those books."

"Or he knew the location of one, such as the wreck of Blackbeard's ship!"

"But isn't that all merely legend?"

"Is it? We know Blackbeard commandeered the French ship *Le Concorde* and the Captain was in possession of some similar gold pieces. And then there were rumors he had met a man who had some kind of contraption for breathing under water."

"I can ask him, but I don't know when I'll see him again." The excitement of William's revelation paled in the sudden realization her heart had been captured by the Captain and now she was another of his hidden treasures waiting for his return.

The expression on her face wasn't lost on William. He locked eyes with her, appearing to see the secrets she wished to keep sealed inside her own emotional vault. "Guess we had better get back to those journals," he suggested when they had finished their wine.

The ticking of the library clock was the only sound indicating time moving on while they did their best to read the lines of the faded ancient script, white-gloved fingertips handling the delicate pages as gingerly as possible.

Madeline asked for the journal after Magdalene's death. Even though the journal details had been rather mundane up to this point, she couldn't bear to risk reading the details of the next voyage. Knowing while he was sailing open blue water, bartering with the natives of the West Indies, and dining on conch and coconuts, his child was dying and his young wife was in distress.

But there were other tumultuous events in the Captain's life. "Oh no, everyone is turning on the

Captain," she declared as she recounted the issues he faced with his friends and neighbors. "They're calling him a traitor because he isn't on board for war with the North. He's afraid they are going to destroy the South and possibly even conscript his son. This is terrible."

She felt more empathy than ever. He had sacrificed so much in order to raise his son after Magdalene's death, and then to think they were trying to turn his son against him and his own beliefs seemed unbearable.

William's face bore a lack of expression. This was clearly not news to him. "I have often heard the tale of how he was considered a turn-coat."

"He's sailing to England to try to find a school for Edward, and possibly wait out the conflict."

William rubbed his chin with the back of his forearm to keep the gloves clean of any perspiration or oils. "It's one of the reasons they came to suspect him of Magdalene's death, though nothing ever came of it. Her father was a West Point-educated military man before becoming a merchant in Charleston. It would seem the Captain lost face with her whole family when he stood up against seceding from the United States over states' rights. He was more diplomatic than corporal."

"Did her family blame him for his wife's death?"

"Probably, though there were never any direct accusations. Just part of the general complaints against him after the conflict started gearing up."

Although the Captain was William's ancestor, Madeline felt she was the only one feeling sympathy right now.

Slowly, page by page, they continued to read with the occasional outburst of discovery. The teen-aged

Edward joined a boarding school, planning to study law. The Captain heard more bad news coming from the south than he did good news. Though he didn't want to leave his son, if he didn't return to Pine Island before the war started, he feared he might not make it through. In the last possible moment, he started stocking his ship for the return voyage.

"Who is William James?" Madeline asked.

"Why?" William peeked up over the page he was having trouble with.

"Well, it says here he 'met the most intriguing William James' and 'spent a great deal on his invention,' but it doesn't say what the invention is. Then it goes right into sailing for home."

"If it's important, there will be more about him. Or when the power comes back on, we can use the internet to search his name."

"Any idea when that might be?" she asked.

"Could be tomorrow since the road is still not passable. It's a nice evening for a sail, what do you say we put these journals away and set out to sea?" He looked sheepish as a boy—or the Captain—when he made the offer.

There was a glint in his eyes when he said *sea* causing Madeline to miss her beloved apparition. She shut the journal carefully and handed it over to William. The symbolism of the Captain's life being in his hands, whether journal or reputation, was not lost on her. "That sounds nice."

He locked the journals away in the library's vault, stowing the keys to the drawer in the Historical Society in there as well, and excused himself to change clothes for the trip around the bay.

"This is my favorite nautical path around Winyah Bay. Many antebellum homes can be seen from the water, as well as the lighthouse, and the bald eagles have returned. Their large nests are clearly visible. You can spot them by looking for the splashes of white crowning their large bodies."

"I imagine the Captain sailed these waters," Madeline said, running her hand in the bay's water just as she had as a child in her father's boat.

"Yeah, I'm sure he did. But he was captive to the weather conditions. No wind, no sailing. I am not very patient."

The evening, perfect for such a cruise around the bay, felt romantic. She remained quiet for most of the journey, contemplative. Water splashed against her forearm, redirected by the slight drag of her fingertips as they dangled from the edge of the craft. It was easy to imagine herself as Magdalene in the dreaminess of the moment.

William killed the engine, afloat in the water in the middle of the bay. "Tell me what happened." His knowing eyes clearly communicated he had sensed a change in her mannerisms.

Snatching her hand from the water, she pulled herself erect. "Why do you think something happened?" She wondered if she could stall, if he would buy the innocent act.

"Oh come on, I'm not a fool. I recognize the faraway gaze of a woman preoccupied with another man. Your certainty he means you no harm is a clear indication the Captain has managed to convey that message to you in a real and believable fashion." He sat facing her, his seat turned toward hers, eyeing her with

186

the precision of a hawk.

"What if something did happen?" she asked, without looking at him directly.

"That would depend on what the 'something' was," he answered. "What did he say? What did you two discuss? Jesus, this is my ancestor, my home, and my obligation! Tell me already."

Madeline couldn't speak. Giant tears rolled down her cheeks. "You wouldn't believe it. I know you wouldn't. There's no point, none at all."

She buried her head in her hands and wept the tears she had been holding in for nearly two decades. The release valve burst open and raw emotion poured forth in its purest form. Madeline screamed at the gulls and fell against the back of the seat as the boat rocked on the water.

William crossed to her, obviously mistaking her outburst for something having occurred during the time he had been away. "Oh my God. What did he do to you?"

****

William knelt by the seat Madeline occupied and tried to pull her into his arms in order to comfort her. It had been a long time since he had allowed anyone to come near his heart, so it felt somewhat unnatural. He had maintained a distance—a respectful detachment, slowly being replaced by affection—but distance all the same.

No something spring-like had bloomed in his chest. His heart was budding along with the dormant azaleas, bursting into a riot of crimson. He felt protective and angry for reasons he couldn't explain.

Madeline's nature wasn't similar to any other

woman he had ever known. She wasn't petite and scatter-brained. She didn't seem to have a standing appointment at the beauty salon or a makeup artist following her around with the best lighting and the newest skin care. She exhibited real beauty—lasting beauty—the kind that couldn't be purchased or salvaged with injections and fillers.

Why hadn't he recognized it until now? It had dipped beneath his radar as effortlessly as the artistic embodiment of elegance slips beneath a designer's overreaching touch.

A giant shadow encompassed their prostrate forms in the sailing vessel. It could have been a pterodactyl or a dragon from yesteryear, its wingspan hugely encompassing the boat along with the sun setting west of it.

They looked heavenward simultaneously and caught the flash of a white-capped eagle. Its beak and focus pointed downward at the two of them bobbing weightless as jellyfish within the enclosure of the boat. A swoop nearly knocked William backward, and he dashed to crank the boat.

"Must be feeling territorial," he commented before gunning the engine and moving along. He didn't try to slow the engine again until they had reached the far side of the North Island, known by the locals as "Shell Island."

Not much existed on the isle except for history. A partial sea wall still held the position where Lafayette had landed when coming to the aid of the first dream-filled Americans. Every time he saw it, William recalled the great effort and sacrifice of so many whose dreams had become reality.

The French Lafayette—for whom parks were named and legends spun—sailed from Europe, spied the same scenery he and Madeline currently enjoyed, and went further inland through the very same Winyah Bay. He eventually made his way to the coastal harbor town of Georgetown—named in honor of the King of England.

"Let's walk." William moored the boat and leapt out to take her hand and lead her along the sand, around the driftwood.

"Where are we?" she asked. It could have been a shipwreck island for all of its loneliness and lack of structures. Whole trees lay in the sand against one another, felled by tides and forces of nature. Giant conch shells pierced the sand. One lay in the crook of a branch.

"This is commonly called Shell Island." He pointed to some noteworthy shells and she dived for them.

With one in each hand she responded, "With obvious reasons."

A certain desolate spot gave rise to William's imagination in ways defying explanation. Like the inside curl of a surfer's wave, it seemed to hold the entire ocean at bay. Shell seekers didn't walk this far inland.

He had only brought one other person here, and that had been many years ago. Now he was leading Madeline there for reasons even he couldn't express. They stopped, awash in silence, in a peace as no other spot in the universe might hold.

"Look around you." William encircled the area with his arm. "Nothing can harm you here."

Madeline glanced around the expanse of sand and

twisted tree trunks. "Do you believe in past lives?"

He didn't answer, but a raised eyebrow indicated he was listening and ready to receive more.

"We have a connection surpassing what can be explained by everyday experiences. I do not know him, cannot know him, yet I understand everything about the Captain in ways I can't articulate. If you had asked me a year ago, or even a month ago, if I believed in spirits and ghosts and things from the veil of the other world beyond sight, I would have said *absolutely not*. Today, I would say, without doubt, I believe it with every cell of my body."

"So you did have a visit from him." William grew silent along with the vacuous atmosphere on the island.

"More than a visit…" Madeline turned from him as she spoke those words.

****

Madeline didn't expect William to believe her, but neither could she bear watching the doubt creeping into his eyes. She wouldn't disclose the intimate nature of her conversation with the Captain. It felt too personal and private. He was a part of her now, and gave her comfort, opening her closed heart to new possibilities.

She counted it as a great gift that the universe had seen fit to heal her broken pieces through the unconventional, and quite ethereal, presence of an apparition. Captain William Gray was as real to her as the man she'd left standing in the circle of sand staring after her. Nobody would take that from her.

****

William's stomach knotted. He knew the moment he saw Madeline sitting on the beach-porch facing the ocean that something appeared different about her whole demeanor. What he couldn't have guessed was it was due to her becoming attached to the apparition of his ancestor.

The last four words she spoke to him, before he watched her skulk off toward the beach and back to the boat, had been nearly-mortal blows. "*More than a visit.*" What did such a statement mean? Had the ghost found a way to be intimate with her without use of a human body? How could that be possible?

Why did the idea bother him? His stomach churned, knotted and raw. He couldn't be jealous, could he?

Yet the minute Madeline's head disappeared beneath his line of view he panicked and raced after her, calling her name. Why did he care so much? All he knew was he wanted her to wear the same expression when she spoke his name as she did when she spoke the Captain's.

Chapter 27

William kept his focus straight ahead. He could see Madeline looking along the horizon, hunting for eagles on the quiet and uneventful boat ride back to Pine Island.

He knew what she wanted to hear. Nonetheless, he couldn't bring himself to agree.

Although he would love to make love to her, he wanted it to be his face, his eyes, his spirit she longed to be with at such a moment, not someone else's, especially not those belonging to a ghost.

And once he allowed such a thing, would he ever know for sure if she saw him through the refracted lens of the apparition or could see him for himself? No, he couldn't—wouldn't—allow it.

****

Madeline felt drained. She welcomed the stillness of the bay's water. She could sense William's turmoil. Who wouldn't feel crazed by this odd turn of events?

Perhaps he would throw her out of the house when they returned to Pine Island. She wouldn't blame him. What help had she been to him?

They were at cross purposes. He wanted her to help the ghost of the Captain to leave, and she wanted him to stay.

They walked slowly back to the house after tying off the boat. Both agreed to just go up to bed.

William held a light for her as they were still without power. He helped her with the candles in her room and lingered for a moment.

She caught him, through the corner of her eye, watching her. He seemed to have something on his mind as he fidgeted in the glow of candlelight.

He rubbed his face with his hands, started to speak, and stopped short. "Well, goodnight, then," he finally said, shutting her door behind him. His footsteps rang out as he headed for his own room.

After he left, Madeline collapsed onto the bed. The temperature in the upstairs room was stifling. She shot back up again to throw open a window and let in a little night air. The rain had washed the atmosphere clean and everything appeared brighter in the heavens.

Lying at an angle so she could stare out the window at the beautiful night sky, she wondered if this was how it felt to be at Pine Island when the Captain and Magdalene lived here. With the window open, she could hear the faint sound of the distant ocean, the undulations of the breath of the sea.

Madeline wasn't sure when she dozed off, but the sound of beeping and humming motors woke her while it was still dark. At first she was confused, but the orangey glow of a night light indicated the power had been restored.

The bedside clock flashed twelve o'clock in neon green. Her senses felt suddenly assaulted. Not once, before the power disruption, had she noticed the continuous hums and the bright artificial intrusions into an otherwise wholly peaceful place.

Why have we done this to ourselves, she wondered, as she grabbed the cords and unplugged everything within her reach. Sure, a hot shower was going to feel divine, but the onslaught of gadgetry—though convenient—was simply too much.

Being so busy with school and work she had kept herself plugged into the worldwide web at all times. The ever-present gadgets needed to connect her to technology never left her side.

She learned the skill of multitasking so efficiently she could do assignments on her laptop while answering e-mails on her phone. Sometimes, she had no clear remembrance of even doing them. It had become robotic. Maybe there were spirits around everyone all of the time but they were too distracted, and too busy, to notice.

The thought of spirits brought her right back around to ruminating about the Captain—not that she ever really ceased to think about him. Now the Captain replaced her laptop and smart phone in her subconscious mind.

He filled the void left by the stream of spam and little reminder pop-ups. He resonated within her, to the point of finding him there even when he wasn't. Seeing him now was no longer a shock, but rather happiness at finding him. Her subconscious mind whispered, *oh there you are; I wondered what kept you.*

When did that happen?

****

William awakened thinking of Madeline and how at home she seemed in his house. She moved with grace and slid around corners as if she knew where they were without having to look. Her eyes caught everything. He often felt naked in her presence, suspecting she could see parts of him even he had never seen.

Why had he been so excited to show her the journals? What had made him take her out on the cruise of the bay, to the spot having previously been his alone? Why was he jealous of an apparition?

He wanted to make her happy and see fire in her eyes. But to let the ghost take over his body seemed outrageous. Then again, maybe it would encourage her desire for him. Maybe she would feel his touch, his flesh against hers and want more.

Or possibly, he might strangle her after they made love and bury her in the graveyard next to Magdalene. Who knew? What if he had no control? He didn't want her harmed, and he especially didn't want to be the one who might exact some menacing act upon her.

Perhaps if the Captain could be exonerated of any involvement in Magdalene's death, William could agree to the possession. It seemed the perfect solution. Solve the mystery of his great-great-great grandmother's death first. Then, if he approved of the outcome, he would acquiesce. He settled it in his mind at least.

Chapter 28

The soft whisper of a breeze tickled Madeline's face. She vaguely recalled opening the window. She hadn't slept well and didn't want to open her eyes, but there it came again, the unmistakable feathery stroke across her face. She smiled, "Captain, is it you?"

The thought of him jolted her upright, eyes widening as they scanned the room. But to her great disappointment it was only the lacy sheer at the window dancing briefly across her cheek, not the spirit of the man she wished to see more than any other.

After indulging in a hot shower, she made her way to the kitchen. William was already there, perfectly groomed for the day. Somehow she found him more approachable the way he had been the day before—a little less fastidious—with stubble on his face, his hair all tousled by the sea breeze, and his shirt hanging out.

"Good morning," he said. "Did you sleep well?"

Madeline crossed to the coffee pot and poured herself a cup. She shook her head in response. "No, not really."

"Me neither," he confessed. Lifting his cup of coffee, he ditched the bright and cheerful expression from his face. "This helps though."

"What are we doing today? Reading through more journals, or independent investigation?"

"I've already been doing a little research this

morning. It seems William James—the man the Captain met in England—did indeed invent a type of underwater breathing device somewhere around 1825. So that would have given him a few years to perfect it before he met my ancestor." He slid a sheet of paper toward her, a printout of a labeled drawing showing a cylindrical iron belt with a copper helmet attached to it.

"That is very Jacques Cousteau."

"It was good for a seven-minute dive, at least, so although you weren't going far with it, you could breathe under water long enough to grab a few pieces of silver." He raised an eyebrow at her.

She instantly perked up. "You think the Captain found *Queen Anne's Revenge* and used this contraption to recover some treasure!"

"Makes sense doesn't it? I mean, before this invention people often went below the surface of the sea using raised and lowered barrels, but there wasn't any way to move freely about and retrieve objects. He might have found the wreckage by accident or by using the barrel technique. And then, with the aid of this little jewel, he pilfered and plundered."

"You make him sound horrible. I don't think it happened in such a manner. I just don't." She sipped her coffee and tried to imagine why the Captain would turn to pilfering wreckage when he had so much going for him.

"I'm simply trying to put the pieces of the puzzle together. And I have a surprise for you." He didn't look at her directly. He seemed to be more interested in the swirling dark liquid in the bottom of his mug.

"A surprise?"

"Yes. I've decided to let your apparition have the

night that you both desire with you. My body is at your service. The only stipulation being we must first solve the mystery of what happened to his wife and be certain he had nothing to do with it. If he so much as hit her with his elbow as they climbed the stairs and she fell over and broke her neck, the deal is off. He must have had absolutely no complicity in it whatsoever." He inhaled a deep breath.

Stunned, Madeline asked, "What changed your mind?"

"Does it matter? You can tell him next time you see him his assistance in solving this mystery will speed up the occurrence of what he desires most."

Once her feet could move again, she sat down next to him. "Yeah, well, I haven't seen him since the storm. Maybe he's moved on."

"He'll be back," William assured her. He handed her some toast and butter. "Sorry, it's the best I could do. We'll need to do some grocery shopping. I don't trust the contents of the refrigerator to be safe."

"No, it's perfect," she commented, thinking more about his first offer and less about the toast.

****

Madeline listened as William called the cleaning lady and asked if she would drive out and take care of the basics for them—laundry, dusting, clearing out the refrigerator—then drive him back into town with her so he could retrieve his car and do a little shopping.

In short time, she arrived with a sack brunch.

"You really think of everything, Lydia," William praised her.

He and Madeline instantly devoured the country ham biscuits and fried apples. "Why don't we work out on the garden porch in order to be out of Lydia's way while she cleans?"

With white cotton gloves and a journal each, they proceeded to the porch. "It was smart to choose this porch," Madeline complimented him. "Saltwater and sand on the seaside could blow in, and the other two are muggy at this time of day."

He leaned against the railing. "You know I wasn't even thinking of that, only about the morning light. It is generally better here without the glare from the water."

Focusing on the pages as best she could, his offer, over toast and coffee, preoccupied her mind. Madeline watched his hands flipping the pages. Even through the gloves—knuckles and tendons popping up against the thin, white cotton—they appeared powerful and strong. She wondered how they would feel trailing the length of her abdomen from neck to thigh, stopping to tweak and tease and stroke as they careened along her body.

William was muscular, indicative at his age of a certain amount of attention to workouts. She watched his thigh muscle pop up and imagined it pressed against hers. Every part of her body responded to the images forming in her mind, and she squirmed in her seat. Could she separate the Captain from William? Would knowing how his body parts felt enmeshed with hers cause her to crave more of the man and less of the apparition?

****

William could feel Madeline's eyes on him. Her stares penetrated his façade of nonchalance.

He wanted to take her to bed right now, but she wanted emotion, and he wasn't sure he had any to offer. All feelings had been bottled and shelved after he nearly died from the heartache of the broken engagement just moments before the wedding.

Yet he longed for her to crave him as badly as she did the ghost who claimed to be the first William of Pine Island. Would she ever look at him with the longing she did for the Captain?

He didn't want to admit the sleepless night he had suffered through was due to thinking about the curves of her body and the expression in her eyes when she spoke of the Captain. He wanted her to gaze at him similarly, to want him in the same way. Perhaps her emotions would transfer in some crazy way if he did allow the apparition to use his body to make love to her.

The pages stopped turning, and the atmosphere on the porch thickened with things unsaid and feelings untethered. If she had been any other visitor to Pine Island, William would have already seduced her, bedded her, and had her begging for more.

Since his last attempt to satisfy those cravings with a local beauty had gone limp—literally—thanks to the apparition, he hadn't tried again. *That's the problem*, he assured himself. *I've gone too long without sexual gratification*. That had to be it.

He shifted positions in the chair, trying to find one which didn't call attention to the raging stiffness begging to be stroked and satisfied. He wanted to make love to Madeline as himself first. *Damn*, he thought, *why didn't I make that part of the deal as well? Just so she'd know the difference.*

A few glasses of Chardonnay and an hour or two of his charm and she would want him. Most did. *No, I don't want her as part of a deal. I want her to want me—the real me, not the future embodiment of her wonderful Captain.* He ground his teeth together, setting his jaw, and tried not to think about her. William shifted again. He just couldn't make it go down this morning, especially with her watching him.

Was she imagining the same thoughts as he? Looking up, he caught her eye. Madeline's mouth flew open and she quickly turned away. What if he walked over to her and rubbed the back of her neck with his forefinger? What if he touched those forbidden places—by accident of course? Would she accept his advances? He decided to try.

He pulled a glove, inside out, from one hand and then the other, placing them and the journal in a lidded plastic tray. Crossing the small space between them seemed to take an eternity. William noticed his legs weren't quite as steady as they should have been, and he flexed his fingers to stop their sudden trembling. "I was just thinking we should take a walk together."

"You want to stop the research and go for a walk?"

"Yes, let's go for a walk."

He stood but a few inches from her. When she looked up, it was right to the area of his clothing giving away his mood. "Is there a reason?"

She'd seen his excitement before he'd quickly turned his back to her. He felt sure of it. "Just need to walk off some stress," he said.

"You walk; I'll read," she answered.

"Come with me," he insisted. "We'll get right back to these in a moment." He reached out to her, offering his hand.

She studied him for a moment before surrendering the journal and the gloves. Placing them with his own, he took them inside to lock up in the study's vault, dropping the key into the desk drawer.

When William returned to the porch, he and Madeline took off along the garden path, meandering through the budding roses, still in their infancy, and the beaten and burnt azaleas, long past their prime. The scent of the wet earth following the rains mixed with the verdant aliveness of the foliage, lending a fresh perspective on its aromas.

"Does it ever flood in here?" Madeline pointed at the flat space of ground lying low behind the walls.

"Only during the worst hurricanes. The sea wall protects more than the house. It saves the floral abundance as well. Once or twice it was nearly wiped out. That's when we added to the wall or changed the garden's landscape."

He avoided her gaze, yet she commanded the gap between them, and he felt himself desiring her once again. On the narrow path, his legs were only inches from hers, his arms swinging within touching distance of hers.

He had the thought to warn her to be careful about tripping over loose rocks. It formed too late. Madeline's feet flew out from beneath her. Instinctively, William grabbed her to prevent a fall, and for a moment his hands were fused to her body. He told himself to release her, but he couldn't.

Madeline steadied herself. "Thank you. I must have slipped on some damp moss. I'm okay now."

As she tugged her arms from his grasp, he dropped his hands, realizing his mistake at continuing to hold onto her. "Be careful," he advised. "These old stones and crevices can be slick when wet."

He regretted his choice of words instantly, hearing

the double meaning and knowing she picked up on it. He hadn't meant anything sexual by them, but it only added to the tension between them.

She blushed, then grinned and lifted an eyebrow. "As many things can be." Bursting into laughter together released them from the physicality of the moment.

William relaxed. The brief spell of humor had cut the tension, and he now felt more at ease. Motioning for her to continue along, he hung back behind her. But he stayed near enough to catch her once again, should another slippery section of the path trip her up.

A breeze blew in, nothing unusual for the area, except this one brought with it a dervish. It might have been a small tornado forming right in front of them. It spun and twisted and finally settled into the shape of a man—a foggy, translucent shadow—but clearly a man.

"He's here," Madeline whispered, turning toward the shape.

William could make out the embodiment, but couldn't clearly identify nor hear it. He supposed it must be the Captain, appearing translucent as haze off the summer's asphalt—a shifting undulating energy field of shapeless outlines one second, regrouping into a human form the next.

Madeline stared at the spot, appearing to see something he could not. She smiled and listened to the personification he couldn't hear. He watched the tilt of her head and the lock of her eyes upon the apparition.

Seeing the spectacle was enough to make the hairs on William's arms stand up. He strained to make out the sounds only Madeline seemed able to understand. "What is he saying?"

"He said we should get back to the house." She looked from one of them to the other.

"Is he afraid of a little competition from a flesh-and-bone man?" William felt his blood boil. How dare this specter dictate to the two of them what they should or should not be doing?

Madeline listened to something else he couldn't hear, and nodded, clearly engaged in a conversation. "I'll tell him." She turned to William. "He says you need to harness your jealousy."

Anger bubbled up within William. Its resulting heat flushed his face, making it burn.

"He said he doesn't blame you..." She turned back to the spirit and seemed to be arguing with him. "No, I don't think he feels that way. No, I don't want to say it. Okay. But..."

"What is it? What is he trying to get you to say?" William glared at her while pointing at the ghost.

"He wants me to tell you he knows you desire me and he doesn't blame you, but that isn't the reason he thinks we should get back to the house. He said the cleaning lady can't be trusted, and that if you were to peek in her purse right now, you would find evidence of it."

The accusation leveled on such a faithful employee incensed William. She had never failed to show up for work, nor had she ever left anything undone. "That's ridiculous! Lydia's been with me for years. She just brought us breakfast and is busy cleaning up our mess."

"The Captain says he's seen her in your study before although he wasn't sure about what she had been doing at the time. Apparently she's pressed your keys into something he describes as similar to a bar of soap, but more malleable." Madeline looked from one to the other.

"Keys? Bar of soap?" he repeated. The stated image formed in his mind, and William understood. Lydia had pressed his keys into a form and had copies molded. But why? "Tell him we'll go right there, and he should come along in the event he can help with things."

Urgency forced them hurriedly back along the path, William's hand on Madeline's arm to steady her across the slippery areas. Snaking along to the ocean side, they slipped into the house through the sea porch, the last place Lydia would expect them to come from.

Stealthy as mice, their shoes deposited outside, they crept along. In such a large house there were many places the cleaning lady could be, and many things she could find of value.

William spied the large tote bag she always carried with her on the table in the main hall. Listening for sounds of her footsteps nearby, and hearing nothing, he inched over to it, with Madeline close behind.

He knew it was despicable for daring to mistrust Lydia solely on the word of an incarnation who haunted the premises. But clearly the bag would be the most likely place for a hidden key mold, so he opened it.

William's heart thundered with the subterfuge. Or was it the nearness of Madeline and the way she had been arousing him? Or perhaps it was the crackle of the ghost whose presence he could see and feel, even if he couldn't hear him.

On first glance nothing looked suspicious. A checkbook wallet, sunglass case, a paperback novel with something sticking out. He lifted the book, its cover that of a man and woman entangled in an embrace.

"A romance novel? Now is hardly the time to be reading," Madeline said. Her voice was low and controlled, but the tone was chastising.

William pointed to the yellow-edged papers sticking out from the edges of the book. He opened it to reveal what he feared they might be. Two precious pages had been torn from the Captain's journals and slipped inside of the paperback. Beneath the book, was a set of wet plaster casts bearing the shapes of skeleton keys and a round vault nook.

William couldn't believe what he was seeing. He placed them all back into the unzipped bag, crept to the door, and then gave it a slam as if they had just entered. "Lydia?" he called out. He yelled again for her. "Lydia, are you upstairs?"

She leaned over the third floor landing, staring down at them from above. "Yes. Did you want something?"

Though anger boiled beneath his cool demeanor, he forced himself to remain calm. "I need to get into town and run a few errands before businesses close for the day. Can you finish up quickly and take me in with you? I hate to interrupt, but the day is getting away from us."

"I'm finishing now," she said with a happy trill in her voice. She bounded down the stairs.

Just as she neared the last few steps, William leaned against the table and knocked her tote bag over, sending the items inside sprawling across the floor.

Lydia gasped at the sight of everything flying hither and yon.

William made sure he grabbed both the novel and the casts. "What are these?" He pulled the pages of the priceless journal from her dog-eared paperback. "What are you doing with these? Where did you find these?"

She raced for and tried to grab them from him. "That's my book. It's nothing really."

Unable to restrain himself any longer, William seethed. "And what about these casts?" He shook them at her. "They certainly resemble the shapes of my vault and skeleton keys. You had better start explaining, and it had better be good."

Snapping out his cell phone, he dialed 9-1 and held his finger over the 1, sending the message he intended to call the police and have a squad car sent out for her.

Lydia immediately began to shake and stutter. "I don't know how it got into my purse. I really don't. You know me. You trust me." Her eyes grew large and round with panic, and she pointed at Madeline. "I...I...can explain. She did it. She wants to get rid of me."

William hit the 1 again and started talking to the communications center. "There's a thief on my property. I need a squad car with a fingerprint kit sent out immediately. Thanks. Yes, she's still here."

Com central apparently assumed he meant the visiting nosy student had now gone to any means to secure her research. "No, she's not the culprit. Please hurry," he added, "before someone gets hurt." Then he hung up the phone.

The cleaning lady burst into tears. "I can't believe you are going to do this to me. I can't believe after all I have done for you...I even brought your damned breakfast...and this is the thanks I get? I've scrubbed your filthy toilets and thrown out half-empty bottles of expensive champagne, and you repay me by calling the cops because that woman planted evidence on me."

William didn't respond.

Lydia kept ranting. One minute she was crying; the next, angry and yelling; bringing to mind something from a television special on split personality disorder.

To her credit, Madeline said nothing, even when being called vile names and accused of planting the pages of the journals.

William had been with her every second of the morning since Lydia's arrival. He had taken the journals from her and placed them in the vault himself. Then they left together and returned together finding the theft and worse—the damage of the irreplaceable journals.

"You'll regret this. She'll rob you blind!" Then more sobbing and pleading. "Why? Why don't you believe me?"

In the midst of the melee, Madeline pulled William to the side. "You know what's going to happen when the police get here, don't you?"

"Yes, of course. They are going to drag her sorry—"

She interrupted him with a wave of her hand in front of his face. "No, that's not what I mean. They are going to collect evidence. They are going to take the casts and the ripped pages—"

It was his turn to interject. "Into evidence! Why didn't I think of that?"

Madeline nodded, biting her lip. "Might want to slip the pages out and put them away. A dusting for fingerprints would ruin them. And there's enough evidence here, with the casts, to press charges."

William placed both hands on Madeline's face, his thumbs caressing her cheeks. He wanted to kiss her, wanted it so badly he could almost feel the soft touch of her lips brushing his. Feeling the tickle of her hair against his nose, he placed his lips close to her ear and whispered into it. "You think of everything."

When the squad cars arrived, they handcuffed Lydia and led her outside. One officer stayed with her while the other, identifying himself as Officer Simpkins, took William and Madeline's statement. After calmly explaining the accidental spilling of the contents of her purse and the findings it led to, William explained the earlier events of the journals missing from the Historical Society.

William could see the seriousness of the crime reflected in the officer's steely eyes. The breach of the society's secure locks would be on the minds of the citizens of Georgetown. Solving this case was paramount for the entire community.

The car with the hand-cuffed cleaning lady in the back seat left the island as she was taken in for questioning.

In spite of his anger at Lydia, William believed her to have been duped into her actions. Money had a way of making people do things they otherwise might not.

Another unit arrived with gloved detectives. While they dusted for fingerprints, William retrieved his keys and laid them in the indentions of the casts, where they fit as snugly as he feared they would. Making no mention of the ripped pages, William turned everything else over to the officials.

One pointed at Madeline. "Who is she, and what is

her role in all of this?"

William placed an arm around her shoulders. "This is Madeline Waters. She is doing some scholarly research on Captain William Gray. We've been working on the history of Pine Island, which is how I discovered the journals were missing in the first place. She has been with me all morning. We came back together, and I knocked over the purse. So we can rule her out, although the woman you've just taken in for questioning wants to blame everyone except herself and whoever put her up to this scheme."

"You don't think she is working alone?" one officer asked.

"Absolutely not. What would she want with Historical Society keys? The general public doesn't even know of the inner vaults' existence. If you press her, you'll get the name of her accomplice. That's the person with something to gain. She probably didn't get more than a week's worth of grocery money for putting her freedom on the line."

"Will you drop the charges against her if she gives up whoever put her up to this?"

William was ready to do whatever it took to get the mastermind behind the theft. "Is that the bargaining chip you'll use with her?"

"Yeah, it will help if there's something in it for her to gain."

"I agree then. If she relinquishes the name of the person who put her up to this, I'll drop the charges against her."

"Are you both going to be around for the next few days, in case we have more questions?"

They nodded.

"What about her car?" Madeline asked.

"We can have it towed, if you want," Officer Simpkins recommended.

"Or I can drive it in and bring mine back," offered William. "Mine has been left in town."

"We'll have to get her permission, but a tow truck is going to be quite expensive for her, so she might agree. You could ride back in with the truck driver. So you won't be inconvenienced, either way," said Simpkins.

"Sure," William agreed.

After placing a call to the precinct, permission was granted. Lydia seemed to realize there was nothing to gain in not allowing access to her vehicle. It was clear to everyone she would never be returning to Pine Island, nor likely to ever work as a cleaning lady in Georgetown again. Her car keys were retrieved from her tote bag and the envoy took off for town.

Chapter 29

When the last car left the Pine Island grounds, the Captain floated down and sat across from Madeline, left alone in the cavernous house.

He didn't have to speak for her to be aware of his presence. She felt his presence in the change of the air—static, chemistry, energy. She turned toward it. "You are here still?" she asked.

His ions began to form into a knowable shape. "Yes my love. I will not abandon you again. You have nothing to fear."

The spark of the Captain's weightless hand, flickering across hers, triggered emotions and desires. They could not be halted by simply wishing them to cease. Yet, she knew he wasn't real. Not in the same way she and William were. She tried to lean against him, his body held together by nothing but an energy field of electrons.

"Yes there is," she said, giving voice to the deepest, most intimate fear of her heart. "I fear the permanent wanting of you and the inability to have it quenched. I am earth, you are heaven. How do we meet?" Her breath quickened, along with her pulse.

"At the horizon," he whispered, blowing across her body and fanning the already intense flame.

The words slipped out in the gale force of his attention. "William agreed to lend his physical body, with one condition—he must be convinced you had nothing to do with your wife's death. And I must have your promise to bring no harm to either of us."

"Then our prayers have been answered. Our night as one body will happen and rapture will be yours and mine forever."

Shaking, Madeline reveled in his passion and his words. "Why do you have this effect on me? Can it be I am your Magdalene resurrected in this body? Does it work that way? And if it does, why have you not returned as someone else?" How could she make sense of the senseless? How could she reason away that which has no reason?

"We have only one spirit and if it learns all in one lifetime, then it does not return. However, few ever do. And you know them by name. They are your spiritual leaders and Messiahs. They need only go around the universe once. The rest of us are doomed to receive our lessons in bits per lifetime. I didn't learn all of mine, yet I didn't trust being released. I stayed lost in the spirit realm searching for the soul of the woman I loved for such a brief time."

"And you believe hers to be in me." Her words came out breathily, sounding as lethargic as a last one might.

"I know it, and I will love it back to life."

"Tell me more about her," Madeline said. Other than having the occasional random recollection of scent, she felt no connection to Magdalene. Surely, if what the Captain said was true, she would have a better sense of his departed wife. "I want to know everything about her. Start with what happened after she recovered from the loss of the first baby."

"When I returned she was a shell of the beautiful young woman I had left. It seemed she had been gutted, and everything happy and cheerful had been removed. She had barely eaten and was so thin I could see her bones beneath the skin. Her eyes had turned into dark hollows. I didn't recognize her." The memory caused his concentration to waver and his form shifted, losing its carefully held-together shape.

Madeline tried to console him while she waited for him to reorganize himself and reappear. Her heart went out to the young woman. "She was depressed. Lots of women have issues when their hormones shift. And especially since she lost the child, I am sure that was her condition."

"Aye. I have learned much about this over the decades, but I knew nothing of its existence at the time. I thought she was gravely ill and brought the doctor out. He said she had melancholia and what she needed was another pregnancy. He left a vial of laudanum drops and also suggested cold baths and invigorating walks. He mentioned a controversial massage therapy—Dr. Swift's female stimulation."

"Female stimulation?"

"He'd reach up their skirts and bring on contractions to get the uterus back in its proper place."

"Orgasm?" Madeline didn't know if she had interpreted it correctly, but what else would bring on contractions.

"I believe so, yes. I felt certain I could take care of that duty myself. After all, a man doesn't spend time in the islands with native beauties, schooled in such techniques, if not to learn how to please a wife." He seemed proud of his sexual escapades.

"And was your wife pleased?" she teased him.

"Aye. Much pleased." He said this with a certain amount of conceit. "From the very first time, and every time thereafter. I was not the sort to just see to my own pleasure, and disregard hers. In fact, I believed the more pleasure she received, the more she would be inclined to offer the same."

"That was very forward thinking for your generation."

"'Tis true, but..."

He sighed and she smiled.

"So I have much to look forward to."

"It has been more than a century since I have lain physically with a woman. You must not expect overly much." Although he seemed to be disclaiming his own prowess, he did so in a jovial manner. Was he simply teasing her?

"What treatments did you use, and which ones worked?" Madeline asked, bringing the conversation back to Magdalene's depression.

"We used the laudanum drops and took long walks. Occasionally I convinced her to dip into the sea with me. I taught her to swim. She seemed much improved, and I stayed with her until Edward was born. She made it to full term, and he was a beautiful baby. But he suffered so when she stopped giving him mother's milk. We were afraid we might lose him as well."

Madeline recalled some facts from her previous research about treatments and cures. Laudanum, a tincture of opium, was available without prescription until the early twentieth century. Used for everything from cough suppressant to pain relief, it was also commonly used for women's ailments. And as an opiate, it would have transmitted through her breast milk. "Was he addicted to the laudanum?"

"We didn't give it to *him*," the Captain snapped, indicating she should know such a thing.

"Yes, you did." She hated to have to be the one to tell him this, but it was true. "You may not have realized it, but if Magdalene was taking the laudanum and breast feeding the baby, then he was getting it through her milk."

"We did not know this. That explains much." He grew quiet and more translucent, almost disappearing.

"Of course you didn't. It wasn't your fault. And Edward was all right after he'd withdrawn from the laudanum?"

The Captain pulled himself back together and grew stronger in his apparition. "Yes. Edward alone survived."

"There were others who didn't?"

"Two more who didn't make it far into the pregnancies, and one who died shortly after her birth. Then I lost Magdalene."

"How did you lose her?" she asked, as he started to fade.

She realized the sad events caused him too much pain to continue with the discussion, so she tried to bring him back by changing the subject. "Don't go; I need to ask you about a couple of pages in your journals."

He thinned into a vapor, a misty form where his body previously existed.

Madeline yelled into the center of the open staircase, looking heavenward, not knowing where he might be, yet sensing him all around her. "Please come back. You were right about William's cleaning lady, and now we need to know what she wanted."

A voice called to her as clearly as one coming from right next to her, though she could not see anyone there. "*Queen Anne's Revenge*. She wants the location of Blackbeard's ship."

Then nothing else came to her. She didn't feel his presence or see his shape. *Had he abandoned her?* But she had gathered some valuable information.

Those journal pages must have indicated the point one of the greatest pirates of all time had run his ship aground, sinking it. There was speculation he had done this on purpose to hide his immense fortune.

And she now knew Magdalene had suffered from depression, and most likely had unknowingly brought on the death of three babies by her own medication. How terribly tragic and sad the whole turn of events had become.

Chapter 30

When William returned, he found Madeline studying nautical charts and sailing quadrants. She seemed excited about something, and that lifted his spirits. He could use a little good news.

After she shared with him the most obvious information Lydia had been seeking, he grabbed the pages barehanded, forgetting the importance of wearing the protective gloves when perusing a delicate manuscript. "Have you any idea how important this discovery could be?"

"What if it is Blackbeard's ship?" she asked. "Doesn't it belong to someone else? Do you get to keep such a gem just because you find it?"

"I have no idea how it works, but I do believe you get to keep at least part of the cache. Why else would there be treasure seekers investing in search and recovery vehicles for underwater dives? And why would someone put Lydia up to tearing these pages out of my journals? Someone knew this information existed and wanted it badly enough to pay my housekeeper for the theft of it, and a copy of the keys only I possessed." He paced the floor.

"Do you suppose the charts and topography are the same as they were then? Are the nautical divisions and measurements the same? I don't understand sailing terminology and sailors' vocabulary. But after all this time, can it be right where the Captain left it?"

"Yes, and no. The quadrants and measurements will be the same, but what is likely to be different is the location of the wreckage from the shoreline."

"I don't get it."

"The place where the Captain found the wreckage could be totally different because the ocean tides move and shift the sands. This island's shorelines have changed much over the years. They say parts of the northern coastline have been transferred to the tip of the Outer Banks and parts of our shoreline are now down around Georgia. So the position of the ship's location, though still mired in the same spot, could be different from the exact location in the Captain's day."

"Oh, I see," she said. "I didn't think about that."

"Well, more importantly, the criminals attempting to steal from me didn't think of it either. But at least we know the identification of one of the culprits."

"Why do you believe there is more than one?"

"Lydia would have no business going into the inner chamber of the Historical Society and no one recalls seeing her there. So she has to be working for someone in the Society."

"Ray?"

He nodded. "You have been paying attention." William considered all the women he had brought out here who couldn't have cared less what he really had to discuss. They'd had one agenda on their mind. And so had he, until now.

"So what do we do about it?"

"Come on. Let's grab a bite to eat. I want you to tell me what you learned about Magdalene." He placed his hand on the small of her back and led her into the kitchen.

The counter was still littered with the bags he'd brought in, having only put away the items requiring refrigeration. Madeline set about placing the various jars, cans, and boxes onto their proper shelves in the pantry.

William tossed some marinade into a container with the tuna steaks and tore open a bag of salad mix. He pulled out the cork of the white Bordeaux and poured each of them a glass.

"So you told the Captain I had agreed to allow him the use my body, I suppose." He tried to toss this out casually, but an underlying edge remained in his voice that even he could hear. William glanced at Madeline's face, checking her expression to see if she picked up on his contempt for the concept.

"Yes, and I explained the conditions. He said it would be no problem, but I don't know. Maybe this is ridiculous, and we shouldn't go through with it. I mean, can we ever be sure what killed her?"

"Backtracking already? Afraid you'll crave more?" He tried teasing to lighten the mood, but she still appeared serious.

"Yes," she answered. Her voice was soft and thoughtful. She wasn't teasing. "That is a concern."

His heart skipped a beat. She was thinking she might yearn for him after a night with his body? The prospect of making love to her at all coursed excitement throughout him, even if during a possession by his ancestor. "Will *I* feel it? Will *I* know it is happening? Will *I* remember it?"

Madeline locked eyes with him. "I don't know. I don't have the answers. I'll ask him."

He kept his eyes on hers. "I would want to remember," he said.

William ran his hand along her cheek, watching her blush beneath his palm. His voice turned husky, thick with desire. "Would you want a man to know you that intimately and not recall every touch?"

He hadn't expected, on their first meeting, to feel anything of the sort for her. Now he was filled with longing.

"Are you in possession of him now?" she asked.

"No, this is all you and me." William lifted her chin and lowered his head toward her parting lips. She trembled slightly, and he knew she felt desire, but was it for him or for his ancestor? He waited for her to meet him, to move the imperceptible inch necessary to press his lips against hers.

She paused a moment too long, and William backed off, afraid to push or to appear too anxious.

****

While William turned his attention to the grilling of the tuna, the Captain swooped down from the staircase and materialized between them. "Tell him I am not amused with his sudden displays of affection," he whispered to Madeline.

She shook her head, a movement she noticed William catching in the corner of his eye.

"Is he here?" he asked, glancing around the room.

She nodded.

"Ask him how we can find out about his wife's death. Ask him if he knows who might have killed her, or if there is a possibility she died from natural causes. Ask him."

"Tell him I hear his questions and I know how she

died. Tell him it's the reason I have been waiting here, frozen in this realm. A mortal sin was committed, and I would rather have died myself than to have disclosed it to a single person. Tell him no child should know such things about his mother. Tell him!"

The edges of the Captain wavered, and Madeline knew he was finding it difficult to hold his concentration together long enough to remain a solid shape as he fumed. Apparently time and distance had not eased the pain of what had happened to his wife.

Madeline didn't repeat his words, she reached out to him. She held her open palms toward him, inviting him to embrace her. "What happened to Magdalene?" she asked, her eyes misting over and the softness of her tone caressing the words. "How did she die? Did it have something to do with the laudanum?"

William made a face. Madeline saw his confusion. Of course he wouldn't know what the question laudanum was about. They had been so busy talking about the pirate ship and the nautical positions of the supposed finding she hadn't taken time to inform him about Magdalene's woes. She didn't have time to stop and fill him in right now.

"I shouldn't have told you about her," the Captain said right before vaporizing. "Maybe you are not Magdalene."

"Captain come back," she called after him.

"What was that all about?" William asked. "What is laudanum? It sounds like some kind of drug. And why would you ask him about it?"

Madeline ignored William's questions and ran up the stairs after the Captain. "Captain, come back, come back. Let's talk about it." But he had gone from recognizable form, if not from the house all together. She limped back to the kitchen where William had proceeded to prepare their dinner.

"Sit," he said, without looking at her.

He sounded troubled, and she feared this predicament between her and the Captain bothered William more than he let on.

He carried the plates to the table where the wine and bread waited for them. "Sit down and tell me all about this." He pulled out her chair and then took his place across from her. Without speaking they passed the bread and the wine.

Continued moments of silence passed between them before she spoke. "Are you sure you want to discuss this over dinner? It is actually rather sad."

"I can handle it," he assured her.

She took a long sip of her wine and then began the retelling of Magdalene's sad story—her miscarriages, stillbirths, depression, and the laudanum drops usage—and the resulting guilt the Captain suffered.

"Do you think she died in childbirth?" he asked.

"Maybe. I don't know. I do know laudanum is derived from opium and can be passed to fetuses and nursing infants. It's possible the medication she took for her depression caused more of the same in the long run."

"Oh my God," he whispered, his face drawn. "How much could one person take before succumbing to the suffering?"

"Not just one person," she reminded him. "The Captain had to watch his wife's descent into a world he couldn't accompany her to, watch his babies die, and raise his one surviving son alone. I'd say there was plenty of suffering to go around."

"We romanticize that era, a time when life seemed simpler and less stressed, but the facts tell us another story altogether. The struggle to survive was a full-time job." William finished his tuna and pushed the plate away.

"We can't let this bring us down. It all happened a long time ago, and there's nothing we can do to change it. If we can figure it all out and give them some peace, then maybe it's all that is required of us."

With an edge of fear reverberating in his voice, he stated, "I don't want you to be alone with him anymore. I'm concerned about what might happen if you get too entangled with this guilt-ridden ghost who thinks you are the reincarnated spirit of his long-dead wife."

"And how will we arrange that? He shows up when he pleases." She pushed her plate back as well.

"We'll stay in the same room. There's one with twin beds, near mine, and I am not going to let you out of my sight."

"What about the deal with him?"

"Do you really want to sleep with this apparition?"

How could she explain she felt as though she already had? "I do have an attachment to him. I don't know quite how to explain it, but he has an effect on me that is—well—supernatural. I think he might be right. Magdalene's spirit might be residing somewhere inside of me."

"But if the Captain knew what caused his wife's death and could clear his name, why didn't he do that back then? It just doesn't make sense."

"I know. That has been bothering me as well."

"Still think he's so honest?"

His intense eyes penetrated hers, communicating his suspicions, until she had to look away. He was right, of course he was, but she didn't want to admit it. "Let's clear the table," she suggested, hoping for the chance to clear her head as well as the dirty dishes.

William insisted they take over the room with the twin beds.

It was large and well-appointed, but still uncomfortable with him only a few feet away beside her. She had felt forced into agreement, the implication being it might be the only way he would agree to continue to work on the project. And they were way too close now to solving many of the riddles concerning the Captain to stop now.

Yet, William was right. If the Captain could have cleared his own name, why hadn't he done so at the time?

It was strange to hear another's breath in the same room with hers. Jacob hadn't slept in the same room with her since he was a small boy. Now she listened to William's smooth, even breaths and wondered how it would feel to have this every night. She watched the corners of the room half-expecting to see the giveaway wisp of light and mist indicating the Captain had returned, but he failed to materialize.

She wondered if he was there, but chose not to present himself in a form she could see. Maybe he wasn't too happy with the idea of the shared room. Tossing and turning until the sky began to turn pink outside of the window, she finally gave up on the idea of getting any sleep.

William didn't even turn over as she crept out of the room, closing the door behind her with an ease guaranteed not to wake him.

Padding to the kitchen to start the morning coffee, Madeline pondered the whole situation. She tried to reconcile the Captain she had come to know with the one who may have been plundering another's sunken ship, and was possibly complicit in his wife's death. The two personalities didn't mesh.

In a flash of brilliance, another idea occurred to her. It would take some convincing, as William didn't want anyone else to know about this strange haunting. Yet, William might be willing in order to bring peace to both he and the Captain.

Mrs. Jenkins, the jeweler, had been anxious to get her hands on some of the rare vintage pieces from Pine Island's vault. As she recalled, Mrs. Jenkins had told her she had the "touch," whatever that was. Perhaps she knew a chant or a prayer or had a bag of herbs they could sprinkle around the house. Maybe she would be willing to search her memory bank for the right potion to cure this fissure in exchange for some of William's treasures.

It's worth a try, she thought.

Chapter 31

William awoke with his back turned to the bed Madeline had slept in. He had fallen asleep rather quickly, given his frustration with the situation and his overall determination to win Madeline for himself. She was obsessed with the apparition of his ancestor, and for some reason that bothered him.

It had been a long time since he had felt such— what did he feel? Was it jealousy? Surely he wasn't jealous of a ghost. Yet the way she referred to the Captain, the faraway expression in her eyes when they discussed him, indicated she had fallen in love with this spirit from the past. Was that the only reason William found her so attractive?

He flipped over on his back and stared up at the ceiling, barely visible in the soft glow of dawn. When *had* he begun to find her appealing? Not in the first moment he saw her, that was for sure. He tried to think backward and pinpoint the exact moment when he had thought of her as more than merely an acquaintance. It all came down to seeing her in love with the specter. He had witnessed enough women in love to know the pensive expression, and what it translated as.

He couldn't even hear her breathing now, as she was such a quiet sleeper. He flipped over again, expecting to see the shape of her body curled up in the bed mere feet from his own. But there was nothing except a pillow and tossed-back covers.

Panic engulfed him. His whole body quivered from its nerve-jangling realization. William jumped up and ran out of the room.

"Madeline! Madeline!" He screamed her name over and over, leaning across the banister in the open staircase before flying downward, unsure whether she was up or down and which direction he should go.

What if the apparition had her? What if she were in danger? Maybe he had lured her to the sea, or to the same place his wife had died. After all, he seemed to believe she was his wife. Perhaps he would want to relive the night she died.

"Madeline," he called, "Madeline!" His feet hit the steps with pronounced thuds. He hadn't taken time to grab shoes or a shirt. The only clothing he had on was a pair of pajama bottoms.

She appeared from the direction of the kitchen, arriving in the hall near the landing at the same time as he hit the last two steps. William didn't stop; he ran for her and embraced her fully in his arms, holding the back of her head to his shoulder with one hand while the other gripped the small of her back.

For a moment neither spoke. He exhaled deeply, relieved to see her. He finally released her enough to ask, "Are you all right?"

"Yes. I was just making some coffee." They were nose to nose—eye to eye.

Her rumpled hair and bags beneath her sleep-deprived eyes gave away her restlessness. William brought his hands around to her cheeks, running his thumbs along her lips, wanting to kiss her, devour her. He leaned forward.

Her lips tantalized him. They landed softly against his. Sensual wisps of nibbles caused her to moan in response.

God help him, but he desired her, wanted to know every inch of her. The minute his lips touched hers, the flame licked the simmering heat born in his groin into full fire.

He pulled her closer into his chest and kissed her more deeply, his tongue flitting across her teeth. Her encircling arms raced up his back as she returned his kisses. He started backing up toward the stairs, wanting to pull her to the room they had shared and make love to her, passion careening them upward.

"Busy this morning, aren't we?" The Captain swooped down upon them from the upper floor landing, his tone accusatory. William and Madeline broke apart at his presence.

"What do you want?" William hurled at the spirit as he tried to push Madeline behind him with one arm.

"I think we all know the answer." He manifested between them, in spite of William's efforts to keep him away, and into the body of Madeline.

William turned in time to see her take a quick breath and gasp.

The visitant quickly made his exit, leaving her trembling in front of William.

The Captain circled back to the stairs in front of both William and Madeline. "She'll be mine—at least for a night, as we have agreed."

William couldn't hide his anger. "I've been rethinking that little deal."

"I have the new coordinates for you. I can help you find *Queen Anne's Revenge*, but then I want my day and night with Magdalene."

"You'll not get it. At least not until we prove you had nothing to do with her death." William engaged directly in conversation with the spirit, and not through Madeline.

She had said nothing to the Captain. It hit suddenly, the realization he could see *and hear* the apparition, too. She tugged on his arm. "William, William do you realize what has happened?"

He turned toward her and threw one arm out, pushing her behind him once more. "I'm protecting you."

"You are talking to the Captain without my aid or translation. You see him yourself, don't you?"

"Of course he does," the spirit replied. "He has actually opened his heart and allowed something new to creep in."

They all three looked from one to the other, astonished at the new development.

"He'll trust me better now that he can hear me, too. Follow me, and we'll solve one thing after the other." The spirit glided to the study and waited for the other two to catch up to him. Once they had, he gave them the new coordinates before disappearing.

"Do you think we can trust him?" William asked.

"Only one way to find out."

Chapter 32

William and Madeline rented scuba equipment and took the boat out to the spot the Captain had told them about. On the horizon they saw another boat tailing them. William was sufficiently suspicious to keep his vessel moving. Steering way off course before dropping anchor, his suspicions were apparently not without merit. The other boat sailed in closer and dropped anchor as well.

"I think we should go back," Madeline said. "People kill others for much less than the location of a sunken ship full of treasure."

"Play along with me," he said. "I want to know who is in that other boat. We'll just pretend we are a couple out diving for fun."

They suited up, and he slipped beneath the surface of the water. But he didn't go far; he simply bobbed back up on the other side of the craft and hid from sight.

On cue, Madeline dropped a pair of binoculars to him, and he tried to identify the people aboard the other vessel. It wasn't Ray, and it definitely wasn't Ray's boat. But he was having trouble determining who it was.

When the two from the other boat dived in, William lifted himself back aboard, pulled up anchor, and gunned it toward their vessel. There was no name on the front of their boat, but there was a number—1289554.

They headed back to their dock with the identification number. Surely if William could find out who was following them, he would know who had put Lydia up to taking the key and the journal pages.

He searched online for the number and had tracked it to a fleet-renting marina in Charleston, South Carolina. Jotting down the name, address, and phone number of the marina, he put the note in his pocket.

He turned to Madeline. "It can be extremely dangerous to go treasure hunting out on the water, away from prying eyes. No witnesses means it's less likely the criminal will get caught."

"Are you going to call the police and give them the marina information and the boat number?"

"No, I'm going down there myself."

"Why? You just said it could be dangerous."

"What would I tell the police? Would I say 'help, someone rented a boat and ended up scuba diving in water near where I was diving?' Does that sound criminal? No. But if I can find out who rented it, maybe I can come up with something a little more solid."

"What if we used the Captain? Perhaps he could find out who is behind this."

"Does it work that way?" He considered it for a minute and then shook his head. "No...no, I am taking care of this myself. You are welcome to ride with me, though."

Madeline didn't hesitate. She jumped into the car with William.

****

Charleston often made Madeline feel both

232

nostalgic and peaceful. It was one of those cities whose old-world charm and first-rate restaurants and hotels merged successfully for a magnificent adventure. Although she and William wouldn't be spending the night, the ambiance immediately rubbed off on her.

"Could you take me by the yellow house?" she asked anticipatorily.

"Which house?" he laughed.

"Magdalene's parents' house by the water. The Captain described it as yellow with long white porches. It's where he first saw her on his excursion here to procure materials for the house on Pine Island. She was strolling along the house's harborside porch." Madeline gazed out of the car window dreamily, imagining the great white sails of his ship and the beautiful young girl in the green dress strolling casually along the porch.

"Is it still there? And would it still be yellow?" he asked.

She wondered. If it still stood, chances were good it bore some resemblance to the original structure. The persnickety historical society of Charleston insisted on authenticity of antebellum period homes. Even the garden designs along the walkways were meant to reflect the graceful bygone era.

"I have no idea," she stuttered. "I don't even know why I asked such a question. Forget it." She waved her hand back and forth in front of her face, regretting the sudden impulse to see the house.

What did she think would happen? Did she think a flashback would occur? Did she think standing on the porch where Magdalene had been raised would ignite the seat of her soul and engorge her memory with sufficient recollections to prove she did indeed belong to the Captain?

"No, this would be one of my ancestral homes, wouldn't it? My great-great-great-grandmother's home? To think that if Magdalene had not taken a stroll when she did, the Captain wouldn't have seen her, and I might not exist. It's staggering, really." William seemed intrigued.

They passed by the lane of tall, multi-storied single houses with wraparound porches, wrought iron fences, and brick walkways snaking along heavily landscaped small yards. On the other side of the flat expanse of road stood a sea-retaining wall holding back a swath of blue water.

Madeline imagined the Captain's ship gliding effortlessly by the gracious homes of the era's wealthy and elite. She could envision genteel ladies posing on the porches in their hoop skirts and multi-layered gowns, hoping to catch a little breeze off the water. Perhaps they held a fan to stir the air, or a parasol in the event they chose to leave the shade of the porch. And suddenly, like a mirage, a yellow house with a white front porch came into view.

"Stop," she called out. "I have to go there."

"Are you insane? We can't just trespass." Although William protested going onto the property, he pulled over into a parking spot and stepped out onto the waterside walkway.

"We could ask them for directions to the marina." It seemed a reasonable plan. Madeline took off, knowing whatever happened, she had to stand on *that* porch and gaze out onto the horizon.

He raced after her. "Wait…hold up!"

But she couldn't. Something from inside her, a

deep longing or magnetized field begging for its companion steel, pulled her forward until the step up onto the porch yielded the view she had longed to see.

The porch was raised above ground level so the eye instinctively skimmed the top of the wall and then out across the water. Her legs propelled her, but not in a normal walking cadence. Her hands found themselves entwined, elbows out at her side. Madeline glided, repeating the bridesmaid's walk she had taken along the aisle a few times.

She stopped and turned as a flash of white caught her eye. Was it a sail? No, it was the head of an eagle, regal and proud, dipping and playing. After a moment, it seemed to stall and stare right at her, its prey. For a second she felt outside of her own body. Voices came to her, but they seemed far away. She was out on the breeze with the eagle. And then it disappeared.

"I'm sorry," she heard William saying to someone.

She turned and caught his figure standing in the doorway opposite an attractive elderly lady in a soft blue seersucker pantsuit. She could have been any number of elderly ladies in the area.

"She's been working on the genealogy of my family line and thinks this house may once have belonged to one of my ancestors. It's absurd really. That house was probably demolished years ago."

They walked toward Madeline, and she met them halfway. "Hi I'm Madeline Waters." She extended her hand, and the lady accepted it with a soft shake, gnarled fingers giving away the arthritis she likely suffered from.

"How do you do? My name is Blanche Cousins."

"Have you lived here for a long time?" she asked.

"About fifty years," the lady said. "We bought the house and remodeled it. Then Hurricane Hugo nearly destroyed it in eighty-nine. That was when we investigated everything concerning the house and remodeled it exactly as it was originally. Ol' Hugo did us all a favor."

"So it didn't always appear as it does now?"

"No, as a matter of fact, I have some pictures of it before it was torn apart. When we started fixing the old place up after the hurricane, a friend found a picture of the house in the historical society's archives. It was a painting that turned up in an estate sale and made its way here. On this very porch was a lovely young girl with long, unkempt hair, wearing a flowing dress and a faraway glint in her eyes. Haunting almost." A shadow seemed to cross the old woman's face. She shook her head and shivered. "Anyway, I knew right then the house had to be painted yellow again, and so we did."

"Thank you," William offered. "We appreciate your time."

He took Madeline by the arm and half-dragged her off the porch and back to the waiting car. "We've got to get to the marina," he reminded her as he clicked open the door locks.

Madeline was in a trance. She knew she had, in fact, just stood on the porch where Magdalene had so besotted the Captain he had wanted more of her. And she had felt the pull of the past meeting the gravitational spin on the future. It had been one of the most amazing feelings she had ever received.

She didn't care that they were headed to the marina and were hunting criminals. She had gone *home* for a moment and now believed the Captain had been right all along. The spirit of Magdalene was inside of her somewhere; somehow.

Chapter 33

At the Marina, a rotund man instantly approached them. "Name's Jerry," he said, offering his hand as way of introduction. "What can I do for ya?"

"We're on our honeymoon," William said, draping his arm around Madeline. "Thinking we might do a little scuba diving off the coast."

"Oh yeah, lots of divin' goin' on 'round these parts," the man said. "I s'pose you'll be needin' a boat."

"Yes. That's why we've come to you."

"Do ya know what kind ya might be interested in?"

Madeline remained quiet. She watched as William scratched at his chin and appeared not to know the first thing about boats.

"Something not too large, maybe like the one a friend rented here." William pulled out the piece of paper and handed it to the attendant.

"Okay, I'll check on that," Jerry said, disappearing inside of the office.

William nudged Madeline, and they followed him inside. She sat across from the man while William stood off to the side, snatching glimpses of the information on the screen. He shook his head at her and she realized he couldn't make out the small print on the monitor.

They didn't have long. She needed to think. How could she help William? It would have to be something calling the salesman away for a minute, giving William the chance to lean in and capture the information they were seeking.

She asked directions to the ladies' room. Picking up a business card from the center desk as she crossed the interior, she walked nonchalantly into the first stall. There she dialed the boat rental agency's number.

"Jerry's Rentals," he answered. "Jerry speakin'."

"Hey Jerry," she said, implying they knew each other. "I think someone just backed into one of the boats out front."

He ran out of the office as fast as his stubby legs would carry him. He didn't take time to secure the computer's screen, and William snapped a photo of the monitor with his smartphone.

When Jerry returned—panting for breath—he wasn't happy. "Damned pranksters." He furrowed his brow as he attempted to remember what he had been doing before he got the summons. "Oh yeah, that's a nice boat. The couple who rented it reminded me a little of you two."

"Oh, in what way?" Madeline asked, having returned from her ruse.

"Middle-aged newlyweds desirin' a little scuba diving," he replied.

"Did they mention where they intended to dive? We've never been out in these waters, so a tip as to where we might want to start would be great." William sounded natural at this kind of information gathering.

Jerry switched screens and brought up a map of the Charleston area then clicked on "enlarge" to widen the coastline and panned out to a spot due south of them. "Yeah right here. You definitely find some pretty nice fish, and maybe some Civil War wreckage."

"Could you print that off for us?" Madeline asked.

"Yeah. We'll come back tomorrow, or the next day, to get one of these beauties." William took Jerry's card and told him he would call before returning. "There's so much to see and do around this area, it might actually be later in the week."

They walked back to their vehicle.

"Let's a get a bite to eat before heading home." William pulled into a tiny lot near *Jestine's,* a nice old south home-style restaurant famous for its fried chicken, fried green tomatoes, and sweet ice tea. It was the type of food Madeline's grandmother had cooked; black-eyed peas, cornbread, turnip greens, and the crispiest fried chicken imaginable.

"You're not saying much," Madeline said as she watched the wheels in William's mind spin and spin. He wasn't at all present in the conversation or even in the meal.

"There's something about the phone number connected to the boat rental that bothers me. I know it, but can't recall to whom it belongs."

"Can we use reverse look-up to see whose it is?"

"Good idea. It says it's a cell phone number from the Georgetown area. I know I know it, but I can't quite put my finger on it." He broke off a piece of corn bread and popped it into his mouth, still wearing the stupefied expression of someone in deep reflection.

"Call it," she suggested.

"No, let's have our dinner, and I'll see if I have it in my contacts list at home. It's someone I know, and that is what worries me."

"What about the chart Jerry said he gave the people

who took out the boat?"

"See,"—he sipped his tea, splaying his hands out in front of him—"there's another thing. The chart's course is all due south of the marina. The boat didn't go south; it went north, up into North Carolina waters. So why drive to Charleston from Georgetown if the intention is to head north with the boat?"

"Covering your tracks, maybe? Not wanting people to know what you are up to?" She cut another slice of the tangy, savory fried green tomato. It tasted scrumptious—real comfort food to her. The only thing missing was her grandmother's hugs.

"Exactly," he agreed. "They passed a lot of places to get a boat, which might make sense if you are sailing south, but to then go north? It doesn't make any sense at all."

The ride back to Georgetown was a quiet one. William appeared to have a lot on his mind.

After too many silent minutes, Madeline asked, "So, who knows about the journals and has access to the vaults at the Historical Society?"

"That's what I keep asking myself," William admitted. "I assumed it was Ray, but his isn't the phone number tied to the rental."

"Do you know any recent newlyweds?"

"No, but they were probably lying about that as well."

They slipped into another uncomfortable silence.

As they neared the Georgetown city limits, William suddenly careened the car toward town.

Madeline didn't ask any questions, she just held on as the car turned down a beautiful tree-lined lane.

William whipped the car into a driveway, asking

her to stay put as he ran up the sidewalk.

At first she thought no one was home, but then a lady appeared at the door and gave William a giant embrace. Madeline watched the two briefly chat and laugh.

He then escorted her over to the car and introduced her as Alex's wife, Helena.

Madeline could tell something was wrong the instant William slid back into the driver's seat. He said nothing, though he had given a hand wave and a big toothy grin to the lady as he pulled away from the house.

Though Madeline hadn't known him long, it was long enough to know the grin plastered there had no emotion behind it. It vanished the instant the car bolted forward.

He drove back out along the same lane before heading toward the center of the town and into a parking lot. "Lock the doors and stay in the car," he ordered, before leaping out to race across the street to the Historical Society.

William yanked on the door, though it didn't budge. He cupped his hands against his face and peered intently through the glass front. There was frantic rapping against the window before he gave up and raced back to the car.

He glanced at his watch before opening the car door. "They're closed already," he announced to Madeline. William shut the door without getting in. He paced the parking lot.

It was humid, the very air seeming to be full of wet, sticky fingers clinging to everything. Madeline opened her door to let in some air. She watched him open his phone case and then shut it. Something about that phone number bugged him.

"Why don't you just dial it?" she shouted across the lot to him.

His head shot up and he stared at her for a moment. "I don't have to. I know whose number it is. But to be certain..." The pacing stopped as he dialed. He stood for an unnatural amount of time staring at his smartphone.

She instinctively knew whatever he had just verified was not good.

His leaden feet trudged across the empty lot and back to the car. He clenched his jaw and the muscles on the side of his face visibly jerked and tightened.

"Who was it?" She dreaded asking, but knew he would eventually have to tell her.

"A good friend," he said through clenched teeth. "Correction," he added, "the chipper voice of a man I used to call *friend*."

"Could there be a mistake?"

"No mistake. The woman I just introduced you to is his wife. She had barely arrived home from work, so she was obviously not the woman who accompanied him on the journey out to sea."

"So who was the mystery lady?" Madeline remembered the woman from the Historical Society. "Could it be Carol Lewis?" It made sense in one way. She did have access to the keys and the vaults. But then why would the journals have wound up in Ray's drawer? No, something still didn't make sense.

William accelerated the car as they whipped along the road. The route was familiar to her now, the stretch of beach, mysterious swampland, dark forest. They were almost to Pine Island before he spoke. "I can't trust anybody," he whispered.

Madeline instantly felt sorry for him. What good was all of the money and land and reputation in the world if there was nobody you could trust to share it with? Here he was, in the second half of his life, and he still had not found the right person to share those things with.

How sad. Yet even as she formed the words in her own head, she realized she was in the same predicament. Her son had his own life now; he rarely came home from college. She had not found anything even remotely resembling a relationship. She worked too many long hours, at the jewelry store, when she wasn't studying for school. So what exactly did she know about sustaining an involvement?

In the garage, William hit the house alarm's deactivator, and they headed along the breezeway. The house had an eerie glow as they walked toward it. Darkness had crept up on them. The soft illumination of the landscaping's lights gave the impression of the house being reflected in a full circle of the moon's circumference.

Madeline stopped and stared at it for a moment. The cupola was out of view from this angle, but she imagined a giant Christmas tree standing in its center, awash in thousands of bright cheery lights. "I bet this place is gorgeous at Christmas," she commented.

"I haven't noticed." William took her by the arm and gently tugged her forward.

She couldn't keep shock from her voice. "You don't decorate it?"

"Only when there is reason to do so. And there

hasn't been a reason in a while." He opened the door and swept his hand forward to indicate he was holding it open for her.

Madeline hesitated. Something inside of her didn't want to go in right then. She couldn't put her finger on what it was, but there was something about the aura of the house, the night, and the confused state of the day, which prevented her from entering.

"Let's go for a walk instead," she suggested.

"Aren't you tired?"

"It might make you feel better."

"Oh, all right." He shut the door back.

"Beach or inlet?" She held her hands out to indicate the choice of directions.

"It doesn't matter. You choose. I am too tired to care."

"I thought you were physically fit," she teased. She noted the irony in his physique—so chiseled and sculpted, though now drained of all energy—and her chubby one, still going strong with plenty of energy left to walk the perimeter of Pine Island.

"Go ahead, poke fun at me. I rarely get over-tired from physical activity. But when I become mentally drained, my whole body seems to cave inward."

She started to recommend the beach when a voice resounded in her ear. *Inlet,* she heard him whisper. She whipped her head around and saw the swirl beside her. The Captain was there, though not in full manifestation.

"Inlet then," she declared. They walked quietly along the sandy path and out to the wooden platform offering itself as a landing before the few steps leading to the dock.

William stopped in his tracks and grabbed her by

the arm.

He pointed to something, and it took her a minute to realize what he was indicating. There were two boats at the dock.

The one which didn't belong to them was eerily similar to the one they had seen with the rental numbers on it. It was too dark to make out the numerals along the boat's top, but it had to be the same one.

"Think that's a coincidence?" he asked.

"Where are the occupants?"

William turned toward her.

She held up a hand, meaning to stop his comment. Madeline stared past William to the ghost she was so fond of.

William followed her gaze and squinted in the general direction of her affectionate haunt.

"They're in the house?" she asked and then turned to William. "They're in—"

"I heard," he interrupted. "And I can make out a shape." He pointed to the fuzzy outline before whipping out his cell phone to call the police department. "Hi, it's William Gray. I need you guys to make a little run out to Pine Island. Got another intruder." Then he turned to Madeline. "If they are in my house, why don't we board their boat?"

"I don't know, maybe that's not such a good idea." Frightened and distressed, this cloak-and-dagger pirate treasure-hunting life was not what she had signed on for. She had only wanted to learn about the man with the vision for human rights and equality in a time unaccustomed to such concepts. He was the man who had haunted her dreams, even before she came to Pine Island, as clearly as he now permeated the old house.

"Oh come on." William took off, and she followed. The spirit of the Captain tried to warn against it, but she most certainly did not want to be left alone on the dock.

They slipped aboard the rented vessel and nosed around the immediate steering and storage areas. Aside from a few nautical maps, there wasn't much noticeable. Then William locked eyes onto an object which appeared to instantly madden him. He grabbed the item before he spat a few curse words and stormed off the boat.

Madeline followed, not knowing what else to do. He raced along; a man on a mission. He tore up the path as energetically as a bull, rage seeping from every stride of his body.

She tried to reason with him, knowing he could be in danger if he stormed into the house and the other couple was armed. Yet there was no stopping him. With the Captain beside her, she somehow felt safe.

William burst through the door, calling out a pair of names. "Alex. Julia. I know you're here. Come on down, Julia, and bring your lover with you." His jaw clenched as he stood in the open center of the house, head turned skyward, spinning in a circle as he watched for some sign of the traitorous pair he obviously had mistakenly thought he knew so well. "I've already called the police. They're on the way."

That announcement spurred a reaction. Two heads appeared over the stairs on the next floor up. William spotted them. "That's right, baby, bring your boyfriend and come on down."

Footsteps thundered on the stairs. The face from the photograph Madeline had seen in the upstairs master suite stared back at them, in real life.

William shook his fist at them, a chain of some sort dangling from his closed fingers.

Madeline saw the man William had called "friend." Alex stood with his arm curled possessively around the shoulders of the woman William had once believed he would spend the rest of his life with. A glance at William revealed his face to be tight with rage and pain.

"Miss me?" he asked, with venom dripping from his voice.

"You wish," the woman sneered.

Madeline, watching the two of them react to each other, had to look away. It was too intrusive; too volatile. So much rage could not be healthy.

"Is Ray in on this, too?" William asked.

Alex laughed. "Oh man," he snickered. "That fool is so gullible. He's on a wild goose chase right now, with a few old coins and a fake map. Lydia had gotten me both of the keys—yours and his—then I lost my copy of yours before I could put the journals back, so that's why she was trying to sneak the mold of your key out again."

"We all share the same housekeeper, but how did you manipulate her into the middle of all of this?"

Madeline thought it smart of William to keep them talking and in the house for as long as possible. This gave the police more time to arrive and apprehend the pair of criminals.

"Well, I guess you could say you have me to thank for that one," Julia said. "I've given her little trinkets over the years and won her trust and loyalty. Of course, I also convinced her it was your fault the wedding didn't go through as planned. That witless pushover felt sorry for me. She believed I deserved a chance to retrieve my belongings—the ones you kept hidden away from me in the vault."

William sounded confused. "There's nothing in my vault belonging to you."

Julia sauntered over to him, laughing. "Of course not. But she didn't know that."

A clicking sound brought all eyes toward Alex. He had pulled out a pistol and cocked back the hammer.

Chapter 34

"Enough," Alex shouted. "As much as I'm enjoying this little reunion, I think we'd better get on with it."

He waved the gun at Madeline and William. "You know what we've come for, and you and your little friend there are going to retrieve it and join us for the dive to find the sunken ship."

William's face contorted with anger, betrayal, and pain. "I'm not going anywhere with you, and I wouldn't give you the journals, if my life depended on it."

"Well, that's good to know," Alex spat, "because it does. And so does hers." Alex grabbed Madeline, holding the gun firmly against her temple. "One false move, one twitch, and you'll get to witness what it looks like when a human life ends in a dramatic fashion."

Fear seized Madeline. She shivered and began to shake uncontrollably. Having arrived at Pine Island for scholarly information, she hadn't expected to be in the midst of clashes over pirate treasure, an undisclosed false friend, a duplicitous former fiancée, a pilfering housekeeper, and a loving ghost. Her mouth went dry—completely arid—convincing her it would never be quenched again.

William kept his cool, while Madeline had never been as frightened in her life. She knew beyond any reasonable doubt they would have to be killed in order for Alex and Julia to get away with the treasure. There was no way they were going to be left here to identify the culprits.

They needed to keep the two lowlifes in the house for as long as possible, hopefully long enough for the police to arrive. She forced her body to go limp in order to give Alex false confidence she was submitting to his plan.

"What about your wife, huh? What about Helena? Does she know about *this one*?" William jerked his head at his ex-fiancée.

Julia didn't even have the decency to appear ashamed. She just stood there, cocky as a mockingbird, smirking so proudly at what she intended to get away with.

"Not a clue. We've set it up for her to think I had a bad accident at sea and disappeared. Then the two of us will take our treasure and retire to a little island in the Caribbean. It's time someone besides you gets a chance at the finer things in life."

Madeline saw the wisp of fog. The Captain was here with them. She knew the only thing holding him back from running through Alex, fierce as a freight train, was the revolver pointed at her head.

For a moment the irony of William having had the chance to get to know his ancestral grandfather filled her with a sense of amazement. How many people got such a chance? But then she realized they might be joining him in the afterlife if she didn't find a way to turn this around, or at least stall until the police arrived.

"I don't recall you suffering in poverty," William snapped at Alex. "In fact, we both had pretty cushy childhoods."

The man's elbow dropped a little, although the gun maintained its proximity to Madeline's temple. "Yeah, that's right. Only, after my dad drank himself to death the family discovered he had mortgaged our ancestral birthright to the hilt. We didn't even get a life raft."

Alex's face reddened. "I don't expect you to understand how crippling it is for a young man to feel so powerless in the face of losing his father, his entire lifestyle, and childhood home. I think I started to hate you immediately, although I wasn't sure why. None of it was your fault, but I still had to watch as your luck and good fortune brought you everything, while I had nothing. You had the good looks, the brains, the backing, the influential lineage, while even my lineage became besmirched. But I could take your fiancée. So I did."

"How *did* you manage to win Miss Money Hungry?" William pointed at his ex-fiancée.

"I comforted her when you were too busy to take the time. Maybe I should show *this one* how much fun I can be." The hand pulling Madeline into his body suddenly dipped along her abdomen and then raced back upward to cup her breast. Grinning at its automatic response, he bragged, "Still got the touch it appears."

"Hey, knock it off!" Julia slapped the back of his head.

Alex turned toward her. His arm moved and the weapon on Madeline's temple slipped. At that exact moment Madeline eye caught the Captain's milky shape approaching from the rear and knew what he was about to do. He rushed into Alex with every possible ounce of power his energy field could entreat. The force of his contact was so violent it sent Madeline off her feet, as well as Alex.

William must have seen him, too. His attention had left Alex and moved to the spot right past him. He grabbed for Madeline, in an effort to steady her, as Alex fell.

When Alex hit the floor, the gun flew from his hand. Madeline watched as William and Julia both scrambled for it. Time crawled during the drama of the race for the weapon.

Somewhere in the distance, a siren became audible. It grew louder, in tiny decibel increments, as the slow-motion dance continued inside the stately manor.

The revolver went airborne in a kind of aerial ballet. Alex fell forward, face first, smacking his head not once, but twice, as it bounced off the floor. He lay motionless as the dance continued without him.

The revolver, its hammer still cocked back, spun around and out as William and Julia dashed toward it. It made contact with one of the graceful support columns and rang out with ear-splitting clarity.

William jerked and flew backward as something powerful slammed into his chest.

Madeline's screams filled her ears, co-mingling with the reverberating shot and the sirens. The whole world seemed to be screaming and shrilly whistling. Her head felt too much pressure. It could explode, surely it could.

****

Madeline's ears filled with stomach-curdling shrieks. Her feet, glued to the floor in the center of the room, kept her grounded in the middle of the circle of bodies and blood. She shook uncontrollably, finding it difficult to hold cupped hands over her ears to stop the shrill noise.

The sirens stopped, but pulsating blue lights flashed through the windows and then the door as it burst inward.

The officers had said something, called out to her, but she couldn't hear above the yells. *Who is screaming?*

Madeline forced her eyes to survey the three bodies lying still and lifeless around her. No noise emanated from any of them. It was in that moment, and with the wide-eyed expressions on the faces of the policemen as they approached her with caution, she realized *she* was the one wailing miserably. Swallowing hard, she forced the sounds of her pain to cease.

"Ma'am," the older of the two officers said, holstering his gun and walking slowly toward her. Madeline noticed the younger man still had his weapon trained on her.

"I am Officer Wharton. And my partner"—he jerked his head at the other man—"is Officer Gaines. We received a call about intruders here at William Gray's estate."

She tried to respond, but words wouldn't form. Madeline feared forcing them might open the shrieking to another round. She instinctively raised her hands, empty of weapons, and surveyed the chaos.

Blood splattered the wall on one side and puddled the floor beneath the body of the woman who almost married William, and might have ended up being the lady of the house. He lay unconscious from the blast to his chest, which had plastered him to the floor. Blood trickled from a wound to his head. The man who had once been an inseparable friend of William's was face-down in another pool of blood.

Chapter 35

The police scanned the carnage. "It's all right. We're here to help," said Officer Gaines, according to his badge, as he inched toward her. "I need you to step over here." He reached out to her as Officer Wharton issued a string of codes into his radio, soliciting back-up and emergency services.

Madeline followed orders. Glad not be required to think, she complied with their commands. When she was taken from the immediate scene, she could still observe Officer Wharton kneeling beside each body, one at a time, checking for pulses. She watched; eager to hear William would be all right.

Finally, words came to her. "How is William? Is he still..." She couldn't make herself say the last word—*alive*.

Silence fell over the center hall as Officer Wharton spoke with the emergency team headed toward them. "We've got two men with sufficient vital signs—pulse, pupil dilation—to assume life. Both appear to have suffered wounds to their heads. The woman however..."—he glanced up at Madeline before finishing—"DOA."

Madeline searched her mental database. DOA? Dead on arrival? Julia was dead? She listened as Officer Wharton supplied the few details he apparently had.

"COD appears to be a bullet to the chest."

COD? He must mean the cause of death. Officer Gaines asked her something, but she hadn't taken in his words. "I'm sorry…" She started to apologize and ask him to repeat whatever he had said. Hearing Officer Wharton mention her, the stark realization she was the prime suspect landed hard upon her.

"…could be the agitated woman we found conscious at the scene, unless another party ran away before we arrived."

Officer Gaines followed her gaze with his own, both now intent on hearing what the older policeman was thinking.

"Not on her," he replied. "If it is the weapon involved, it is on the floor several feet from the suspect." A pause as he appeared to be listening. "I don't know. She was a bit crazed when we arrived. Probably threw it after firing."

The shaking returned. Of course she appeared suspicious. She was the only one still standing when the police arrived.

Officer Wharton turned his attention to William as he began to stir.

"Madeline!" he screamed.

"Yes," Madeline yelled, snapping out of her daze. She slipped from Officer Gaines' attention, breaking into tears as she ran to William. The younger policeman held out his arm as a barrier to stop her from reaching the injured man.

Wharton placed his hand onto the outstretched arm of his partner, pushing it downward and giving a nod to indicate they should let her go.

"Listen to what they say," she heard him whisper

as she knelt beside William.

"Are you all right? I was so scared for you." She wept as he tried to raise his head.

"My head," he said, lifting a hand to his forehead. "It feels like it has a small sofa resting on it."

"You'd better lie still," the policeman advised. "Help is on the way."

"He knocked me out of the way," William moaned through clenched teeth. "He saved me."

"Of course he did. Of course he did." She stroked his forehead and the sides of his face.

"Who, ma'am? Who knocked him out of the way? Was there a third man?" Officer Gaines asked.

She stared up at him, unsure how to answer. She shook her head. They would never understand the concept of the ghost of Captain William Gray saving his own heir.

William tried pushing up on his elbows. He looked at Officer Wharton. "Did you get the two of them? Please tell me they didn't get away."

Madeline's composure returned with her assurance William was alive and expected to live. "Lie back down. Everybody's here. Everyone's accounted for."

"Okay," he muttered, settling down.

Officer Gaines tapped Madeline on the arm. "Can we see you for a minute?"

She started to rise and William grabbed her. "Please…stay with me."

"She's not going anywhere," the policeman assured him. "I only need a brief statement."

"It's okay," she said to William, before following the policeman to the settee by the door where Officer Wharton waited.

"We got a call about intruders here at Pine Island," Wharton said. "Can you fill us in on the time line?"

She tried to be brief but succinct. "We returned from a walk and saw a strange boat at the dock. As we approached the house, we heard the intruders inside. That's when William called for assistance. We managed to get caught by them, resulting in a gun to my head." She began to shake again, feeling the ghost of the icy revolver against her temple once more. Her hand went instinctively to the place tingling with sensory memory.

"It's all right, we're here now. Go on."

"They demanded the contents of William's vault. They said they would be taking us with them. I think they would have killed us and dumped our bodies." She trembled, her hands shaking. "Guess we came close to being shark chow."

"Do you know who they are?"

"Yes. The man is Alex Hamilton, one of William's friends. In fact, William recently spent the night with Alex and his wife in their home. I met her just today." She paused a moment. "She seemed a really pleasant lady. I can't imagine the pain she doesn't know yet is on its way to her. Not only was her husband seeing another woman, but he was a criminal. He planned on faking his death and escaping to the Caribbean never to see her again. She would have mourned, waiting on news of a body washing ashore. How cruel! What kind of a man does such a thing?"

The two policemen exchanged strange expressions, absorbing the gist of what had just happened.

"The dead woman was once engaged to marry William. She…" The words fell away.

"How did she end up with a bullet in her chest?" one of the policemen asked.

"They were arguing and the woman yanked at Alex. The gun went airborne during the brawl, and everybody raced for it. It hit the column and discharged. I thought...I saw..."

"What did you see, or think you saw?" Officer Gaines encouraged.

"I feared the stray bullet hit William, but it must have hit the woman."

"What are the chances of a stray bullet from an airborne revolver piercing someone's heart?" Officer Wharton theorized.

"All vacuums seek filling," Madeline answered coldly.

The policeman raised an eyebrow, obviously wanting more than a philosophical answer.

"Do you really think it hit her in the heart?" Madeline thought of the irony of Julia's death. "It was already a cold, dead thing, I think. The bullet only made it official," she said.

Her eyes glazed over with the evening's trauma. The sound of the shot reverberating through the cavernous entrance replayed in her brain.

****

Her heart? The bullet had come to a halt in her heart? Madeline was still stunned by the realization.

Julia had wounded William nearly as fatally as a shot to the heart. He had been cold ever since— heartless even. Now Julia had suffered a mortal wound to her own heart in the very house she could have been the queen of.

Madeline kept thinking about this as the officers

took a statement from William. They had wanted to wait until he had been seen by the medics, but he insisted on clearing Madeline from their suspicions.

He mirrored the officer's question. "How did I wind up unconscious? I guess I fell while racing for the gun; slapped my forehead on the floor pretty hard."

The second wail of sirens—faint at first, but growing louder—approached Pine Island. The emergency vehicles' flashing lights illuminated the entire atmosphere.

Madeline rushed back to William's side. "I want to accompany him to the hospital."

"Stay here," William told her. "I'll probably just need a few stitches and then I'll catch a ride back."

"I could follow the ambulance and drive you back out here. Besides, I don't want to be alone." So many questions filled her mind, things she had never considered before.

The entire ground floor was now a crime scene. More vehicles arrived, bringing well-dressed, rubber glove-wearing detectives who carried plastic bags as they walked carefully into the fray.

Officer Wharton approached. "Ms. Waters, you need to accompany us into town. You may want to pack an overnight bag. It's probably best if you plan to stay elsewhere for a few nights."

She nodded, understanding the house was now off limits to them. Madeline glanced around at what had been serene surroundings before the melee broke loose. Yellow tape spilled across the entire floor, giving the impression of the room being toilet papered with skinny yellow ribbon.

"Should I get a few of his things as well?"

The policeman nodded.

She crept up the stairs seeking the basics to get them by. The Captain appeared beside her as soon as she left the open stairwell and entered her room. His calming spirit bestowed a feeling of safety she had not been in possession of for the last hour or so of her life.

"You saved us both," she said, thanking him for his efforts. "If it hadn't been for you, I know we would both be dead."

"Maybe it will be good karma for my spirit," he whispered as she felt his comforting aura surround her.

"Can you go with us, or will you stay here?"

"I can do either, but I don't think you need me to go with you and William. I'll hang around here and see what I can learn. But do not fear. If anything or anyone tries to harm you, I'll know. I will be there in a flash."

The electrical static of his aura slipped slightly inside of her outer shell of flesh. His comfort, love, and confidence that all would be well, accompanied it. She was able to let go of the fear that had her gripped in its fist.

He exited and reappeared on the other side of the room. "I'll watch over the house as I've done for all of the years since my demise. And I'll watch after you, as well, until yours." Then he disappeared.

Great drops of tears rolled down her cheeks. She had never experienced such love or devotion. How had she earned or deserved it?

After tossing a few things into her bag, she seized a few of William's, their cell phone chargers, laptop computers, and some toiletries. Then she rejoined the disturbance in the center of the house.

"Ready?" Officer Gaines asked.

She nodded.

"Who plans to drive you into town?"

"I can drive myself," she answered, suddenly feeling calm from the reassurances of the Captain.

Medics strapped William to a gurney, rolled him out of the house, and into the back of a waiting ambulance. Alex was also strapped down and accompanied by an officer. Madeline was sure that as soon as he was treated and well enough to leave the hospital, he would be taken to face a laundry list of charges.

Officer Gaines asked, "Do you have a residence in town?"

"Yes," she replied, and jotted the address down for him. "That's my apartment—not quite as glamorous as all this, but safe and secure."

Officer Wharton stared at her strangely, his eyebrows furrowing in a surprised expression. "Are you sure you are fit to drive? This has been a rough night, to say the least. And earlier, in the midst of the ruckus—"

She held up a hand. "I understand your concerns and agree that I have probably not given you any reason to believe I am a rational person. But it's over now and I have to sensibly consider William's needs. I don't think he'll be up to hiking around Georgetown until his head heals."

"That sounds very rational indeed. But—"

"I know. My hysteria emanated from thinking William might be…might not…you know what I mean." She ran a hand across her face, trying to wipe away the visual memory of his still body lying face-down on the floor. "He seems okay, so I can relax a bit. I'm sorry if my momentary panic got the better of my usual good senses."

"That's understandable, ma'am, given the circumstances." He surveyed her for a minute, holding her in his gaze as if he could see the secrets she withheld. Appearing convinced, he finally gave in. "All right. Get the keys and follow the ambulance with your flashers on."

They left Pine Island in a procession of vehicles— police car, ambulance, Madeline, another police car, another ambulance carrying Alex and an officer inside, and one of the many detectives in a black sedan bringing up the rear.

Madeline glanced back at the glow of the house. There were as many flashing lights still perched in its yard as were careening toward town. It was surreal to be involved in such a calamity, and yet she felt a sense of peace she couldn't explain. It had to be the Captain's influence, she reasoned.

Chapter 36

Madeline drove straight to the hospital. Marking time in the emergency waiting room, she saw Alex's wife enter. Helena Hamilton barely resembled the woman she had met earlier that afternoon. Her face, contorted and swollen from crying, now seemed more shocked than grieving.

Madeline felt immense sorrow for her. She had apparently lost everything she held true about her life, and her marriage, in the course of a few terrible minutes.

The accompanying officers presumably took her to the room where her husband was being prepped for surgery. It was doubtful anything of substance would be gleaned from the injured man.

Scant minutes passed before the doors to the emergency room swung open once again, and Helena returned to the area where Madeline waited.

Though she felt nothing but anger and hostility toward Alex, her empathy for his wife softened her fury. "How is he?"

"Apparently, several bones in Alex's face will have to be repaired. He wasn't able to talk...was having difficulty breathing." She gasped. "What the hell just happened to my life?"

Madeline could only shake her head. How do you answer such a question? "When William's better, maybe he can help you make sense of all of this," she offered.

"There is no sense to be had. This is madness. Maybe that isn't my husband; maybe it is someone who merely resembles him. Yes, that's it. The man back there can't be my husband."

Helena paused, her eyes moving back and forth in a rapid cycle. "My husband is William's best friend in the world…always has been. And he has never cheated on me. I know the sex hasn't been what it once was, but he wouldn't stray. No, that's it. It isn't him."

She let out a deep breath, and Madeline said nothing. She supposed it was common to go into a state of denial. Perhaps that was just where Helena needed to be in this moment.

A "crash cart" was called to the back and both women stared at each other. Which room was it for? Whose life lay in the balance? Fear seized Madeline. *What if William doesn't make it?* What if his head injury was worse than the medical team had assessed? People died from less. Brains swelled and died from the pressure.

Madeline's heart squeezed and fought against the fist of panic tightly grasping it. The commotion of people in paper-covered shoes and caps, and long coats running in and out of the swinging doors held the two women's attention as surely as a dramatic-action play at the theater. The only difference being lives depended on whether or not they were granted a second act.

It seemed an eternity before the doors opened again. Wheels rolled against the smooth tile flooring and William appeared with a bandage on his head and a hooked-up intravenous fluids bag hanging from the wheel chair's attachment.

Both women ran to him with a barrage of questions. He took one of their hands in each of his and tried to comfort them with gentle caresses.

His enormous courage didn't last. The strain of the past day had taken its toll on him as well. Giant tears passed from beneath the strong lids that had held back emotion since the day his bride-to-be had walked out on him.

"We've been living a lie," he told the woman who wanted assurance that the man who was responsible for all of this was not her husband, and his friend. "He didn't love either of us."

He wept, and she laid her head next to his, her body seized by shaking sobs.

"Do you want me to leave you two alone for a minute?" Madeline asked.

"No, I want you to stay." He still gripped one of her hands. "They want to keep me overnight to make sure my brain isn't swelling. Hopefully I should be released tomorrow."

She nodded. Helena lifted her head and asked the question—the one whose answer would either stop the pain or intensify it. "Was it my husband? Was it really Alex?"

He nodded, solidifying the crushing blow.

The doors behind them swung open again. The doctor who had been working with Alex asked who was there for him. They all turned toward him.

"I'm sorry," he offered. "His air passages swelled shut. While we worked on a tracheal tube, his lungs collapsed. Apparently they had been punctured by broken ribs." He paused. "These are the kinds of injuries usually sustained when dropping from heights. He must have hit the floor harder than anyone imagined. I'm truly sorry."

Madeline's mind filled with the image of the Captain slamming his energy field into the man's body. It had indeed appeared as damaging as the type of violent fall the doctor characterized. But he couldn't have done less, given the dire consequences they had been in.

"It's better this way," his wife said. "I'm glad I won't have to hear the truth come directly from him." She pulled herself up and headed for the exit.

Madeline ran after her. "Come stay with me," she pleaded. "Don't go back home tonight."

"No. I have to face this alone. I'll have to go back eventually." She patted Madeline's hand. "But thank you for the offer."

An officer escorted her to the door.

The corpse of the man who had once been a loving husband and good friend rolled past in a covered body bag. The hospital could do nothing else for him.

Madeline returned to her apartment after William was settled into a hospital room. She scrolled through television shows and shopping networks, trying to find some way of releasing the tension valve threatening to overwhelm her. Infomercials, an eighties drama with big-haired, overly-made-up women, black and white movies, seventies sitcoms, news scrolls—she saw it then.

Television trucks camped out at Pine Island. Their lives had been reduced to television drama. She snapped the set off, waited a few minutes, then switched it back on. It was still there under the heading:

Breaking News.

She couldn't stop watching, yet it horrified her. She finally managed to shut it off for the night. Her mind picked up where the television couldn't go, and made it worse.

It replayed the moments of sheer terror when she thought she was about to be killed. And then when she feared William had been, as the shot rang out and he'd flown across the room and against the floor. The sight of the explosive blood spray and the limp arm of the woman he had so loved. There seemed to be no escape from the living and reliving of the events.

Madeline finally gave up and went out onto the balcony. It was a beautiful night across Georgetown, belying the horror that had happened only a short distance away. The harbor, magnificent with its silver steaks across the water, followed the boardwalk. Silently promising a calming environment, it begged to be walked. Grabbing a jacket and some shoes, she headed out.

Something glowed over her head, a flash of white. Glancing upward, she spied an eagle balanced on the night breeze. Its eyes focused keenly on her. She watched as its wings slanted and spread, offering its peace to her as it neared.

Whatever fear lay between bird and man lifted for a moment as the beautiful bald eagle landed on the boardwalk railing. It looked at her, tilted its head, and gazed outward indicating it had something to say. Then, soft as a baby's breath, she heard a female voice say, "Never fear, I am always with you."

She didn't recognize it, but the words were the same ones the Captain often spoke. The bird flew off, brushing her cheek with the soft feathery tip of a wing as its giant span opened up. Once the beautiful eagle was out of sight, Madeline returned to her room, turned off the light, and slept peacefully.

Chapter 37

The whole town buzzed with crazy excitement the next day. News crews filled every parking lot and café. People were being interviewed about their firsthand knowledge of the strange occurrence. It had everything to make a good story—wealthy characters, love and friendship gone awry, betrayal, greed, death, destruction—and it all happened in a beautiful southern coastal town many people hadn't even heard of.

Sandwiched between Charleston and Myrtle Beach, Georgetown was the opposite of either, while possessing the best of both. William worried at what this might do the community. Those who felt robbed by the elite of the area might see Alex as a type of pirate figure akin to the revered Blackbeard. His death could elevate him in a way which would never have occurred had he lived to face the nasty charges.

William was released from the hospital and brought by police car to Madeline's apartment, as promised. Madeline stayed out of sight until he was locked in and curtains pulled, safe from the cameras and prying eyes. The last thing he wanted was to subject her as being another of the characters in the love quadrangle drama. There were enough players already.

He decided to bring the conversation back to the thing they had been working on before all hell broke loose. What happened to Magdalene, and how could they prove it? "Well, you see how quickly people can turn on you when they think there is a treasure somewhere they can rob from you. Perhaps it was the Captain's best friend." William couldn't seem get past Alex and Julia's betrayal.

"Or maybe she took too much laudanum?"

"Yeah, I forgot about that. Remind me again. Why was she taking the laudanum?" His memory had gaps—not uncommon for someone with a concussion.

Madeline reminded him about the lost babies and Magdalene's subsequent depression. The cure in that day and time probably brought on the loss of more of her babies. Edward was lucky to have survived.

"What else have I forgotten about?"

"Do you remember giving the Captain permission to occupy your physical body for one full day—and night?" She raised an eyebrow, staring at him with lust in her eyes.

He understood the facial expression. It wasn't meant for him, but for the Captain. The realization made him seethe. "No."

"Well you did," she said. "And I believe you do still remember."

"This is crazy. Besides, we haven't proved what—or who—killed Magdalene."

"Aha!" She pointed her index finger at him. "You do remember. You're just saying you don't because you've changed your mind."

"I don't think I'll ever be convinced of his lack of culpability." William shook his head.

"What if I knew someone who could help us with this?"

His brows furrowed toward each other. He felt his

eyes narrow. "What exactly do you mean? I don't want to reveal this information to anyone, so bringing in a seer or a psychic—"

"Listen, and don't say a word until I finish talking. Agreed?"

He took a deep breath. "I'll try, but no promises."

"I know a woman; a very trustworthy woman who would never want her connection to the art of voodoo to be known. She would stand to lose more than you if this information leaked out. She'll want something from you, too."

"Something from me? What could I have—?"

Madeline interrupted. "I need your word this time. Though I have no contract to make you sign, as you required of me on our first meeting."

William recalled the chasm of mistrust. But he'd felt the hired photographer should be sanctioned by the promising legal ramifications of disclosure. "I'm sorry, but I believed it necessary, given the subject."

"I'll take your word, William Gray, but I must hear you say it. You must promise not to give away this woman's identity."

"Yes, of course. You have my word."

"It's the jeweler, Mrs. Jenkins."

****

William stared at Madeline. "A jeweler? You mean the local jewelry shop owner on Main Street?"

"Yes. She handles quite a bit of estate jewelry. She'd like to purchase a few of the famed Gray pieces. It would mean a lot to her business."

"Okay, whatever. I'm sure I can come up with something. But how can she help us?"

"She's a descendent of the Gullahs. She told me

she had 'the touch.' Maybe she would know a chant, a prayer, or have some other remedies to release Magdalene and the Captain, so they can move on to the next life."

Even as she said the words, part of her hoped Mrs. Jenkins wouldn't have such a thing. Did she really want to lose the Captain? Perhaps William would say no. She could tell he was averse to such things.

"It's worth a shot. Call her," he said with a determined glint in his eye.

****

Madeline walked the few blocks to Jenkins Jewelry Store. She took her time, going over and over the way in which she might present the situation to Mrs. Jenkins. Her worst fear was that the woman would think she was poking fun at her after her admission of accompanying her grandmother, when she was a child, to the market in Charleston.

She reached the corner and stalled. How was she going to explain all of this to Mrs. Jenkins? A thought occurred to her and she gathered her courage, forcing her feet to carry her onward through the glass door with the tinkling bell.

"Welcome to Jenkins Jewelry." The woman glanced up. A smile broke across her slightly wrinkled face as she raced toward Madeline. "Oh it's you," she cried out.

Madeline grabbed the older lady and gave her a big hug. "Hi! I was in town after the...incident."

"Oh yes. I heard it on the news." She frowned. "Nasty bit of business. Thank God you weren't hurt."

Madeline couldn't find the words. She feared her attempted smile appeared more as a sneer.

"You weren't hurt, were you?" Mrs. Jenkins surveyed her face. "Something's going on with you. I can see it in your eyes."

"Yes, there is something bothering me. I…we need your help. But first I must have your word to keep this between us and William Gray."

"William Gray? Is he all right? You know those concussions can be worse…"

Madeline waved her hand back and forth. "It's not the concussion. It's something else."

"This sounds serious." Mrs. Jenkins walked over to the door and flipped the sign over to, *Sorry, we are closed.*

"No, don't close the store. What if you miss a sale?"

"Nobody's coming around here today. They're too busy talking about what happened out at Pine Island. The only reason they'd want in is if they see you in here and recognized you from the news stories. I haven't sold anything in two days." She entwined her fingers and straightened them again.

"I'm so sorry. This is such a mess." Madeline buried her head in her hands, pushing against her temples with the heels of her palms.

Mrs. Jenkins patted her on the arm. "Now don't get maudlin on me. Truth is sales have been slipping for some time. The estate jewelry you photographed for me was my last-ditch effort to make a decent profit. But, without well-known names behind it, most of it barely brought what I purchased it for."

"What if I could get you a few of the Gray's vintage pieces?"

Her hands flew to her mouth. "Really? You got

William Gray to agree to allow me to sell some of his family's jewelry?"

Madeline nodded. "He might even throw in a French coin or two from Blackbeard's ship. Would that be famous enough to get you back on track?"

"Blackbeard's ship? Where on earth would he get such rare treasure?"

"Do I have your word you will accept what I am about to say, and that you'll keep it between us?"

"Of course," she sputtered.

"The first William Gray, the Captain, may have found Blackbeard's ship. His journals, the ones starting the whole fracas out at Pine Island, had coordinates for the find. Accounts of the day have him in possession of items suspected to have been from *Le Concorde*, or *Queen Anne's Revenge* as we've come to know it."

"But how...? Sorry," Mrs. Jenkins said, catching herself before asking a question, as she had promised not to do so.

"So here is where I need you to be really open-minded..." Tension threatened to choke the words out of Madeline.

Mrs. Jenkins nodded. "Okay."

"Do you remember how preoccupied I was after the initial meeting with William Gray?"

She nodded again.

"And when I asked you if you believed in ghosts?"

"Yes, I remember."

"The spirit of Captain William Gray *is* haunting Pine Island. I've not only seen him, I've talked with and touched him." She searched the lady's face for signs of disbelief. Thankfully, she appeared to be keeping whatever suppositions she had in check.

"He thinks the spirit of his wife, Magdalene, is inside me."

Mrs. Jenkins snapped to attention, her gaze becoming intense. "Inside you? How exactly?"

"Well, I can't say, except sometimes I do have memories I shouldn't have. I can smell things that aren't in the house such as lemons and pineapple, both items he used to bring back to Magdalene after a sea voyage. We have a weird connection and..." She debated whether or not to tell the rest.

"And what?" Mrs. Jenkins' face was solemn. She wasn't taking this as a joke.

"And I feel attracted to him, emotionally and sexually."

"You feel attracted to a ghost?"

"He jumps into William's body sometimes. He's saved me from nearly drowning. He was even there the night of the shooting. If it hadn't been for him..."

Mrs. Jenkins eyebrows crinkled inward toward her nose. Her eyes narrowed, as did her lips. "Boo hags," she whispered.

Madeline had never heard the term before. "What did you say?"

"Boo hags. They are spirits who occupy human bodies, walk around in their skin. They can leave you tired, crazy, even vegetative. This has to end. You cannot allow them to keep using your flesh."

"But..."

"No buts, dear—none." Mrs. Jenkins' eyes had grown into huge, dark saucers with small circles of white around them. Her lips were drawn into a taut line across her face. She reached out across the table and snatched Madeline's hands. "Do you hear me?"

Madeline inhaled sharply. "Yes, but I need to finish telling you everything."

"There's more?"

"The Captain wants use of William's body for twenty-four hours. He wants to spend a whole day and night with me."

Mrs. Jenkins hit the table with the flat of her palm so hard it reverberated throughout the store. "A full twenty-four hours?"

"Yes, that's what he's asked for."

"What has he dangled in front of you? What does he give in exchange?"

"The truth that would clear his name in connection with Magdalene's death, and the location of the ship rumored to be Blackbeard's."

"That squatter!" Mrs. Jenkins jumped up and paced the floor. "You can't do this. You aren't even considering it, surely." She grabbed Madeline by the shoulders. "Tell me you aren't considering it!"

Madeline's spine began to tingle as fear crept up it, instantly chilling her body. She shivered. "I was…yes…actually…"

"No, no, no. You mustn't do this thing. Stop it Madeline. Don't let the boo hags near you again."

"They won't harm us. He's promised. I can feel his great love for me. I—"

Mrs. Jenkins gave her a gentle shake. "You've seen him possess the body of William Gray?"

"Yes, and get thrown out. William hates it when he does that."

"As he should," she enunciated with passion. "If you allow them twenty-four hours with your bodies, you will never get them back. You'll be lost Madeline.

You and William will take the place of the Captain and Magdalene in the afterlife, and they will walk the earth again in your flesh."

The words fell as a guillotine upon Madeline, slicing away the story she had been telling herself, rendering the fantasy dead. She couldn't believe it. "No, no. He loves me," she protested.

"He loves Magdalene."

"He saved me from drowning. He pushed William away from me. He—"

"Your dead body won't do him any good. And an unwilling one won't gain him time enough for the conversion to take place. He was winning your trust, that's all. You listen to me. Do not engage with any more encouragement for this spirit."

"But what else can I do?"

"You're going to send him back where he belongs. And you're going to send his wife back with him, too."

"But she isn't here. She doesn't possess me."

"You just said you smelled aromas sensitive to her. You said you had feelings for this apparition. These aren't your memories Madeline, and they are not your feelings. They belong to Magdalene and the Captain. And if you don't send them back, I'm afraid it's going to be too late."

Madeline considered what Mrs. Jenkins was saying. "If what you are saying is true, then how do we send them back? Can you help us do that?"

"I don't know." She released Madeline and collapsed in the chair with such exhausted flurry it appeared all of the air in her lungs had just been sucked out of her. Her hands fell into her lap, where they lay as her head shook back and forth. "It's been such a long time." She looked away and Madeline watched her eyes refocus on something she couldn't see, likely some memory from her past.

Madeline knelt beside her, taking one of her hands in her own and lifted it upward. "You said you had 'the touch.' Your grandmother taught you about potions and chants."

"If she were here I'd go straight to her. But now…"

"Do we need to go down to Charleston?"

"Yes—immediately. Come on, we can take my car." With that thought, Sarah Jenkins found her second wind and grabbed her purse and keys.

****

Madeline didn't hesitate. She jumped into the car with Mrs. Jenkins, and the two of them set out for Charleston. As she drove, Mrs. Jenkins spat out a series of things they would need, each item appearing to rise up from some place so deep within her it seemed to come as a surprise every time she thought of something new.

"Root doctor," she said, hands gripping the steering wheel.

Madeline used her smart phone to type the list into an application meant for taking notes.

"A spell caster and a charm weaver," she added.

"There is such a person as a spell caster?"

"Oh yes. The spell caster is a very important position in the Gullah community."

Madeline couldn't hide her surprise. "Really? Still?"

Mrs. Jenkins' back stiffened. "You know, if you're going to come to me for help and accept the practices of my people, then you can't thumb your nose at our

280

traditions."

"Oh…I didn't mean…" She stopped talking, thinking about what she'd said. Her implication had indicated shock at such things existing in the modern world. Yet she *had* gone to Mrs. Jenkins for her aid, expecting help from nontraditional methods. Of course it sounded offensive. "I'm sorry. This has me a bit strung out."

"Me, too. Didn't mean to snap."

Her friend gave her a smile, but Madeline knew it was forced. It then occurred to her the process could prove hazardous. "Can this be dangerous to you?"

"You saw him blow through a man hard enough to kill the intruder. You say he used his energy to save you from drowning. What do you think?"

A cold trickle of fear coursed through Madeline's veins. "Turn around. I won't put you in danger. I trusted him. I didn't see things winding up like this. I shouldn't have come to you."

Mrs. Jenkins exhaled for a long time. "He needed you to trust him, and he made sure you did. Maybe the wave shoving you under was also part of his doing. He might even have placed the information into Alex's ear as to what might be found in his journal. Why else would Alex have known exactly where to look?"

"I don't know. He didn't have a chance to say." The older lady had a valid point. How had Alex known about the journals and what he might find in them?

They continued in silence for a while before Mrs. Jenkins had another idea to add to the list. "Straw brooms—thick, old-fashioned ones with lots of straw—none of this rubber and plastic so popular with today's youth."

"Got it," Madeline replied, "thick, straw brooms."

"And sieves, the more holes the better."

"Sieves. Old-fashioned ones, too?"

"Yes."

"Uncrossing spells and indigo ink."

Madeline typed the two things into her phone app.

They were nearing Charleston. Mrs. Jenkins navigated the turns leading into the area.

They weren't taking the same roads Madeline normally arrived in Charleston by. They were headed out to the swamp, if memory served.

"A piece of white fabric and a crystal—pure and clear," she suddenly said.

Madeline quickly added these items. Staring out of the passenger window, she was reminded of the day she and William had traveled here, arriving by the waterfront.

She had seen the yellow house and felt certain she was the reincarnation of Magdalene, the Captain's long-dead wife. Now she wondered why she had been so eager to believe the stories the Captain whispered in her ear. Was it because he had made her feel alive again in ways no man since her brief marriage had? Was it the possibility of having a connection to something lasting and beautiful?

The road turned into a sandy bar leading into the forest. Thick black pines with cones the size of coconuts lined their path. Vegetation draped from the overhanging limbs, but it wasn't romantic Spanish moss. It favored ivy and creeper, possibly some wild grapevine in the thick mixture winding around and around the trunks from the ground upward.

Roots popped up into the road, forming speed

bumps. The car bounced over them, groaning with each thud as they inched further and further into the dark forest.

Fear seized Madeline. She wanted to ask if Mrs. Jenkins knew where they were going, but of course she did. Nobody would come out to this place without meaning to.

They were pulling to a stop. Madeline glanced around at a cottage perched high, on stilts, above the swamp water. A foot bridge ran from the end of the sandy road, over the water, and out to the sloped porch of the cottage. She grasped the car's door handle, prepared to exit.

"No. Stay put," Mrs. Jenkins commanded.

"I won't let you go in by yourself," she said, glancing around at the cypress knees popping up around the cottage. "You are going to do as I say. You're in my old stomping ground now. Trust me."

"I do, but…"

"Lock the doors behind me and don't unlock them for anyone but me. This may take a little time."

"But who—?" The door opened and shut so quickly Madeline didn't get to finish her question.

She could only watch as the lady she thought of as being older and frail, summoned courage and tenacity. Mrs. Jenkins seemed a spry young girl as she navigated the rickety swinging bridge.

Madeline hit the lock button, though she didn't expect to see anyone else out this far in the swamp. With eyes glued to the cottage door, she waited patiently.

Fear continued to bubble up—its long-reaching tendrils dipping onto her scalp and showering her with prickly sensations. The urge to flee came over her. She closed her eyes and tried to take deep, cleansing breaths. When she opened them again, it was much darker in the forest, a great black cloud having swallowed the sun. Zigzag shapes were all she could make out of creatures winding their way across the path to the swamp's dark waters.

Something sprang up from the darkness, making a splash as it forced its huge, long body into the air, swinging its tail around. Madeline squirmed in her seat as she watched the now-discernible alligator seize whatever creature it had knocked off balance and pull it down into the murky depths.

Hurry Mrs. Jenkins, she whispered to herself. *Please hurry.*

Time dragged on. Inside the car, the air grew hot and sticky. The humidity of the southern climate was accentuated even further in damp, swampy marshes. Too many insects popped against the windows to even suggest cracking one to let in a bit of fresh air. Madeline wiped the sweat from her forehead and scratched around for something to fan herself with.

Snatching a brochure of the recent auction from its nest above the visor, she shook her wrist back and forth, stirring a little manufactured breeze. *What is taking so long?*

A flash of light immersed the cottage in brightness for a split second. Barely a glimpse, a small window into the space beyond the door, but it instantly heightened Madeline's fear. What looked to be cages of birds and animals lined the walls, one of which stood open. A rather large person—she couldn't tell whether it was a man or a woman—gripped one of the birds in a giant hand, the other held a bowl beneath its bleeding throat.

Madeline began to shake as the surrounding light muted once again. What if she had to rescue Mrs. Jenkins? How would she do it? What would she use?

Think, she commanded herself. But she couldn't think; couldn't reason. What were they doing in that cottage above the swamp water? How could anyone live out here amongst the snakes, alligators, and relentless insects?

A crack of lightning split the heavens. Its electricity shot toward the cottage, illuminating it once again. The bird in the hand of the stranger flew away. Surely it was a different bird from the one she had seen offering its blood into a bowl moments before.

The feathered creature appeared to take the darkness with it as it disappeared into the sky, the clouds peeling back in its wake. With the black clouds rolling away, the sinister surroundings regained a bit of charm, especially given the cottage's bright indigo door. It swung open and Mrs. Jenkins' slight figure appeared, carrying a brown paper bag and a small cloth sack.

Madeline sighed with relief, hitting the unlock button.

Her cohort opened the door and hit the trunk release, securing her newly obtained items in the back of the car. Crawling behind the wheel, calm and collected, she backed around a clump of roots and steered the vehicle back onto the main road.

"What's the matter with you?" she asked Madeline.

"Me? What's….*me*?" If what she had seen through the window during cracks of lightning was any indication of what was going on inside of the cottage, Mrs. Jenkins should know the answer.

"You're all wet. Did you get out of the car? I told you to stay inside with the doors locked." Her voice had an obviously alarmed edge to it that she then tried to hide.

"It's sweat." She subconsciously swiped at the strands of hair sticking to her forehead and tugged at the blouse clinging to her damp chest. "You were in the cottage for a really long time. What was going on in there?" She quickly caught herself, waving her hand back and forth. "No, no, don't tell me. I don't want to know."

"I left the keys. Why didn't you use the air conditioner to cool the air?"

Madeline told herself she was an idiot. She hadn't thought about that. "I'm not in my right mind," she answered, knowing with certainty she couldn't be. Ghosts, possessions, voodoo, root doctors; this didn't exist in the seen world—the sane world.

"Well you had better get it together. I'm going to need you bright and collected by the time we get all of this back to Pine Island."

She nodded and peered out of the window as the brightly-colored houses of the main downtown area of Charleston popped into view. They slowed to a crawl behind a horse-drawn carriage. The clip-clop of its hooves seemed more of the Captain's era than of theirs.

Mrs. Jenkins popped into and out of several short streets and back alleys—places Madeline wouldn't have thought of as leading anywhere. She pulled to a stop, parking in a non-designated area. "It's fine," she said, before Madeline could question her.

The unique market entrance was framed by a double set of steps with ornate wrought iron railings wrapped in a green patina. The steps appeared to be in a perpetual competition for the porch with its four stately rounded columns. An archway between the two flights of stairs led into a lower level of shops. Mrs. Jenkins caught Madeline's eyes and jerked her head toward it.

"Around the side," she said before disappearing.

Madeline had to nearly run to keep up with her, unusually spry for her age, friend. She caught up and tried to stay in her shadow, not knowing what sorts of things she might ask for.

The shopkeepers immediately recognized Mrs. Jenkins, several calling out to her in greeting. Madeline knew she sometimes obtained jewelry from a craftsman in Charleston to sell in her store.

The city had plenty of artisans devoted to one-of-a-kind baubles, as well as every other type of artistic expression—photography, oil paintings, pottery, soaps and candles, clothing, yarn shops, and of course, the ubiquitous sweetgrass baskets made into all shapes and sizes.

Madeline couldn't resist watching one of the craftsmen at work, nimble fingers taking the darker shards of long, dry grass and weaving it in and out between other lighter colored ones.

Mrs. Jenkins tugged at her. "Come on. You can watch the basket weavers another day."

Near the back of the marketplace, in a small stall lacking tourist encouragement from the elderly woman manning the station, Mrs. Jenkins halted. She said something in a language Madeline didn't understand.

The woman jerked her head at Madeline, cutting

her eyes in her direction. Though she turned her chin toward Mrs. Jenkins, she continued to stare at Madeline. After some more unidentifiable words were exchanged, the woman appeared to be satisfied with whatever Mrs. Jenkins had told her. "In the back," she muttered.

Madeline fell into step behind the two women.

"Not you." The old woman pointed at Madeline with one gnarled finger. Its long nail curved downward, as hooked as a talon.

"Madeline, can you watch the front for us?" Mrs. Jenkins' requested. It dimmed the exclusion of the older woman's command.

"Certainly," she replied, knowing it made no difference. Whatever was stored in the back was not for an outsider's eyes.

****

"William? William, come quickly." Madeline called out to him as she hurriedly threw open the door to her apartment. "William?"

No answer, though both she and Mrs. Jenkins waited silently for his reply.

"Isn't he here?" Mrs. Jenkins asked.

"I suppose not." She looked around, as she replied.

"There—on the table!" Mrs. Jenkins pointed to a sheet of paper folded in half, resting tipi-fashion against the table's smooth oak top. Madeline's name was scribbled across the front.

Madeline yanked it up, scanning it quickly. "Oh no. He's gone out to Pine Island."

"I thought you said he didn't have a car here."

"He didn't. The note says he caught a ride with the cleaning crew going out to scrub up the mess."

"We'd better get out there fast. The Captain probably knows we are on to him by now."

Madeline gave the door a tug behind them. They raced back to her car. The concerned expression on Mrs. Jenkins' face alarmed her.

"Mrs. Jenkins?" she asked.

"Hmm...?" She was still clearly far away in thought.

"How does a spirit become malicious in the afterlife, if it was good and kind in its own time?"

"You're confusing two different concepts. The Captain may have been a wonderful person. He may not mean harm to anyone. Yet, whatever he has been seeking these many years now seems attainable. His quest is likely not to intentionally *cause* harm, but to *alleviate* his pain. And possibly hers as well."

"And William and I just happen to be in the way?"

"You and William *are* the way."

Chapter 38

The cleaning crew sent out to Pine Island had scrubbed away the outwardly visible signs of a crime having occurred, but a wall of memories hit William as soon as he entered the ground floor. He threw open all four of the double sets of doors leading outside in an attempt to rid the house of the odor of disinfectant.

He wanted to smell the salt marshes and the sea mist and the verdant green of the garden's bounty, not the chemicals used to remove the dried blood of his long-ago fiancée, along with his lifetime friend's.

He couldn't think of Alex as anything else. As far as William had been concerned, he had been his friend for every second of his life since memory served…until that fateful night just days ago.

And Julia? What had Julia been? At least she'd had the decency not to continue to pose as a person who cared about him.

How had he missed the signs of their involvement?

William walked out onto the garden porch, drinking in the lushness of its aromas, trying to put the bad memories to bed. They were both gone—Alex and Julia—and he had to move forward as best he could.

He walked back into the house, knowing one more room needed cleaning. There was no point in keeping the master suite locked in the past, a false past.

He had wasted so many years feeling responsible

for Julia's abandonment. Now he knew the awful truth. She had never loved him. At least, not as he had loved her.

His thoughts returned to Alex. Apparently his friend had begun to resent him when Alex's father died. How had his family's downward spiral been William's fault? It wasn't, of course. But he had paid the price for it anyway.

Now there was one more thing to do. He had to clear out the one room that held years of pain and false hopes, the one serving as the repository of something unpleasant—hurt feelings, broken hearts, and shattered dreams. There was no point in keeping the shrine any longer.

Inhaling a sharp breath, William sensed the whole world operating through a haze—a heat glare off asphalt in the middle of the summer.

He wondered about the entire parade of women he had been intimate with. Would even one of them have had the fortitude to withstand the drama and horror of what Madeline had managed to bear? He doubted it.

Having picked those female companions based solely on looks and sex appeal, he'd thrown back anyone with less than model perfection. He had been little more than a trophy fisherman. It was shameful, and he felt the sting of his shallow behavior.

He had assumed people envied his bevy of beautiful young dates. Now in his forties, and with the perspective of the last few weeks, they all seemed pathetic. He *felt* pathetic.

Grabbing a bucket filled with cleaning supplies, he jogged up to the master suite. It was cathartic to have a physical project to work on.

Most of the house had double interior walls, the only way to run plumbing and electricity without wiring and pipes being visible. The long line of owners had not added closets to the bedrooms. The original feel of the house was in keeping with the time period in which it was built. Instead they had turned one small room on each floor into a large storage room for all types of items needed on that floor, including rows of rods for hanging seasonal clothing and ball gowns.

The Grays had maintained the giant wardrobes or armoires handcrafted and purchased for Gray Estate by the original owner—the Captain himself. The furnishings in the master suite had been passed down generationally.

With the exception of one set of owners who had wished to stay on the bottom floor near the kitchen, every owner of Pine Island had stayed in this room for at least some portion of their lives. Some had traded the upstairs room for one on the lower floor in their golden years, but almost all had started out in this very space. The adjoining bath had taken on various restorations and would soon need another. But the master suite itself—besides dust and dirt—was in good condition.

William threw himself into the stripping of timeworn coverings, coughing as the dust sprang to life, filling his nostrils with fusty hopes and even staler memories. He battled with the windows, stuck as tightly to their jambs as he had been to his past.

"Here, let me help you with that."

"Sure," William agreed, not even flinching at the appearance of the ghostly apparition.

The windows flew up and fresh air filled the musty room, thickening with the sudden spray of energy that went with the Captain being in the room. The milky form of his body solidified into an almost identifiable man. He shifted his shape onto the now bare bed. "Are you going to allow me the one full day and night I have asked you for?"

"It's a possibility," William agreed. "As soon as I can be sure you had nothing to do with Magdalene's death."

"You're wanting proof?" The apparition grew more solid in form as he stared at William.

"Yes. I need something to assure me you mean no harm to either Madeline or myself."

The Captain glided to the armoire. "The proof is here, in all its horror. You'll find it behind a false back. All will be revealed. It is not only proof of my innocence, but of my constant search for her spirit. When you find it you will know why I have been unable to leave this world and join her in the next."

William's heart pounded as he watched the storm occurring in the room. The Captain had transformed himself into a dervish and blown everything—dust, tattered clothes, shoes, books, papers, unopened gifts, sheets—out into the floor. Finally the backing of the armoire began to pull away from the sturdy wardrobe, and the spirit of the Captain vanished.

For a moment William was powerless to move. Tentatively, he stepped forward and grasped the back, pulling it toward him from one loose edge. It protested from the many years of remaining in one spot. Finally it loosened.

Behind the board was another thin slice of wood tied to something with marine rope. He pulled it out and the roping disintegrated letting the two sides of boarding open to reveal another journal—one he had never seen before.

He carefully carried it to the study, donning the gloves he had used to examine the other journals and began to read. William didn't question how he suddenly seemed able to decipher the ancient handwriting with ease. If he considered it at all, it was in supposing he had adapted to its strange spellings and looped lettering.

Every word made sense to him suddenly. He devoured the pages describing the Captain's life in the eighteen hundreds. The Captain had been a skillful and learned man for the age, always longing for more knowledge. In this journal he had kept drawings of things newly invented. Among them was the makings of the diving belt designed by William James—the man he had mentioned meeting in the other journal.

Also chronicled were the dates of the deaths of the children he and Magdalene had lost, and his despair over them.

There were notations of his fears concerning his seafaring lifestyle. He couldn't make a living unless he went to sea, but if he went to sea, he feared losing his wife—a terrible dilemma for this proud man. That was when the Captain began to search for local ways to do both.

He decided to make his own diving belt in order to retrieve enough of Blackbeard's treasure to support them. After many failed attempts—whose plans were also there—he managed to make an apparatus that appeared to work. When the tide was out for the winter, scraping back as much sand and revealing as much as the sea would allow, he made the cold plunge and began to plunder *Queen Anne's Revenge*.

The Captain couldn't sell the antique gold, with the French fleur-de-lis, in the surrounding area. Too many people would have caught on, and his discovery might have fallen into the hands of some other would-be thief. No, he sailed to the tip of Florida, and at times even to the Cuban island, in order to trade for things he could bring back to sell.

He was pleased not to have to leave Magdalene for long periods of time. But he did leave her for a few days intermittently. After one such voyage, he returned to find her body free of all life.

His handwriting changed after that entry. It wasn't as carefully constructed, and it was a bit harder to make out the words. William tried to decipher key words and scribbled them onto a tablet of yellow paper. Then he filled in the less obvious words between, coming up with the most obvious conclusions.

Magdalene had sent their son to her parents' house, along with the nurse the Captain had left to care for them. She had just lost another baby, and her despair was too great. She penned a note—in her own soft writing, he recalled—apologizing to him for her inability to be a fit wife and mother. Edward was past the age of needing a breast to feed him. He would be fine with his father and the nurse. The spirits of her dead babies called to her.

William's heart ached for the couple. She had loved her husband, still loved him, and that love was meant to release him from the bondage of having an insufficient wife. She had written:

You will be better off without me. You deserve better. I be little more than the anchor thou doust set to the ocean floor. And the babies haveth naught to care for them. I must go to them.

She drank the laudanum, all of it. The empty bottle was lying beside her stiff body.

"Oh my God," William exclaimed, realizing what it meant. "So she committed suicide?" He glanced around the room. "Is that it Captain? Is that what happened?"

A voice inside of him whispered, "Y*es*."

****

Madeline and Mrs. Jenkins raced up to the Gray Estate's driveway-facing porch. Madeline was too worried to observe courtesy. She yanked open the door, holding it for the older lady, and the two entered with a tote bag of ingredients meant to help usher the spirits of the Captain and Magdalene back to their own realm.

"Are you sure about this?" Madeline asked.

"Don't get soft on me now. I'm going to need your strength."

"Madeline? Is that you?" William's voice wafted down the staircase, followed by the sound of footfalls on steps.

"Are you all right?" she called out. "I was worried when I didn't find you at the apartment."

"More than," he chirped.

Madeline stepped into the center of the room and watched him descend. It wasn't William she was seeing, but rather a flashback of the last time she had been in the old house threatening to smother her. She imagined Alex's face as he leaned over the railing, his sneering at William, the joy in his voice at having caused William pain.

The columns were washed free of the offensive red stains; the floor was no longer puddled with the blood of three people who had once been close friends. Nevertheless, it was all captured in Madeline's mind, as vivid in her memory as when the bodies were still lying prostrate around her.

Hands clamped down on her shoulders. "Madeline? Are *you* all right?"

She gazed up into his sky-blue eyes and saw the concern there for her. "Yes. Sorry. It's just…" Turning back to face the scene of the crime, she only saw the gleaming hall. "Well…my imagination, I suppose."

William put his arms around her, pulling her into his chest. Both hands caressed her back as he buried his face in her hair.

"Madeline, come back over here, please," Mrs. Jenkins said.

"No," William said, not bothering to even glance up. "I don't want to let you go."

Her voice took on an edge of urgency. "Now," the older lady ordered.

"William, I want to introduce you to someone." Madeline slipped her hands against his chest and gave a gentle push.

"Later," he said. "Right now I just want to hold you in my arms. Oh, how I've missed you."

"Captain?" Madeline squealed with delight, forgetting about her friend's warnings. "Is that you?" She knew it was before he answered; could feel her heart leap with the recognition.

"Yes," he whispered; his breath a gentle butterfly stroke against her cheek. "I've been waiting for this moment and no Geechee Priestess is going to interfere."

The hair on Madeline's neck prickled. Frightened shivers ran down her spine, turning her insides to mush.

"Geechee Priestess?" She tried to push against him again, but he had her in a vice-grip. "I haven't introduced her. This is Mrs. Jenkins, the lady from the jewelry store."

"I know who she be," he growled. "And it isn't my jewelry she's come for. Better tell her to leave. She can come back tomorrow."

Madeline sensed a change in the spirit. He was too confident in William's body. The threat of being evicted didn't flutter between them as it usually had. "William gave you permission to use his body? You must have proved your innocence to him."

"Aye. And now, my love, you and I will be as we have longed for. I will take you as my wife once more."

"Madeline," Mrs. Jenkins repeated. "Madeline, now!"

The Captain twisted toward the voice, and Madeline was able to push free. She started to run toward her friend, but his energy captured her, making her feel trapped in a heavy wind.

Mrs. Jenkins' hand was buried in the tote bag. She pulled it out and threw white powder at William's body.

A puff of smoke surrounded them and something smelling of sulfur filled Madeline's nostrils. The energy field broke and Madeline took the opportunity to escape the Captain's hold.

"Stay behind me," Mrs. Jenkins ordered. She mumbled a few words and threw another handful of powder in front of William's body.

A loud groan escaped his lips, followed by every door to the outside flying open with pronounced bangs. A whirlwind zipped through the center of the hall, and a clap of thunder shook the house.

Mrs. Jenkins kept chanting. The words had a French-Creole sound to them, though Madeline understood nothing being uttered.

William writhed and shuddered and then became still. A grin slid across his face as his eyes fixed on something just beyond her.

Madeline turned to see what he had found to smile about. The sheer outline of a young woman with flowing hair and a gauzy gown filled the doorway.

"Mrs. Jenkins?" She poked her on the arm. "You'd better turn around," she warned.

Before the older woman could pivot, the shadow closed the gap between them with unnatural speed. The ghostly body pressed up against Madeline and a cold froth washed over her.

"Now, Mrs. Jenkins!" she squealed.

The spirit of Magdalene laughed, the sound filling Madeline's ears with its tinny trilling.

Mrs. Jenkins kept chanting and tossing the powder.

Madeline's skin began to tingle and tiny currents seemed to run the length of her body. It popped and sizzled, though instead of issuing warmth, it carried into her a dry frigid iciness. Her body was slowly turning to stone.

"No!" she said. "Get out of me!"

Mrs. Jenkins, without breaking her concentration on William, tossed a bit of the sulfuric powder toward her. Madeline's body shook, and the spirit trying to merge with her lost its hold. She didn't waste a minute leaning in to Mrs. Jenkins' side.

"It's Magdalene. She's here."

"Come, my darling," the Captain said.

The spirit of his long-dead wife wafted around him

in a vapor.

"What a pity," Madeline said, as the Captain tried to capture the ghost in his rock-hard human hands. "Now she is here, and you, in your human form, cannot touch her."

"She will take your form," he growled, "and we will exist in these bodies until they collapse from our abuse."

"I will never give her permission to use my body—*never*!"

He walked toward them, the shadow of his wife clinging to him. "But you already have, my darling. And her memories have already started their gentle transmission. Do ye not remember the day in the cemetery, kneeling by the marker, when the wisp of her entered your hand?"

Madeline did recall the moment, on the day she and William had taken the rubbing. The cold finger had risen from the stone and passed through her. She had assumed it dissipated. Apparently it had only drifted, untethered, throughout her body.

"Reach into my pocket Madeline," Mrs. Jenkins whispered, bringing her out of her confusion. "Take the linen-wrapped crystals and place them near your heart."

Madeline did as she requested, pulling out a small bundle with three stones inside. She stuffed it into her bra.

"Now hold up this cross," she commanded, handing one to Madeline. "Touch it to William's forehead when he gets close enough to allow it."

Fear gripped her, but Madeline overruled it, palming the cross, feeling its smooth shape against her fingers.

"Come to me," the Captain cooed, returning to his seductive sweetness now that he needed her to complete his plan. "You know I love you. You already know the things I can make you feel." His countenance softened.

Madeline felt her resolve slipping as she recalled the moments they had shared, the deep love she had felt rising in her heart for the apparition. He held out his hand and she lost her fear of him, inching toward him.

"That's right. That's right, my darling. Come to me." He licked his lips as she neared.

Madeline was torn between two realities. She had longed to be loved, to feel love and desire. He had given those emotions to her. She wanted to experience the fullness of such a longing begging to be quenched.

He laughed and nodded. "Yes, yes, here we are." The vapor surrounding him began to glow, then slowly it peeled away and wafted toward her. "Say the word, and we'll be together. Say 'yes.'"

Madeline understood with sudden clarity. It wasn't *her* he was in love with. He had seen her desperate need for affection and had used it against her. Filling her with the feelings of adoration and protection, desire and its fulfillment, he had given her just enough to tease her into acquiescing to this exchange of bodies.

Mrs. Jenkins had been right all along. The Captain didn't love her, he loved Magdalene. And *she* had convinced William to allow the Captain to attain his life on earth once more.

Summoning every ounce of courage she could muster, she smiled and walked forward.

Chapter 39

The Captain laughed as the spirit of his wife bumped up against Madeline's form. "Oh, yes," he cooed, licking his lips with obvious anticipation.

Madeline reached out to him and he leaned in. Without hesitation, she lifted her hand to his forehead, touching the cross to his flesh. He let out a howl and jumped backward. Mrs. Jenkins walked forward, issuing new commands in her strange tongue.

Icy shards attacked Madeline's body, but she maintained the contact. "Take her," she yelled out to the Captain. "Take your wife and go back to the other world together. Gather her up and leave. Get out of William's body."

Mrs. Jenkins reached into the bag again and pulled out a bird. It was a dove, a gray mourning dove. Its throat was stained red indicating a previous injury to its neck.

Madeline thought back to their visit to the swamp and the scene outside of the cottage. *No, it can't be the same bird.*

With a spray of sing-song words, Mrs. Jenkins took another item from the bag. Its needle-like blade stabbed into the poor creature's wound, dousing William's body with its blood. "Into the bird," she commanded. "Leave this body and fly back to your realm. Here is your vehicle. Into the bird."

William's body began to shake. The whole house trembled. Madeline feared it might crumble beneath the vibrations.

Darkness fell, just as it had in the swamp. Wind blew against their bodies, a hurricane inside of the four walls. Lightning split the sky, illuminating the windows with a bluish stripe of intense brightness. Without blinking, Mrs. Jenkins continued to issue commands, vacillating between the strange Gullah and that of common English.

Magdalene appeared to tire of forcing her energy onto Madeline. Her spirit materialized, but wasn't strong enough to lift Madeline's hand from William's forehead. The cross glowed against his skull.

She opened her mouth and screamed. The high-pitched, blood-curdling screech filled Madeline's ears. It numbed her from head to toe, yet she refused to drop her arm.

William began to glow, a neon green vapor pouring from his body.

The spirit of Magdalene shrieked even louder, but eventually tired of it. She reached into Madeline's chest, her smoky fingers threading through her body with ease.

Madeline gasped as a chill set into her. She didn't know what to do and hoped Mrs. Jenkins had some magic in her bag for this. The entire lower floor glimmered with the emanating green glow from William's body. It lifted outward, pushing his chest open and forward.

Madeline closed her eyes. Not seeing the apparition of Magdalene made it easier for her to remain steadfastly glued to William's forehead. The stab to her chest grew more painful and the trickle of fog comprising Magdalene's fingers fumbled around her ribs, chilling them.

Madeline's heart began to race and her breathing increased. The cold turned to fire, the pain was intense.

Magdalene's hand fell upon her heart and squeezed. Madeline seized beneath the firm, icy grip. Her heart stopped beating and she grabbed her chest, unable to breathe. The room began to spin.

And then another scream filled the air. Madeline supposed it was her own as she dropped to her knees. The cross fell from her hand and skidded with a tinkle across the floor. Feathers blew across her line of vision. *Did someone just slice open a pillow?* She landed hard and ceased moving.

****

When Madeline opened her eyes, the worried faces of William and Mrs. Jenkins hovered above her. "What happened?" she asked, pushing up onto her elbows.

"You wouldn't believe it if we told you," William said.

"Are you kidding? I think I would believe anything after the last few days."

Mrs. Jenkins rested an arm behind her, bolstering her attempt to sit up. "You've had a bit of a shock. It could have been worse if you hadn't been wearing the protective crystals near your heart."

She remembered then. "The ghost of Magdalene…" Madeline recalled the frosty hand reaching beyond her breastbone, clutching her heart in a vice grip.

"When she came into contact with the crystals, her form dissipated. She nearly blew up. At that point the

304

Captain flew to her, releasing William, to join her in the afterlife."

"There was a bird…" Madeline's memory kicked up the recollection of the dove, its throat rusty from the ordeal.

"That bird has taken him to join his beloved."

"Into the afterlife? The bird carried him into the next world?" Madeline was confused about the way all of this voodoo worked.

"The dove was already dead, as well. It just didn't know it. The Captain needed his wings to go after Magdalene. There was no reason to stay here in William's body."

"He didn't love me after all," Madeline lamented.

"He would have, if he had met you in this life." William spoke softly, but his words carried a punch.

"How was he able to convince you he had nothing to do with Magdalene's death?"

William recounted the scene in the master suite, the emptying of the armoire, the missing journal.

"She ended her own life." Mrs. Jenkins rubbed her chin.

"So why didn't he simply show the letter to everyone back then? Why didn't he clear his own name?"

Mrs. Jenkins glanced between the two of them. "Because suicide was an unforgiveable sin back then. You couldn't be buried in a holy cemetery or be given last rites, nor expect the promise of heaven. He couldn't let anyone know she had died by her own hand, or she would have been condemned by all. And he couldn't live with that."

William nodded. "Even the Captain must have

believed in the lack of redemption for those who committed suicide, as he did bury her outside of the cemetery confines."

"She must have believed it, too. That's why she didn't move on to the next world." Mrs. Jenkins shook her head.

Madeline began to feel sorry for the couple's predicament. "And when he died, he expected to find her waiting for him. But she was trapped here, clueless about her ability to release the pain binding her to that time, that age."

William glanced around the room. "Do you think they're gone now? Or will they return?"

"Only time will tell. But they aren't here now, so I'd advise the pair of you to get some of that indigo blue paint I brought with me. Paint it on to all of the doors opening to the outside." Mrs. Jenkins retrieved the pot of paint and set it prominently on the table by the forest entrance. "And I'd put a bit of it on the cupola too," she added. "It will send the message to any other haunts wanting to find a place to perch that you know how to rid yourself of their kind."

"I'll get the paint brushes right away," William agreed.

"In that case, my work is done. I'll just leave you two to your chores."

"Wait," William called out. "I have something for you." His footsteps echoed loudly as he mounted the stairs.

Madeline stretched, pulling the linen-wrapped bundle of crystals from their nesting place. "What's in here?"

"Don't open it. They've been blessed with a

protection charm. You never know when you'll need them again."

"So, this is what stopped Magdalene from finishing me off."

"Magdalene needed you. She wouldn't have killed you, but she would have rendered you unconscious before inhabiting your body."

"And after twenty-four hours?"

"You would be turned to stone inside of your own flesh and bones and she would have been living the life you were meant to live."

The thought of how close she and William had come to losing their existences made Madeline shiver. "How can I ever thank you?" she asked.

The sound of William's footsteps, as he descended again, carried to them. "How's this for a thank you?" He held out a couple of boxes to Mrs. Jenkins.

She took the first one and opened it, revealing a necklace of sapphires and diamonds.

"They were a wedding gift to Magdalene, upon her marriage to the Captain." He pointed to another of the boxes. "And that is the ill-fated set of rings meant for Julia and me, along with a few antique silver coins. One piece is thought to have come from *Le Concorde*."

Mrs. Jenkins rolled them around in her hands, caressing them with the same care one might give to a baby. "These are priceless. I can't take them."

"Can and will. They are for you, for your help in saving us from the clutches of those two ill-fated lovers. Perhaps we have set destiny to right."

"I have to admit, the publicity of auctioning these treasures wouldn't do me any harm. But there should be some worthy cause to give the proceeds to."

"You could send Madeline to England to finish her dissertation. She won't admit it, but I think that is the next step in her research."

"No, oh no." Madeline shook her head. "I won't allow it. You won't go selling your family jewels to send me anywhere."

"How about a refuge for birds then? Doves, hawks, eagles?"

"Now that has symmetry to it—selling a necklace given to Magdalene by the Captain and using it to profit the birds they may have turned into."

"It's settled then. Mrs. Jenkins will set up the auction, and you and I will set up the aviary foundation." William concluded his sentence with finality, leaving nothing to argument.

William and Madeline watched from the threshold as Mrs. Jenkins pulled away from the gate. "Guess we'd better get to painting," Madeline said, after the image of her friend and guardian angel's car could no longer be made out.

"Not yet," William said. "There's more in the last journal; more equally tantalizing material."

Madeline paused for a moment. She recalled something Mrs. Jenkins had said. "Is this the journal with the map to the hidden location of the ship thought to be Blackbeard's?"

William nodded. "I think so."

"So why did Alex think it was in the vault? And how did he know you had this information, when even you didn't know about it?"

William started to speak and then stopped, shaking his head and shifting his eyes. "That's a darned good question, Madeline. How did he?"

"Mrs. Jenkins thought the Captain might have planted the idea. Is that possible?"

"Why would he? What would he gain?"

"I don't know. Perhaps he thought removing your friends from you would set you on a desperate course. Maybe he wanted the treasure for himself. Knowing it had shifted over time, conceivably he might think Alex would do the leg work for him. Who can say?"

William squinted off to his right, his head tilted as if receiving a satellite signal. "There's something else here. There has to be."

With that they both headed to the upstairs room, gathering up the journal and two sets of gloves on the way down. It was hard to understand every word but they continued to plough through the pages as best they could, taking breaks when necessary to clear their heads and correct blurred vision.

It appeared that respect for the Captain—a valued asset in his era—waned after the death of Magdalene. Some superstitious people considered the loss of so many babies, and then his wife, to be bad omens. Some called it the work of the devil.

There was talk about the wild, loose ways the two of them had carried on. Magdalene had been seen on the shore without proper attire. She had worn her nightgown to the beach—scandalous for the time.

"But it's a private beach, even now. What on earth would it have been then?" William reasoned. "Who would have even seen them all the way out here?"

Madeline had more perspective and knowledge about the mores of the people of that era. "Probably the help. Maybe even the doctor. People would have spoken only behind their backs, initially. It seems ridiculous now, but not for the eighteen hundreds."

They continued to read. When the Captain enrolled Edward in a European school, the neighbors looked upon that as scandalous, as well. Why wasn't their method of schooling good enough? What was he hiding? He couldn't seem to win for losing.

The people of the Charleston area had all sided with Magdalene's family in their efforts to bring Edward back to Charleston—to live and be raised by them. They began to blame the Captain for Magdalene's death.

The people of Georgetown weren't much better. They felt shunned by his lack of fitting into their way of life. Why didn't he get a few slaves and farm the fields in the same manner as everyone else? He had perfect land for growing indigo, rice, and cotton. Why did he insist on being different? He wasn't behaving as they did and didn't fit in, which ended most associations with him.

But no one seemed to be able to find any concrete reason to throw him off his own property. They couldn't prove he had anything to do with his wife's death, especially since he was at sea when it happened. They couldn't connect him to dark arts and voodoo, though the area was thick with it. Anything one could want to charm up a spell could be found at the Charleston market or in a hut of a voodoo priestess deep in the cypress swamp. They couldn't even prove he was a pirate—which could have resulted in a stretched neck. But they were always trying to do one or the other, and the stress on the man must have been terrible.

Madeline's heart ached for him, in spite of his plot

to assume her and William's identities. He had suffered through immense pain and agony. If only things had been different, what could he have accomplished?

After another break, she and William continued to read.

Tensions were building. President Lincoln had declared the South's slavery practices couldn't expand into the western territory. The Captain's neighbors felt threatened by that. He feared both their bravado and threats of secession from the union. He tried to talk to sense into them whenever possible, but it was useless.

They already thought him to be guilty of numerous sins, now they added traitor to the list. If he was truly of the south, if he believed in State's Rights, sovereign destiny of their land, and the pursuit of their happiness as they saw fit, then he would be solidly behind the Confederacy.

He worried, especially for the coastline. By the time the first shot was fired at Fort Sumter, it was too late for him to have any influence. The Union's naval brigade poured into Georgetown and quickly took control without much resistance. They occupied the North Island and only allowed a certain amount of travel along the waterway, and only then with the proper paperwork.

The Captain was so scorned by the populace the Union officers felt he must be a Union sympathizer and left him alone. He posed no threat—a man alone.

The only gray he could lay claim to, was in his name, not in a uniform. He was neither blue nor gray. It was worse than being the enemy. The enemy would have been respected—hated, but respected. The lack of belonging to either was not seen as the mark of a gentleman. It was reviled.

Madeline had to stop and pace the floor. "It's hard to read past this. I can't imagine the amount of suffering this man endured."

"I feel it, too," William added. "I feel Magdalene's pain, the Captain's pain, and quite a bit of my own. Perhaps we should just burn the whole place down," he suggested. "It appears nobody has ever been happy here."

"Were your parents happy here?" Madeline asked.

"Well, yes, I think so."

"And your grandparents?" she continued.

He gave her *the look*, the one that said he got her meaning. "Yeah, I get your point. Just because a couple of us have had difficulty finding peace in this environment doesn't mean every generation has."

"Let's put the journal away. I don't think I can take anymore."

"No, let's keep reading. Once we've finished, we can put it away for good."

****

According to the newly revealed journal, news of the destruction of many southern cities had reached Georgetown. Winyah Bay was being used to house Union warships. During the last months of the war, the Union's General Sherman began a campaign of major destruction, burning cities and plantations. The news of what was happening in surrounding cities of Columbia and Atlanta reached Georgetown.

The Captain couldn't take it anymore. Though he did not believe in slavery, he did believe in States' Rights and many of the other articles of secession as outlined by Jefferson Davis' call for division. Most of all he was firmly against the destructive methods that hurt innocent people.

News of rape, pillage, plunder, arson, subscription of young boys—all reached him and buoyed him up to a level of hostility he had never felt before. He heard the Union planned an attack using the ships docked in Georgetown's harbor. He thought of the men who had taken over their city and their doubtful claims to be protecting it from harm. It was unconscionable. Captain William Gray decided to take measures into his own hands.

Pretending to only be fishing, he slipped his diving belt on and proceeded to steal a torpedo from a Confederate ship commandeered by the Union naval forces. He then anchored the explosive device into the opening of the bay, should one of the ships in Georgetown's harbor attempt to make it out into the water for another attack on his neighbors.

As long as everyone behaved as they declared they would, no harm would come to anyone.

But the *USS Harvest Moon* was ordered to Charleston. On the way out of the harbor on March 1, 1865, it struck the concealed mine. The hole blown in the ship caused it to sink in under five minutes. A steward, John Hazard, was killed. The remaining men made it to safety.

The weight of the man's death caused the Captain great pain and suffering. Although the following month would see the surrender of General Lee in Virginia, and with that the virtual end of the war that had dragged on for four years, the south was still, and would be, suffering through the period of reconstruction and beyond.

The Captain felt himself a failure in all categories of his life. All that was left for him was to capture his wife's tormented soul and return it to the spirit world, with his own.

"How do you suppose he intended to capture her soul?" William asked.

"You'll have to ask him," Madeline replied, not really sure what, in the eighteen hundreds, the religious considerations were about that sort of thing.

"So he killed someone, after all?" William rubbed his chin. "At least if we can believe the implications of everything we have just read. I wonder why he didn't admit to planting the mine. It probably would have made his neighbors love and respect him. Since it was during the war, he wouldn't have been held accountable for a death. It was an act of war."

Static electricity crackled in the background. Madeline jumped, not sure if one of the apparitions was about to reappear. She rubbed her arms, trying to ward off the goosebumps threatening to prickle her skin. "War or not, he did kill a man. He'd left his wife alone to die by her own hands—an unforgiveable act back then. Also he had ladled laudanum into his wife's mouth, which may have led to the deaths of many of the fetuses. He knows this now and may feel unfit for an afterlife."

William reached around her and closed the journal. "So where does this lead, now the mystery has been solved?"

The electricity reappeared, only this time it generated within Madeline's flesh, just beneath the skin. She practically vibrated from the nearness of William. For the first time since arriving at Pine Island, she was openly thinking of his body as something other than a possible receptacle for her to be able to touch a man long dead.

Madeline told herself there was no use imagining a relationship between them. He had made his revulsion to her clear. The only time he touched her was in response to the Captain's possession of his body. Even when he had been released from the hospital and stayed the night at her house, he didn't try to make physical contact with her.

She thought back to the parade of women he had been with; all gorgeous, long-legged, beauties without a wrinkle or an ounce of fat. Though she had lost a few pounds due to the trauma of the recent events, she would always be just a little bit chubby. And she would always have hair that didn't cooperate with humid weather; and it was always humid seaside in the south.

"I guess it leads to me packing up and heading back to the mainland."

Chapter 40

William gave Madeline permission to use the newly revealed journal to complete her thesis, and she agreed to return it when she finished.

Watching her pack the sweaters they had fought over on the night she last attempted to leave, he had a strong urge to yank them from her arms and return them to the chest of drawers again. Instead, he carried down the heaviest of the bags for her while she proceeded to her car with the carefully folded gowns she had brought for the Azalea Ball over her arms. She carried them as though they were the precious treasure from *Queen Anne's Revenge*.

He winced at the memory of how horrible he had been then, treating her as a means to an end rather than with the respect of one human being to another. He cringed too at the way he had allowed his guests to mock her vintage gown, while pretending not to hear their giggles.

Now that it was too late, he realized he had always known there was something special about Madeline's way of carrying herself, in spite of her financial position. She didn't need the latest couture to make her feel worthy. She simply brought worthiness to everything she touched.

Madeline's wreck of a car rebelled against her attempts to crank it. The starter dragged—tired and lethargic as it growled and groaned—and the battery seemed in need of a long nap.

"Maybe it's a sign," William said, not altogether unhappy about its refusal to cooperate with her departure from Pine Island.

"A sign of what?" she asked. "That I have neglected it for too long?"

He chuckled, suddenly feeling nervous at the absence of knowing what to say.

"Would it be too much of an imposition for you to drive me into town?" She peered up at him.

Her wide-eyed expression was one he would never be able to refuse. "Of course not," he answered. The thought whipped about his mind that this would give him a little more time, and he might find the words to tell her how he felt about her.

William stared straight ahead at the road in front of them. Fear of rejection prevented him from begging her to stay and finish her thesis at Pine Island, even though he wanted it more than he could articulate.

This emotional attachment to her frightened him. It had been a long time since he'd let anyone near his fragile heart. If only she could convince him she wanted to stay, that she wouldn't refuse his attentions, then he could risk exposing his true feelings.

Every mile accented the urgency. His inner voice kept imploring him to pull over and explain. But he couldn't seem to find the right place—a place both forgiving and peaceful. So he kept driving, and suddenly they were outside of her apartment on the edge of town.

"Thank you for everything." Madeline extended her hand to him.

He started to accept the handshake, but before he knew it he had grabbed her in an embrace. Inhaling the lavender scent of her hair and feeling the warmth of being so near her enticed him. All he could think of was the way they fit together—the glimpse of passion in her face and the softness of her body wrapped around his.

His mind implored hers to ask him to stay for a while. Maybe if they weren't standing awkwardly on her stoop, he could find the courage to confess his feelings.

****

Madeline felt William's embrace as surely as if it came from the Captain. Its energy coursed through her body in ways that made her want to beg him to come in for the night. But she realized it was probably only sensory memory—her body responding to the physical body the Captain had so often used to delight her with.

She still felt bruised by the knowledge he hadn't loved her either. He had only been enticing her emotions to win her trust. *Men! I can't even trust dead ones*.

But the Captain was long gone, and soon William would be too. She peeled herself free from his arms. "I'll call a mechanic first thing in the morning. I'll have my car towed as quickly as possible, to get it out of your way."

"You…I…it's not…" William couldn't seem to get any words out in a coherent manner. He stood there, stammering, as she opened the door.

Madeline crossed the threshold into the world she lived in, and shut the door behind her with only a slight wave of her hand.

Chapter 41

Madeline threw herself into her work. Her paper nearly finished itself.

She worked overtime at the jewelry store, photographing pieces for Mrs. Jenkins's upcoming auction. It was gathering steam, receiving a lot of press. Thinking the attention would bring in the right buyers to pay a hefty sum for their treasures, several people wanted to add their items to the collection. Mrs. Jenkins' cut should be awesome.

Madeline's ears perked up at every mention of William's name. Georgetown's rumor mill suggested he was working on a project for a bald eagle preserve on the island. She found herself thinking about him far too often, wondering what he was doing.

Would he undertake the growing of his own vineyard, and make his own wine? Would he start dating his usual string of socialites again now that the hauntings had ceased? Her body cringed at the thought. Could he possibly revert to his previous behavior, after all they had been through?

She ran shaking fingers through her hair, cupped her face with her palms, and tried to get the memory of him from her mind. There was no point in longing for him. It was only the sensory memory of feeling his body, while under the influence of the Captain, next to hers. She couldn't fathom her heartache was anything other than what had happened with the apparition.

****

William missed Madeline more than he could ever have imagined a person could be missed—even more than with Julia's departure. He yearned for her quiet presence in the house, and the way she found joy even in the broken parts of him.

He couldn't pass the conch shell she left from their foray out to Shell Island on the hall table without a pang of grief for her. Trying to conjure up reasons to call her, he simply lacked the courage.

So much in his life had changed. He could never go back to being the playboy he had been, settling for women that sort of behavior attracted. It was too shallow. Living through the ordeal had left him wanting more substance in his next relationship.

Feeling the need to escape from Pine Island's reservoir of memories. both good and bad, he drove into town to check on Alex's wife. Helena wasn't doing well either. The shock of her husband's secret life and horrid plans had been a nasty blow. Recovery was difficult, too difficult for most to ever fathom.

William took her to lunch to discuss her future plans and to offer his assistance. She was shattered, a shadow of her previous self, and his heart broke for her.

"How did this happen to us?" Helena asked William over crab dip at his favorite little deli.

"I don't know. I didn't even know Julia and Alex talked to each other. What a fool I was, huh?"

"That makes two of us," she said sadly. "At least you and Julia weren't currently involved. How long do you think this was going on?"

"Since before our scheduled wedding date. Alex

made a comment about taking her from me on the night…when…" He dropped the sentence, not wanting to say the words.

They stared down at their cold plates. The meaning was clear, whether or not the words were spoken. Helena began to cry and William slipped onto the bench seat beside her, pulling her against his shoulder to comfort her.

"It will never be the same," she wept. "We're broken forever."

Chapter 42

Madeline had some errands to run downtown. Remembering the food they had eaten out at Pine Island, she decided to stop at the deli William mentioned and get a bit of the crab salad she had found so delicious.

As she neared the door, she glanced through the window and seeing William, smiled. Maybe they could have lunch together.

She stretched out one hand to wave, reaching for the door with the other one. That's when she saw him sit down beside a woman and pull her into his arms. Stunned, Madeline watched them together.

When he pulled away, she saw it was Alex's wife. Were they seeing each other? No doubt they could help each other through their losses. It made sense—shared childhoods, shared grief, shared betrayal. They had much in common.

Yet it made her sad to see them together. Why did she care? She chastised herself and walked into a different restaurant for a sandwich and a glass of wine.

****

Graduation approached and Madeline could hardly wait to hold the degree declaring her worthy of a *position*—not just a job. She could take this degree and apply for an advanced degree at colleges and universities throughout the southeast.

Yet, she kept thinking about the bald eagles and the preserve William was trying to get started. That was what she really wanted to do—work for the birds' preservation out on the secluded North Island.

She called herself "crazy," and lectured herself about the long years and hard work she had devoted to getting her degree. The probability was she was only searching for a reason to go back to the North Island, and back to Pine Island.

The night of the graduation approached. She wasn't the only older student getting a degree, but definitely in the minority.

She was, however, the most famous. Madeline's thesis on Captain William Gray had gone viral. She was now widely recognized for bringing to light the revelations of the newly discovered journal, and its historical link to the torpedo that had stopped another Union attack on Charleston. Granted that hadn't been the Captain's mission in placing the mine, but the media had typically put its own twist on the news—it sounded good when replayed.

His accepting blame for the death of his wife, though she had taken too much laudanum and been poisoned by her own hand, made her a local hit. And it made the Captain a long-suffering hero.

The people of Georgetown were thrilled to have a new legend to brag about. They demanded a "Captain Gray Day." Restaurants started naming entrees after him, hoteliers named suites in their establishments after him, and they set forth plans to name a new park after him.

Parts of the thesis had been published nationally in magazines and newspapers, especially across the south.

The fact the Captain had left the torpedo anchored at the mouth of the bay could be translated to mean he might have also been trying to protect the Union fleet from a Confederate attack. At least that was the northern publications' answer to his quest. And then they began to declare he was also a Union hero, even if his actions had the undesirable effect of sinking their ship. It seemed everyone loved the story of the unlikely hero.

On the night of the graduation, the stadium filled with proud parents, spouses, friends, grandparents, and in some instances...children. Madeline had hoped Jacob would be able to make it, but he had his own college exams, and the round trip distance was too great for him to manage.

She understood, and yet still felt incredibly lonely when she realized there would be no one special there to cheer her name when it was called to receive her degree. Although she supposed she would have to consider Mrs. Jenkins special.

After all, Madeline might not be here to receive her degree if not for her friend's interventions. She'd said she would be there as nothing made her prouder than to see Madeline succeed, even though it meant it wasn't likely she would continue to work at the jewelry store.

A host of dignitaries—at least they were considered such in their community—gave relatively short messages to the graduating class. Then Mayor Hyman came to the podium and began, much to Madeline's surprise, to talk about a subject dear to her heart.

"Nothing touches the hearts and minds of a community faster than a determined woman going after what she wants, and elevating others in her quest to do so. One of our graduates, here with us tonight, has done this for the entire city of Georgetown. She pointed out that history had been an unfair judge of another upstanding citizen of this area, one who lived and prospered in the eighteen hundreds. That man did so without bending to the socially acceptable methods of the day that appall us now. Most of you know I am speaking about the great hero and sea captain, William Gray."

Applause resounded. Mayor Hyman held up his hands after a few moments of letting the audience cheer their newfound hero.

"Captain Gray refused to engage in the practice of slavery, yet he thrived and his estate is still one of the nicest in Georgetown. Our Captain would not accept breathing beneath the water wasn't possible for mankind, so he brought back plans for a contraption from England that helped him to achieve that very feat. William Gray declined to disclose his wife's suicide at a time in history when it was considered an unforgiveable sin, even at the cost of his own reputation, because he didn't want her memory besmirched. He rejected the idea a man alone couldn't raise a fine son, and never remarried. Captain Gray repudiated the war effort, yet used his ship and particular talents to protect human lives. The one life that was lost on the *USS Harvest Moon* troubled him forever."

More applause.

"We have here in the audience today, Captain William Gray's only surviving heir, and namesake, William Gray—stand up William."

Applause and bravos went up. Madeline felt her heart thundering in her chest. She'd had no idea William would be here, nor that the mayor intended to speak about her work. She hoped all the acclamations would soon die down. These things usually did.

"The great people of Georgetown have earmarked funds for a bald eagle preserve, and we intend to form that foundation based out on the North Island. It will be named The Captain William Gray American Eagle Preserve."

More ovations sounded.

"And I want to put you"—he pointed at William—"and the *she-ro* who made this honor possible—our very own Madeline Waters—in charge of running this foundation. Stand up, please, Madeline."

Madeline was dumbfounded. She stood erect among the sea of caps and gowns, feeling proud of her work, and also shaking at the sight of William. She immediately sat back down, hoping to disappear before she burst into tears.

Even from a distance, the sight of William's dark curls brought every memory rushing back. Her mouth went dry and her pounding heart drowned out the sound of the applause and the cheers.

"Ladies and gentlemen, this is what it means to receive an education. You take what you have learned and use it to right wrongs, unearth new truths, lift up a society, asking for nothing but scholarly recognition. You see today what a difference one of these graduates has already made for her community. I call on each of you to take what you have learned from your time in this institution of learning, and use it well."

Wild applause resounded across the field. Tears

dropped down Madeline's cheeks as the college's poet laureate read his work. She tried to calm herself for the long walk to receive her diploma.

After the graduation ceremony ended, people mulled around hugging and taking pictures with their relatives, classmates, and friends.

Madeline tried to slip out of the stadium, unnoticed, to no avail. William waited at the exit for her. He surprised her with a giant hug and a smile. These melted her heart all over again.

She hadn't seen him since the day in the restaurant with Helena. She peeked behind him to see if Alex's widow had accompanied him to the graduation.

"You really are a *she-ro*," he said, stroking her under the chin.

"Thanks...thank you for coming. I didn't know all of this...I mean...I'm surprised..." She didn't know what to say.

He eyed her expectantly, his charm emanating in the same manner it had when the Captain had taken over his body.

She found a smile, in spite of herself.

"Madeline, do you have dinner plans tonight?"

"Actually no, I don't have any plans."

"Then have dinner with me. We can celebrate your graduation and talk about this proposed foundation that you and I seem to have been volunteered for." He put both hands on her shoulders.

The heat from his fingertips ran through her body conducting the connection between them as electrical currents might. "Sure," she managed to say.

He burst into a grin and took her by the arm. "Is there any special place you wish to go?"

"Yes." She was not used to asking for what she wanted, but decided it was time to start. "I would love to go back out to Pine Island, and see it all one more time."

"Great idea! We can pick up dinner and wine and take it with us. If you'd care to ride out with me, I can wait on you. In fact, why don't you pack on overnight bag and stay over. You can have your old room. We could cruise around the North Island in the morning."

Madeline tried to remain calm, though she wanted to see the island again more than anything in the world. "Well, if you're sure it won't be too much trouble."

"It's settled then. I don't mind that at all."

"Great. Maybe you could pick up dinner while I gather an overnight case and get out of this graduation *uniform*." She tugged at the polyester gown. It was a little secret among the graduates that the heat and humidity of the south demanded virtual nudity beneath the graduation robes.

Mrs. Jenkins had driven her over. Madeline found her and begged her forgiveness for leaving her to drive home alone. She seemed happy at the news Madeline was accompanying William Gray back to Pine Island.

She slipped a small package into Madeline's hands. "For you. I'm very proud of you. In fact, I couldn't be prouder if you were my own daughter."

Madeline grabbed her, pulling her in tight for a hug. "I'd be honored to be your daughter. You do have the touch, Mrs. Jenkins—the loving touch."

"Maybe it's time you called me something besides Mrs. Jenkins. How about just Sarah?"

"I'd love that."

Mrs. Jenkins took her by both shoulders, searching

deeply into her eyes. "Am I detecting a broken heart?"

"It's obvious?"

"William's here. He's taking you for a celebratory dinner; wants you to stay over. Sounds like making up to me."

"It's not William…I mean…it's…sensory memory, or something…"

"Oh honey, don't be so sure." Mrs. Jenkins wore wisdom the way her customers wore her jewelry. It oozed from her, leaving Madeline unable to argue her point. "Give him a fair chance," she advised. "You may be surprised at what unfurls."

They exchanged hugs and cheek kisses before the older lady disappeared. Madeline watched her jaunt off toward the parking lot, replaying her words in her head. *What had she meant? Does she think I'm in love with William?*

****

William dropped Madeline off at her apartment and returned within the hour. The back of his car, with the loosely-wrapped finds from the deli, emanated a pleasingly delicious aroma. Wine bottles and whole loaves of two different kinds of freshly baked bread stuck out of the canvas bags.

William tossed her purse into the back and opened the car door for her. She marveled at how far they had come since their first meeting. She actually enjoyed his company now.

On the drive out to Pine Island, they kept the conversation light, discussing the craziness surrounding her thesis.

It was hard to keep her mind on her work though. Each movement of William's hands on the steering wheel made her remember the deftness of his touch and the way those same hands had danced over her body. His smile tore at her heart and she had trouble discerning between the Captain and William. Which one had she fallen so desperately in love with? Did it matter? She could have neither.

Chapter 43

The minute Madeline saw the long-standing live oaks, lining the drive, and the dripping beards of Spanish moss, she felt herself slip into another world. *It could be the eighteen hundreds out here*, she thought. The house popped into view and the memory of her first meeting the Captain in the cupola rushed back to her. Would she see him again? Did she want to after the horrible realization of his using her?

William carried the sacks of food, and Madeline her overnight bag, as they walked into the house. For a split second, as she scanned the center of the ground floor, she recalled the horror of the bloody scene on the night of the shooting. But then it wicked away, as William glided up beside her and started talking.

"If you want to put your things in your room, I'll set out dinner. Or if you'd prefer, we can take it down to the beach."

She could tell he was nervous. Perhaps he thought she would misunderstand his intentions. Maybe he was worried she had misunderstood his reason for asking her to Pine Island. Obviously it was a business proposition. She needed to be clear in her mind about that.

It would be far too romantic to sit on a beach drinking wine and eating prosciutto. She didn't know how she might react. Madeline lied, "I think eating here is better. I don't care much for sand in my food."

She climbed the stairs and pushed open the door, recalling every night she had lain in the bed and watched for the Captain. Then of course there was that last night, the final night. Sitting down on the bed, the tears that had played cat-and-mouse began to rack her body. What was she doing here? Hadn't she suffered enough?

Suddenly, through the open window, a wisp of smoke spun into being. Madeline sensed she was no longer alone. "Captain? Is it you?" Fear crept up her spine as she swiped at her cheeks, trying to wick away the tears. She backed toward the door.

His energy formed and focused into the shape of a man as he smiled and whispered, "Yes, it is me. Do not fear. I mean you no harm."

Memories of the attraction and how she had fallen for his declarations of love pushed the fear away, replacing it with hurt and anger. "Why did you do it? Why did you use me so cruelly?" Her efforts at wiping away the tears were useless. She now cried harder. "Have you come back to finish me off?"

He shivered, fading as he shimmered away. "I will not hurt you. I only returned this once to tell you I am sorry, and that I have found what I was seeking. Now you must do the same."

She shook her head. "Seeking? I was only seeking information, and I have accomplished that." Momentarily forgetting to be frightened of him, she bragged, "You're a bit of a hero now."

"Yes, for now. All that fades with time— everything but love. It never fades, Madeline. True love grows stronger every day, and for it, you will do things you shouldn't. But I think you were seeking it, too, not just the information."

"You only think that because you succeeded in making me love you. I believed you when you said you loved me."

"I can only beg forgiveness. Now I must go with my mate. She waits for me, and yours waits for you, downstairs."

"What do you mean?"

"Oh my dear, you have given me everything. And I have given you nothing. But the one downstairs has all the love in the world for you. You see, you freed us, and now Magdalene and I can be together throughout eternity. Now you must find your own true love."

He started fading. "Goodbye Madeline. Take care of my grandson, and my house." And then he was gone.

Madeline ran to the window and peered out to see a pair of eagles gliding low in the sky. She collapsed on the bed. The hot tears that had leaked from her eyes now ran, swift as a waterfall, down her cheeks. What did this mean—any of this?

Chapter 44

William waited for Madeline to return to the kitchen. He laid out the deli trays of fine cheeses, tiny ham biscuits, a bowl of caviar with a mother-of-pearl spoon, melon, strawberries, the best champagne, and her favorite—crab salad. *What is keeping her?* he wondered.

He walked to the stairs and called up to her. "Madeline, is anything wrong?" He waited for a moment and heard no response. "Madeline?"

Maybe she fell, or got sick or…the possibilities frightened him. The thought she might be in danger alarmed him enough to send him spiraling up the staircase, taking the steps two by two.

"Madeline? Madeline, are you all right?" He rapped his knuckles against the door. Hearing the sounds of her crying from the other side, he raced in and grabbed her in a full body embrace. "What's wrong, Madeline?"

"I'm sorry…" She hiccoughed. "The Captain…was here."

William jumped up and glanced around. "Did he harm you? Are you okay?"

"It's all right. He said he is where he needs to be, and we are here where we should be. All is set to right."

William stroked her face. "And you did it. You made it all right."

"Then why...do I feel so bad?"

"You've missed him. And I've missed you. Maybe we could comfort each other." He kissed her on the forehead and stroked her back.

She felt the tears drying and took a few deep breaths. "He said something I don't quite understand. He said 'the man who loves you is downstairs.' What do you think he meant by that?"

William felt crushed, as if the whole ceiling had just caved in on him. He had wanted to be the one to tell her, and only when the time was right. He pushed himself off the bed and crossed the room.

"I have been trying to find a way to tell you. I...I can't..."

"Just say it."

"I think I'm in love with you."

"Oh my God! I have to get out of here," Madeline cried. She ran for the door.

William froze in place by the window, feeling the rejection he had feared facing. She had never pretended to care about him. It had always been about the Captain. He was merely the vessel through which she thought the Captain could make love to her.

He heard the door slam and finally sprang to life, running after her, calling her name. It was starting to get dark, and he couldn't see which way she'd gone. He called and called and headed out each path. Suddenly an eagle appeared and clipped past him flying toward the beach. Sensing he should follow it, he ran along the beach path. He could barely make out the white head of the regal bird as it headed along the water's edge.

****

"Madeline," the sea whispered in her ear.

"Madeline, turn around. The man who loves you is right behind you." The eagle soared seaward. Obeying, she turned, landing squarely in William's arms.

He held her tightly to him, his fingers gripping her hair and his tears wetting her cheeks. "Please don't run from me. I love you. You mean everything. Please give me a chance."

"I...I..." The words wouldn't come, but her eyes locked on William's and she saw the spirit of the man she had loved all along.

He leaned in, his lips softly touching hers, and then slowly exploring her in a way that melted her heart and her resolve.

"Is it possible we are meant for each other?" she asked.

"Yes, Madeline, I believe it is," he answered with confidence.

They walked back to the house, arms tightly around each other. They didn't stop at the kitchen but headed straight for the stairs.

He pulled her into the master suite. "This will be our room. Its bad memories no longer hold any power over me." Shutting the door, he began to undress her, tenderly kissing each spot as it revealed itself.

Madeline returned his ardent kisses and pulled at his clothing. This time there was no doubt about the identity of the man making love to her. It was all William, and she shuddered as his lips found hers. He moaned as she reached for his pants to unzip them. She felt his fullness there, just waiting for her.

"I love you, Madeline," he whispered as he parted her and slipped into her depths. She gasped and peered into the eyes of the man, not the ghost. "I love you too,

William Gray."

In the distance, two eagles played, two souls soared and crossed the bay headed out to the far North Island.

Chapter 45

Madeline drove through the gates at Pine Island on the first day of summer. The house was buzzing with caterers, photographers, and parking valets. Her car was packed with all of her belongings. The Halston off-white column she had worn on her first night at Pine Island—and gifted to her by Mrs. Jenkins, Sarah to her now—was to be her wedding dress.

She knew enough to feel proud of her vintage gown, the same one the shallow and vain women had laughed about at the Azalea Ball. Madeline still couldn't spend money frivolously. There had been too many years of struggle and penny-pinching to suddenly abandon frugality.

She had made one rather large splurge, although she thought of it as an investment in her soon-to-be-husband's happiness. It should be arriving on a truck shortly after the ceremony—her wedding gift to William.

William met her at the door, sweeping her into an embrace. He seemed so calm and happy planting kisses on her cheeks and along her neck. "How is my bride this morning?"

Madeline laughed. "I am very happy."

"Wonderful. I'll have your belongings taken up to the suite, and then I'll meet you out on the morning porch."

338

He released her and she watched him head off to his study for last minute preparations.

"Hello there," the photographer called out to her. "I was wondering if there was any place special, or unusual, in the house that you might wish to pose for a wedding album picture."

Madeline started to say any place within Pine Island would be special, but then she thought of the cupola and asked him to meet her there. Once she was fully dressed, she took the stairs all the way to the top.

It was already getting warm. It would be hot before the day was over. Lifting a hand to cover her eyes, she peered out across the water. A pair of eagles swooped low and flew with their wings tipped down across the marsh. On the opposite side of the house, a stream of cars poured in from the inland entrance.

The photographer snapped a few shots of her standing by the windows before they walked down to the porch where William waited.

It was a beautiful morning wedding. The party afterward carried on for the entire day, from porch to porch. Madeline's gift to William arrived to great ceremony—a juice press, the old-timey kind they could use to turn grapes into wine.

"It's time to start your winery, don't you think? And here's a list of vineyards who can supply us with grapes." She handed him the names and phone numbers of possible suppliers.

He sputtered and grinned. For a moment he was totally lost—not just in the press, but in the possibilities it presented.

Madeline watched him with joy. She had never thought to see him as happy.

"I have a gift for you as well," he said, once he could pull himself away from his press. He pulled a card from his pocket and presented it to her.

As she pulled it from the envelope, two airline tickets fell out. She read the destination. "London? We're going to England for our honeymoon?"

William laughed. "We're going for the summer, so you can further your research."

For the first time in her life, Madeline was speechless. Every dream was coming to fruition.

"Do you like it?" William asked.

"I love it; I love you." She embraced him as the tears fell—happy tears.

"Hey, look at this," the photographer called out to them. He sounded excited. "Come over here."

William and Madeline walked to the computer screen where he had uploaded some pictures for them to peruse. He was pointing to several of them. "If I didn't know better, I'd swear you had a ghost at the ceremony." In several of the pictures, a shadowy shape stood between William and Madeline. "It's probably a reflection of William. I don't know how it happened."

William and Madeline laughed. "We'll tell you about our ghost someday," William said.

"Yes, we'll definitely want full-sized shots of the ones with the ghost," Madeline assured him. She thought of her failed mission to capture the Captain in her pictures and, by way of stream of consciousness, of William's complete capture of her heart.

"Who's going to look after the house while we're away?" William whispered. "I gave the help the summer off."

"Oh, William, I don't think we ever have to worry

about Gray Estate. It's in good hands." She pointed to the computer's picture with the haunting image in the background.

William led her away through a spray of white rose petals. They raced into their future with no tethers to the past and no ghost standing between them—except for the shadowy image in their wedding pictures.

A word about the author...

Renee Johnson has contributed to Bonjour Paris, an online travel website; Storyhouse—where she won second place for travel story of the year two years in a row; and received an honorable mention in a travel essay contest from Study Abroad. Only then did she begin to pursue her true passion for fiction, one which started when she was only nine years old.

After placing third in Indiana's Golden Opportunity Contest for romantic/suspense in 2013, she signed with The Wild Rose Press for *Acquisition*, a sassy southern novel full of intrigue and secrets.

Renee blogs at two sites: http://writingfeemail.com for personal observations and photography, and http://reneejohnsonwrites.com where she focuses on the craft of writing.

She lives in North Carolina with her husband Tony and a very spoiled German Shepherd named Gretel. Renee is a member of Romance Writers of America, North Carolina Writers Network, and She Writes.

http://twitter.com/@writingfeemail
http://www.facebook.com/renee.johnson.549436